WHAT ONE WOULDN'T DO

An Anthology on the Lengths One Might Go To

Edited by

SCOTT J. MOSES

What One Wouldn't Do
Published by Scott J. Moses

Cover Art/Design: George C. Cotronis

Editor/Proofreader: Rachel Oestreich, Owner/Editor of The Wallflower Editing, LLC

Interior Formatting/Design: Scott J. Moses

CONTENTS

INTRODUCTION

LAUREL HIGHTOWER

***A brief caveat—I'm lucky enough to have a story chosen for inclusion in this anthology. In the same way an author might review a full anthology, excluding their own contribution, my words below are only meant to encompass the writers with whom I share this Table of Contents, not my own story.*

Before releasing my novella, *Crossroads,* I never knew grief horror was a thing. I'd written a sad story, centering around devastating loss and the subsequent fallout, but it wasn't until a few people read it and gave it a label that I learned of the subgenre. That's been one of the wonderful things about immersing myself in the indie horror community—exposure to subgenres and sub-subgenres I never dreamed of—it's another way I feel connected, a path to a shelf that contains exactly the story I'm looking for.

Yet even knowing the nomenclature, I'm still hard put to define grief horror. It's a question I get a lot, after people read my work, and I'm never sure how to answer it because I didn't set out to write grief horror. When Scott Moses announced the call for this anthology and approached me about writing the introduction, I was honored and more than a little intimidated. Whereas Scott wrote an entire short story collection centering around grief horror (it's excellent by the way—check out *Hunger Pangs*) it seemed a thing I'd fallen into by accident, not a subject I felt qualified to introduce. I figured I could wing it, relying on the stories within to guide me, but when it came down to writing a contribution, I shrank from the task. After all, hadn't I already tapped that well? What more did I have to say about the entwined nature of deep mourning and the terrible places it can take us?

But another joy of this community is being exposed to diverse and wonderful authors, folks whose minds reach farther than mine, travel paths I never knew were there. Settling in to read the full manuscript, I knew from page one that Scott had a hit on his hands.

Seeing as how he took on the arduous task of reading every submission he received, only he knows the true breadth of horror's reach into the dark world of grief. All I can say is, through a combination of his keen eye and the incredible quality of stories shared by fearless and talented authors, you hold in your hands an anthology that will defy all your expectations. A beautifully blended mix of tones and subject matter, of poetry and prose, there is something to touch the heart of every reader on the pages within. This is the horror genre at its most effective: exploring and evoking deep emotional reactions, whether through quiet horror, body horror, or a splatterpunk lens.

Grief is a deep, dark, looming shadow, the threads of which seep into our beings, tighten around our hearts, and change our very souls. There is grief for the death of a loved one, certainly, and the stories within that take that tack each do so with raw authenticity—loss is personal, as are the ways we mourn it. Beyond that, there is grief for who we used to be, or who we might have been. For a peace we once knew that we can't recover, no matter how hard we try. For a relationship or a future now out of reach. For a sacrifice, made or not made. When you really dig into the concept, as these authors have done with gusto, you realize how broad and individualized the experience of grief is.

So, too, are the things we're capable of doing to mitigate that grief—the titular question of what one wouldn't do was a masterstroke on Scott's part. For within our own hearts and minds, let alone the far reach of what-if that the horror genre grants us, the possibilities are limitless. We may say, in perfect truth at the time we utter the words, that we would never steal, or take up necromancy, or drag someone back over the divide between life and death over and over. That we would never remove a person's autonomy, never torture a human being, become someone we don't recognize in the mirror, or travel across time and worlds to alter a life path. That we would never kill. But in the grip of it, in the throes of unimaginable grief that pierces our very souls. . .well, what wouldn't one do?

Laurel Hightower
Lexington, KY
July 7, 2021

WITH ANIMALS

J.A.W. MCCARTHY

The first time Ezra brings me back, thirty seagulls fall from the sky.

I open my eyes to him crouched over me, palms and knees sunk into the sand, his face stretched and stilled in a mixture of disbelief and triumph as a swarm of those giant birds swirl in the gray sky overhead. Their frenzied squawking signals some kind of pending disaster—their own demise, they seem to intuit—not my rebirth.

"Lou? Louise? Can you hear me?" he asks. His breath is sour with burnt coffee and a stomach that hasn't seen much else. "Are you okay?"

"What the. . . ?" I murmur, lifting my head.

Before I can sit all the way up, Ezra scoops his hands under my back and brings me to his chest, holding me gently as if he's afraid he might squeeze this new life out of me. My eyes struggle to focus against the worn cotton weave of his shirt. Perspiration clings to his chin, softening the scratch of his stubble against my cheek. Four, five days of growth? I know him well enough, saw him through puberty and the uncertain stretch after, to know what he can grow when he wants and what will grow when he stops caring.

Ezra's face is the last thing I remember, a clean-shaven relief after the unruly forest he'd sported since his girlfriend broke up with him eight months ago. It was as if he'd emerged from the wilds of grief with a machete he'd fashioned on the last day before a controlled burn. I'd called him Baby-Butt Face and he'd flipped me off as I drove away from his apartment.

"Why are we at the beach?" I ask, my eyes adjusting to the blurs of pink, red, green, all the bright colors dotting the gray sand and sky. People on beach towels, hands hovering over paper boats of French fries and foil-wrapped burritos, protecting their snacks from the frenzied seagulls circling above. Ezra and I learned long ago to never bring anything more than brown-bagged beers to the beach.

"I thought it would be quiet," he says. "It's seven-thirty in the morning. Where did all these people come from? Who the fuck has french fries at seven-thirty in the morning?"

I laugh then cough, spitting up an acrid mixture of bile and blood onto Ezra's shoulder. I stay with my cheek pressed to his throat. My skin swallows his sweat, and I feel my flesh plump, a fresh rush of blood forcing open collapsed veins, sea air thick with salt and wet rot inflating my lungs, my body splitting awake like ice under hot liquid. I realize what I'm wearing—my funeral dress—is the bridesmaid's dress from my cousin's wedding four years ago, the fluffy blush-pink number my mother cooed over as I scratched at my forearms and reached for my jeans. I haven't spoken to her in over a year, but of course she had the final say in what I would wear for all eternity.

The squawking overhead intensifies. I wipe my mouth on Ezra's sleeve and look up. Has the world always been this loud, this bright?

Then the first seagull falls.

A hard plop into the sand just three feet from where we sit, throwing up a dusting that catches on my lips. Dead before it even fell out of the sky. Then another, right next to a woman asleep on her towel several yards away. A hush falls over the beach. Bodies still, heads tilt up, fingers point. The screaming starts with the man unlucky enough to have the next seagull land in his lap.

Those birds come down hard in a fit of feathers and open beaks, their own screams cut short as the swirl overhead folds into blurs of white and gray, slicing through the sky to break the mirror of water below. Food wrappers and six-packs are abandoned in the sand as people flee for the parking lot. Seagulls rain down on coolers and car hoods, slapping against asphalt as traffic grinds to a halt in the distance. Ezra and I are the only people who remain, staring up in horror as we hold each other.

Thirty in total. When we're alone, after I can stand, we walk the beach and count them all.

"It's. . . it's kinda what I thought it would be," I say, taking the beer Ezra offers me. He settles on the opposite end of the couch so we're both turned toward each other, knees steepled, toes butting toes. Thirteen hours back, surrounded by small animals trotting past and weaving around my legs in his apartment, the fecund scent of their skin and breath pulling into my lungs and going right back out to them—I'm part of the circle again, a loop I never found inside my own apartment filled with books and unpaid bills and the plants I never could keep alive. Even after a hot shower and a set of Ezra's clean sweats—and the satisfaction of stuffing that godawful bridesmaid monstrosity in the garbage—it still doesn't feel like a rebirth. All I know is that whatever space between life and death I now occupy, I want to stay here.

"Like when you're falling asleep," I attempt to explain. "Your mind slows and. . . it's vague, you know? It fades. Like when you dream you're watching TV. You're invested in what you're seeing, but you're out of your body. You're you, but you don't matter. Nothing matters."

Ezra's eyes widen above his beer bottle as he takes a swig. "So were you looking down on the world, watching the whole time?"

"Don't worry, I didn't see you jerking off. I did see you crying over me, though."

"Perv. I did all my crying in the shower."

I pull a pillow from behind my back and throw it at him. At that a small black cat skitters out from the side of the couch, her claws clacking against the hardwood. When she comes within reach, I scoop her up and hold her in my lap.

"Well, you're new. Who are you?"

"That's Daphne," Ezra says. "I found her on the side of the road yesterday morning. She's doing really good so far."

I hold the cat aloft, scanning her from head to tail. The right side of her mouth hangs a little crooked, but otherwise she looks healthy. Intact. She squirms in my hands until I put her back down. If she's like any of the other dozens of animals Ezra has brought back from the dead over the years, she will be gone again in days, maybe weeks if she's lucky. He's getting better and better at this resurrection thing, but even the smallest of mice never last more than a couple of months, not even after its weight in bees or moths fall to their demise.

"I'm the biggest thing you've ever brought back," I say.

"What about that German shepherd last year? He made it three weeks."

"Ezra, I'm not—"

"Don't worry, Lou," he cuts me off. "I wouldn't have done this if I didn't believe it would work this time. I feel really good about this."

We both know that's a lie.

I stretch my leg across the couch, hooking my foot under his bent knee. "Whatever happens. . . I know I'm on borrowed time. It's not so bad. I know what's out there now. I'm not afraid."

I jiggle his leg with my foot, but he doesn't smile. His features are set, dark eyes focused on my face so that I wonder if my ear is hanging loose from my head like that rabbit he brought back four years ago. I've avoided mirrors all day; I don't need to see my already pale skin take on the waxy sheen of death. It's bad enough that Ezra has to see me fall apart piece by piece.

"After you. . . after the accident. . . " Ezra's mouth wavers and his gaze shifts down. He takes a deep breath before continuing. "I kept thinking about you alone in the dark. I just knew. I knew you weren't up on some cloud playing the harp and eating chocolate gelato. I know it's not like that and I couldn't stand—"

"You thought I was in hell, then? You really think I'm that big of an asshole?" I flash a grin, prodding his leg again. Even Riley the rabbit bouncing across the floor in front of us, humping his little beach ball, doesn't elicit a laugh.

"You remember that time in third grade when Davey Sherwood locked me in the janitor's closet? He blocked the door and I couldn't get out, and the fucking light switch—the bulb was dead. I gave up and sat down, and I felt like I couldn't breathe, like I was suffocating. Then you came in, and you sat with me. How long were we in there? You were so afraid of the dark, but you stayed with me until I could breathe again. I was afraid being dead is like that. I didn't want you to go through that. I didn't want you to be alone in the dark."

"Jesus, Ezra. . . " I scoot across the couch, leaning back against his tented shins. He wipes his arm roughly over his eyes then turns so that I can't see his whole face. "Seriously, it wasn't bad," I assure him, grabbing his arm and draping it over my shoulder. "Being dead, it's quiet. It's a relief. Everything just falls away, like the world doesn't exist either. You're not missing anything. You don't care. It's peaceful."

He gives a rueful little chuckle. "How can you be so casual? You were fucking *dead*!"

"How can *you* be so casual, Mr. Messiah, my lord and savior?"

He hooks his arm around my throat, pretending to choke me, then kisses the top of my head. "Okay, okay, we don't have to talk about it. You need to eat. Wanna order a pizza?"

At my agreement he slips out from under me, swinging his long legs over the edge of the couch. His cats Jax and Butters scatter from the rug. Rodney the basset hound—resurrected in the empty lot behind the 7-11 three weeks ago and still going strong—lifts his head then promptly goes back to sleep under the coffee table. The new black cat, Daphne, watches from the top of the bookcase as Ezra takes a step forward then freezes, his knee dipping into a lopsided lunge as his face contorts in pain.

"What is it?" I ask.

He waves me off, already limping toward the kitchen. "Nothing. My leg's asleep."

I lie back in the warm crater of the cushion he vacated, the seat I used to joke smells like farts. I'm too tired to grab a pillow and it feels good to stretch out, as if I haven't had all the room in the universe when I was dead less than a day ago. The truth is, I'm afraid to fall asleep. Exhaustion has been creeping in throughout the day, but I've been able to hold it off as long as Ezra is with me. He's left me alone only to use the bathroom, always talking to me through the door as if he's afraid I'll vanish without his eyes on me, without the sound of his voice. We've seen it happen with the countless animals he's resurrected, all those shiny eyes and fuzzy little heads growing heavy, never knowing which time would be the final sleep. No matter how many new animals he brings into his home, it never gets any easier, and he never gets any less attached. He knows and he's right.

I struggle to focus on the dark green ceiling, my eyes tracing the spiderwebs draped in the corners. Ezra's voice carries as he paces the kitchen on his phone.

"Peppers, goat cheese. . . hey, Lou, do you want caramelized onions too?"

My mouth forms a *yes*; I feel it, I hear it in my mind. *And extra parmesan.*

"Lou?"

I blink hard. The green ceiling darkens around the edges of my vision, closing in. The sound of my name, the quickening slap of sneakers against the hardwoods, the crack of the phone hitting the floor. A hand gripping my shoulder, shaking, grabbing at pieces of my body as it floats away. I'm watching through the rearview mirror of my car, staring at Ezra's clean baby face, an irritated pink blushing his brown skin where his beard used to be, his right hand up and flipping me off. Then it's the same as last time, the darkness that means I'm gone.

I wasn't honest with Ezra. Yes, your mind slows, and it's vague, but you're still aware; there's never a moment when you're not aware that you are fucking dead. There is nothing to see or hear or touch. You have nothing to crack the silence, not even your own voice. It's quiet, but it's not a relief. You know you're alone in the dark.

This time, though, it's different. I'm still in the infinite dark and I'm still aware, but—maybe because I got a second life, maybe because I'm an abomination, maybe because there's a different place for those who die again—I'm not alone this time.

They squawk, but it's not the frenzy I remember, more like an exploratory call, a game of Marco Polo where everyone is blindfolded. Their webbed feet slap against what sounds like water. There's the whispered whoosh of their wings slicing through air or whatever it is that binds us to this new gravity. Though I can't feel my body—only the muscle memory of a bodiless mind—I can sense them closing in, the heat they make encircling me as they gather at the sound of each other's voices. Every cry, every ruffle of nonexistent feathers is unique. I count them all.

Thirty seagulls, all waiting for me in the dark.

The second time Ezra brings me back, sixteen trees and a horse fall to the ground.

I open my eyes to a dry, brown field, the sky above blinding white with no clouds. There's a whiff of sulfur and burnt wood in the air, like right after a close lightning strike. Ezra is on his knees at my side, turned away from me. It takes until the blood reaches my extremities for me to realize he is holding my hand.

"How long?" I ask.

Ezra doesn't answer. I sit up, pulling on his arm as a counterweight.

The field is vast, nothing but summer-fried, overgrown grass from the one-lane dirt road to the smattering of spindly trees marking the horizon. A small white farmhouse and barn stand in front of the tree line. Ezra and I passed many fields like this on childhood road trips, and we'd always marveled at the cows, the sheep, the horses that lingered along the fences watching us the same as we watched them. Fields like these—even the dead ones—always support some kind of life. There are always animals.

Once my eyes fully focus, I see what Ezra is looking at, what is right in front of us.

We're ringed by tree stumps, white oaks all jagged and broken off at various heights, some with the roots ripped up from the dusty soil. Their tops lay behind them in a starburst of singed branches and blackened leaves, as if thrown back by an explosion. Beyond these dead trees, a chestnut horse lies on her side, mouth open, head thrown back, hooves sunk in the thick grooves she left in the dirt.

"I checked before I brought you," Ezra says, eyes fixed on the horse. "There was no one here. Then, out of nowhere. . . it was too late."

I turn my hand beneath his and squeeze. His palm is cold and wet. He swallows hard, still staring at that horse, unable to look away from what he's inadvertently done, same as he stared at his guinea pigs dead in their cage the first and only time he resurrected an animal in his home.

"You couldn't have known," I say.

He helps me to my feet, but he has more trouble standing than I do. I notice his limp as we pick our way around the fallen trees and the tall grass, and I wonder how he got me out of his apartment, into the car, then into the middle of this field. He bites the insides of his cheeks with every other step, but he doesn't say a word.

I last twenty-four hours. Ezra still won't let me out of his sight, but this time I'm the one following him from room to room, talking through doors, trying to muster everything I've ever wanted to say to him before I'm gone again. He says he's fine, even as he wraps his knee, cracking jokes about the high school football injury that never was, how my ass is going to break his back next time.

We eat lunch and dinner. I cook, like all the times I tried to take care of him. I know it's close to twenty-four hours because the sky looks the same as it did in that quiet field of dead trees, that particular kind of mid-morning light after the pink edges of dawn have burned away to the promise of an overcast day. We stay up all night talking, and as I slip away—Daphne asleep on my chest, Jax and Butters curled together on Ezra's lap, Rodney snoring at our feet—I think about about how happy I am here, how I'd be satisfied with an eternity of days like this, each a lifetime encapsulated into a few hours where I'm with my best friend, this is home, and there are no angry bosses or landlords or parking tickets waiting for me in another place.

I don't remember my eyes closing, but the edges go dark as I'm telling Ezra about the seagulls that were with me.

I'm fine with this. There's a safety in knowing that I'll likely be back, that I'll get to finish the conversation or task that was so brutally truncated the last time death claimed me.

I don't know if the trees are in the darkness with me. I have no body, no way to see or reach out and touch them. The only smell here is both clean and acrid, like ozone.

The horse is here, though. I feel her close, a rich heat the same as a gathering of all those resurrected animals in Ezra's apartment. As she approaches, I brace myself for her hate, her knowing I'm the reason she is here, but that feeling never materializes. Unlike the seagulls, the horse has no one of her own kind to answer her. She nudges me, and for a brief moment I have edges, a way to feel. I'm not alone.

Turns out I wasn't lying to Ezra. It's not so bad.

The third time Ezra brings me back, a crow crashes onto the asphalt.

I open my eyes to another gray sky, just a few shades lighter than the parking lot of the abandoned Sears off Highway 99. A tower crane hovers at the far end, and in front of the building a land-use action sign advertises a new multi-unit mixed-use building. The last time Ezra and I were here we were teenagers, getting high late at night on the loading dock, thinking we could see city stars.

Wind rocks the crow's body between the faded white lines of the parking space next to us. Tits up, both little feet curled into its black feathers.

"You can't do anything about the birds," Ezra says.

It's automatic, him helping me to my feet, but this time he falls back, catching himself on a bent knee and a palm slammed hard against the ground. I try to help him up, but he refuses me. When he rises, he cradles his right arm against his chest. His limp is more pronounced as we walk to the car.

"So your arm," I say. "It's like your leg?"

"I'm fine," he says.

One crow. What will that get me, then? An hour? I've been counting the minutes of my life in dead animals, and now it will be in pieces of Ezra's body.

"It's not worth it, Ezra. I'm not your responsibility."

We get in the car, but he doesn't start the engine right away. He winces as he reaches for his seatbelt, his face and throat coated with sweat. The sedan fills with the icy spice of his deodorant, his musk fighting its way from under, and a musty sourness that I realize is my own odor. My body breaking down.

He catches me looking at him. "I said I'm fine."

"Bullshit! First your knee, now your arm? You can't tell me this isn't related."

Ezra's eyes are red, set in dark bags that weigh down his Baby-Butt face. The stubble is closing in on full-scruff, long enough to creep into the black curls that peek from around the back of his neck. How long was I gone this time, in the dark with that horse?

"I can do this, Lou," he insists, eyes fixed on the rearview mirror. He keeps his arm curled against his side. "What's the fucking point of me having this ability if I don't use it?"

"What's the point if it kills you?"

"Are you saying you don't want to live?"

I don't know.

"What about your animals?" I ask, twisting in my seat, trying to get him to look at me instead of the dead crow in the rearview mirror. "What happens to them when you're falling apart, when you can't take care of them? What if you don't get better?"

"Most of them are on borrowed time anyway."

"Why me, then? It's not like I'm out there serving my community, saving the world. I've been dead how many times now? I told you, I'm not afraid. It's peaceful and—"

"That's not true, Lou. Don't lie for my sake." Hand shaking, he pushes his key into the ignition and turns, eyes now focused there as the engine rattles to life. "I see it in the animals I bring back. I see it in their eyes when they start to slip, when their time is up. That fear, that fucking *terror* when they realize they have to go back to the dark."

He moves his hand to put the car into gear, but his arm

won't cooperate. I recognize the pain on his face, same as when I broke my wrist in the seventh grade.

"You're gonna have to drive," he says.

I die again two hours later, while Ezra's stretched out on the couch. He's still insisting he's fine, says he doesn't want to talk about it anymore, but it's not like he can talk anyway; every word becomes more and more garbled as his jaw seems to unhinge on one side, a swelling that mottles his skin from under his lip to his cheek. Jax and Butters circle him, then tuck themselves one under each of his arms. Ezra falls asleep, and I slip away right after finding Riley dead in the bathroom, next to his beach ball.

The crow is waiting for me when I reach the darkness. Her caws are insistent, piercing. She makes sure I know I'm the reason she's here.

The final time Ezra brings me back, no animals fall.

I open my eyes to the pale yellow ceiling of the stairwell in Ezra's building. I'm partially sitting up, my ass on the landing and my head tipped back onto a stair, the metal edges of the risers digging into my back. My shoulders and arms ache. I feel bruised all over, the result of a full-body tumble.

"Ezra?" I'm slow to right myself. It hurts to turn my head.

Ezra is lying on the landing above me; I recognize the waffle-patterned soles of his shoes and his fingertips curled into his palms. I can't quite walk yet, so I crawl up the stairs on my hands and knees. His eyes are open, but his expression is soft, peaceful. I know what I'm seeing, the clouds that have settled over his pupils—I saw the same thing with so many of his animals, was struck time and time again by the truth in the cliché.

With a busted knee and a busted arm, unable to speak, he dragged me out of his apartment full of animals into this stairwell with walls thick enough to protect the occupants on the other side. He didn't want me to be alone in the dark, but he died alone in the fucking stairwell of this building.

"Stubborn asshole," I whisper, curling my body around his. I press my nose into the hollow of his throat, inhaling the brine cooling on his skin. All I can think about is that janitor's closet in third grade and how long it took me to find him.

I last thirty-eight days this time. I wasn't prepared; it's too much without Ezra. We never talked about the future beyond each of those days he brought me back. I never asked if my apartment, my things, were still there. We never discussed how or if we would tell the other people in my life.

I stay in Ezra's apartment and care for his animals. I revel in their heat, surrounded by the comfort of their beating hearts until they slip away one by one. Daphne first, her little body deflating on my chest while I'm watching a movie. Rodney goes quietly at my feet, on a rare night I allow myself to fall asleep with the confidence that I'll wake up again. Butters never rouses from an afternoon nap in his favorite window. When I feel my time drawing to a close, I give Jax, the only animal that was never resurrected, to a neighbor.

Borrowed time. We both said it.

The last time I die is in Ezra's bed, watching the sun burn up an ink-blue sky.

In the darkness, I expand until I have edges. I search.

Even without sight or sound, it doesn't take long for me to realize I'm not alone. I reach until I feel Ezra in the dark.

As with many of my stories, "With Animals" started with a first line, a vague notion of where it might go, and not much else. I wanted to tell a necromancy story from the point of view of the resurrected person, and let my characters develop and lead me from there. What I got was an ending much different from the darker one I envisioned halfway through. This is a story about friendship and the price paid when two people are willing to do anything for each other.

The title is taken from the Mark Lanegan and Duke Garwood song of the same name. It's a favorite, and as I found myself listening to it over and over again while writing, all the pieces fell into place.

J.A.W. McCarthy
Seattle, WA
June 5, 2021

J.A.W. McCarthy's short fiction has appeared in numerous publications, including *Vastarien, LampLight, Apparition Lit, Tales to Terrify*, and *The Best Horror of the Year Vol 13* (ed. Ellen Datlow). Her debut collection *Sometimes We're Cruel and Other Stories* will be published by Cemetery Gates Media in August 2021. She lives with her husband and assistant cats in the Pacific Northwest, where she gets most of her ideas late at night, while she's trying to sleep. You can call her Jen on Twitter and Instagram @JAWMcCarthy, and find out more at www.jawmccarthy.com.

THE GRIEVOUS ART OF COMPULSION

AVRA MARGARITI

Sleep, sweet son, and dream what you like best.
This, I whispered in your ear during the latest siege
of our jeweled city, our home for all your young life.
How could I stand idle and watch you weep
as the liquid fire put the sun to shame?
Schoolhouse ruins, ominous mist,
a multiplication of death in ditches.
How was I to know you'd never wish to leave
the dreamland I wove for you in a spell
of dread devotion?

Vainly, I tried to coax you back to me
with promises and curses, wetting your forehead,
maneuvering atrophic limbs.
My only son, forever lost to the gods
of slumber.

Your father—violin virtuoso and renowned composer—had
suffered a similar fate at my luckless hands.
Play something for me, I had told him

palms resting over my convex belly.
How was I to know he would play himself to death?
Fingers blistering and bleeding, yet never once
relinquishing rosined bow and strings,
sweat a beadwork on his forehead, dripping
on the polished wood instrument
as his own organs gave out.
I tried to pry his violin away, ordered him to stop,
but afterward I could do naught but watch him
waste away. Only his plangent music lingered,
a haunted violin attached to its cadaver
through flesh and fluids.

You are still and placid now, sweet son,
but I remember how you once danced inside me
to the final staves of your father's swan song.

In Athens, sometimes you look at the sky and it's burning red and liquid from some distant summer wildfire. When I used to play a musical instrument, I was urged to spend hours on end hunched over the keys, never mind my cramping fingers. Sleep is the getaway of many an escapist (and I am one of them).

Avra Margariti
Athens, Greece
June 4, 2021 (the small hours)

Avra Margariti is a queer author, Greek sea monster, and Pushcart-nominated poet with a fondness for the dark and the darling. Avra's work haunts publications such as

Vastarien, Asimov's, Liminality, Arsenika, The Future Fire, Space and Time, Eye to the Telescope, and *Glittership. The Saint of Witches,* Avra's debut collection of horror poetry, is forthcoming from Weasel Press. You can find Avra on Twitter (@avramargariti).

MOIRA AND ELLIE

MARISCA PICHETTE

Radha got her imaginary friend before me. We were walking home from school on Tuesday when she stopped and stared at the fence. I kept walking until I realized she wasn't with me anymore. When I looked back, she was smiling.

"What's your name?"

Obviously, she wasn't talking to me. We'd known each other since we were babies. Still, a part of me wished she were. I didn't have an imaginary friend, not yet. I was almost eight. Radha was just a little over seven-and-a-half.

Some people got theirs as early as four. For others, it didn't happen till they were nine. Radha and I had been waiting, counting the months as they passed, looking everywhere for our imaginaries. We didn't mind that we were getting a little old, 'cause we were together.

Until now.

Radha giggled, a low, treacherous sound. She faced the fence, cow parsley and goldenrod leaning through the chain-link. I wondered what her imaginary looked like.

She looked at me, joy and surprise filling her face. "Jenna!"

I walked back to her, my stomach twisted and empty. I wanted to get home to dinner. I didn't want to stay, hearing one half of a conversation I couldn't be part of. Radha beamed. "Her name is Xin!"

Not really sure what to do, I forced a smile at the blank spot in front of the fence. "I have to get home," I said. I left Radha with her imaginary and ran the rest of the way.

That first week, Radha ignored me. She tried not to, asking me to come with her when Xin wanted to show her the places she used to play when she was alive. We went to the old school and an overgrown soccer field. Xin led Radha and Radha led me through the trees to a rock that her imaginary remembered standing on, pretending to be a queen. From the places we went I could tell that Xin had died a long time ago, though not really, *really* long. Not like Fran's imaginary, Judith. According to Fran, Judith didn't recognize any of the places around here. Only the distant hills hadn't changed since her death.

Eventually I got tired of following Radha around. I went straight home after school and sat in the living room, cutting pictures out of the catalogues my mom let pile up on the coffee table. I cut out trees and animals and some people, but mostly other things. With a glue stick I pasted the images to my notebooks and folders, covering them completely. I liked the pictures.

My mom told me what to call what I had made: collage.

I stopped talking to Radha, but I don't think she minded. She spent all her time with Xin. Sometimes I heard her in the hallway at school, speaking words from another language to the blankness in front of her. It weirded me out, and I stayed even farther away.

The school has a rule: imaginaries are permitted in classes, but we can't talk to them. Some imaginaries like to come back to school, remember what it was like when they were alive. They hear the familiar lessons and maybe they talk to each other. I actually don't know if imaginaries can see other imaginaries. I know they can all see us. We just can't see them. Except *our* imaginary, but I don't have one yet.

Some of the imaginaries, like Fran's Judith, are so old that being at school is new to them. The lessons are like magic, talking about things they never learned about when they were alive. I wondered what it would be like for them to see a college class. Maybe they would learn even more. But the imaginaries disappear before we're old enough to go to college. They never stay past a twelfth birthday.

My mom said that this was because the imaginaries had to go before you got too old for them. Imaginaries had to stay close in age to us, and when we got too old they disappeared. I wondered where they went when they left. Did they come back for someone else? I'd never heard of them remembering other people. Maybe they just came once, and then went away.

One day when I walked home, Radha stayed at the school with Xin. She'd had her for a couple of months now. I turned eight yesterday.

Something was wrong when I got home. I could hear crying. When I followed the sound I found my sister, Matilda, in her room, lying across her bed. Her hair flopped around her head. She was lying on her stomach, her face buried in the covers.

I stood in the doorway, not sure what to do. Matilda never cried. She was tough, beating up other kids when they commented on how her body was bigger than theirs. She had started getting boobs, swelling from her chest to match her size, which made her look older than her classmates, and also made her angrier. My sister was eleven-and-a-half. I loved Matilda, but sometimes she scared me.

Her imaginary scared me too. I couldn't see him, of course, but Matilda talked to him a lot, especially at night. He made her do things. I didn't like it.

"Matilda?" I said. I was still standing in the doorway, in case she yelled at me to go away. Or started talking to Klaus.

"H-he's gone," she mumbled into the bed. Her shoulders shook. I crossed my arms, holding tight.

"Who?" But I knew who.

"Klaus. He. . . he went away."

Matilda went quiet, her face still hidden. I backed out of her room and went to my own. I wasn't sure why her crying made me happy. Not really happy, just. . .

I didn't have an imaginary. At least Matilda didn't either.

Lots of imaginaries don't remember how they died. Maybe it's too scary for them to remember. Some are older than others, but they all died young. Sometimes it was illness, like with Judith. Fran said she was thin and pale and wore a white dress that looked like a wedding gown, or a shroud. Judith didn't remember dying, Fran said, but she remembered being very sick.

Sometimes they killed themselves. I didn't like those ones. Sometimes accidents happened, or didn't. But imaginaries looked the way they remembered looking, so you never saw the blood. You didn't see them like they were buried. Or not.

Everything I knew about imaginaries came from my friends. They talked about theirs all the time, comparing personalities and experiences. Xin was bubbly, but Judith was quiet and shy. Klaus was mean. I was glad he was gone. Maybe Matilda would be nicer.

The day after Matilda lost her imaginary, I got mine. I was at school, in the bathroom. I flushed the toilet and went to the sink and there was a girl standing next to it. She had eyes that seemed to droop on the ends, pulling at her face. Her skin was almost yellowish, her hair very short. I had never seen her before.

I glanced at her, then washed my hands. She didn't seem to be in the bathroom for a reason. She wasn't looking in the mirror or using the stalls. She was just standing there, looking at me.

I finished washing my hands and stuck them under the air blower. It roared to life and the girl flinched, her eyes widening at the sound. I pulled my hands away, guilty for scaring her. "Sorry," I said, though the machine continued to blow air where my hands had just been.

She didn't look at the blower, her gaze still fixed on me. It made my head itch.

"Um." I waited, but she didn't seem to want to say anything. I almost walked out of the bathroom, left her there. But there are ways to introduce yourself, even when you're not sure whether you should.

"I'm Jenna. What's your name?"

She blinked, her face lightening. "Moira."

When she said it, I heard it somewhere other than my ears. It was like she was speaking more from her eyes than her mouth, and I was hearing through my eyes too.

"Are. . . are you an imaginary? I mean—" my heart beating —"are you *my* imaginary?"

Shyly, she nodded. She looked real enough, not fuzzy or anything that told me she wasn't really there. I reached out, wondering if I could touch her. My hand passed over her shoulder, and I almost twitched back. She felt like a leaf on a tree, smooth and hard but thin. When I tried to hold on, her smoothness slipped away from my hand, like trying to grab hold of a leaf when you couldn't find the edge.

"How old are you?"

Moira's sloping eyes drifted, thoughts or memories pulling her away before she returned. I heard that it could feel weird for imaginaries when they first appeared after their death. They didn't know how the world had changed, or how much time had gone by.

"I'm ten," Moira said with her gaze.

I brought her back to class with me, but I couldn't talk to her. I sat at my desk and she stood beside me, watching our teacher with no particular interest. For the rest of the history lesson I never once looked at Mr. Williams. I examined Moira, her strangely sad face and her shorn hair. Her clothes were old-fashioned, not *really* old. She wore a faded red dress that looked like cotton, with tiny yellow flowers all over it. Her shoes were scuffed, little brown boots that would be too small for me, even though she was older.

When class finally ended I jumped up and rushed over to Radha. She was already talking to Xin, and when she saw me surprise dotted her face. We hadn't spoken in weeks.

"Radha, I met my imaginary."

Her eyes widened. She looked around the classroom, even though she wouldn't be able to see Moira any more than I could see Xin. "Where are they? What's their name?"

I looked at Moira. She'd followed me over to Radha. "Her name is Moira. She's ten."

Radha grinned. "Hi, Moira!" she said to the space next to me, almost exactly where Moira was standing. "I'm Radha. This"—she gestured to the space to the left of her—"is Xin. She's six."

Moira stared at the space. From her expression, I couldn't really tell if she could see Xin or not. "How did you die?" she asked, her voice almost a whisper, almost asking no one. But I knew then that she was talking to Xin. She could see her, just like Radha.

I looked at the space, then at Radha. Radha was looking at

the space where Xin stood, her brow rumpled in confusion. "What?" she said.

"Moira asked how Xin died," I felt compelled to explain, though I didn't know if Radha was confused by Xin's silent reply or something else her imaginary had said, something unrelated to Moira or death.

Radha looked at me, sharp and cold. "It's not nice to make her remember. Moira should know better."

She grabbed her backpack and left the classroom. I stayed behind, staring at the space that almost definitely no longer held Xin, who surely followed Radha everywhere. Was it rude to ask? Imaginaries appeared right after they died. It was the last thing they experienced before they came to us. Why shouldn't they talk about it? It's what they all had in common.

I wanted to know how Moira died. But maybe she didn't remember.

Instead, I said, "Let's go home. You can see my house."

Moira liked my room, I think. She wandered around looking at the pictures and the glow-in-the-dark stars on the ceiling. I showed her my notebooks and folders with the collages I'd made, and she even smiled. After that, I wasn't sure what to do with her.

"Do you need somewhere to sleep?"

She seemed confused. "I don't."

"Don't sleep?"

She shook her head, a jerky motion. I sat on my bed, cross-legged and holding my feet. She stood by the window. She looked just like anybody else. The light didn't go through her, but she didn't cast a shadow either. It was like she was a paper doll pasted to a background with only the illusion of light. She looked real, but didn't really touch anything. The light didn't know she was there, so it didn't make a shadow for her.

"What happened to your hair?" I asked.

Moira touched her head, her face taking on that thin, confused look again. Maybe there was more that she couldn't remember, besides her death. "It got shaved off," she said.

I touched my own hair. "How? Who did it?"

She didn't answer.

Matilda didn't come to dinner that night, so I didn't introduce her to Moira. She must have been sulking. Matilda would hate finding out that I had an imaginary now, so soon after she lost Klaus. I didn't really care. I told my parents about Moira and my mom was happy that I'd finally gotten an imaginary.

"I remember mine," she said, smiling. "His name was Yves."

"What was he like?" My mom had talked a little about her imaginary before, but I never paid a lot of attention. I was always thinking about Klaus, the only other boy imaginary I knew. I was afraid all boy imaginaries were like him. It wasn't until I got my own imaginary that I wanted to know more.

"He was quiet. I think he was around your age. He liked to read a lot. I used to open books for him and flip the pages so he could learn all sorts of things. I got him when I was five, and he would read aloud to me, if I would flip the pages." Her eyes shone with the memory.

"How did he die?"

Mom shook her head. "I don't know."

We finished dinner, my dad talking about other things.

He had to wait to meet his imaginary. Boys didn't get them until they were old. Their imaginaries came when their own memories started fading, when they needed help walking and seeing and using the bathroom. Before my grandfather died, he had an imaginary named Helen. He used to talk to her all the time, even when we came to visit. I don't think he knew she wasn't alive. She stayed with him right until he died. The nurse said he was talking to Helen at the end. It made my mom feel happy, that he hadn't been alone.

But it didn't always happen that way. Some of the kids at school were born boys but weren't meant to be. They met imaginaries when they were young, like girls.

My mom had a friend who wasn't a boy or a girl. I asked them if they ever got an imaginary. They said that they got more than one, that they had one when they were little, then it left and they grew older and met one again, one who had died as an adult. They said that when they got really old, they were sure they would meet another, one who was old like them.

I thought about this, about being able to see imaginaries who hadn't died when they were little. What was it like when they'd died in college, or after having kids of their own? Men had imaginaries who had lived entire lives. Did they still not remember how they died? Could they still have killed themselves, like some of the young imaginaries did?

After dinner I went upstairs, Moira following. She didn't say anything, didn't ask me anything. I wished she'd talk more. Radha talked a lot. I wondered how Xin had died.

When I got in bed Moira stayed standing by the window, neither blocking nor letting the moonlight past.

On my first weekend with Moira, we walked to the ice cream shop from my house. It wasn't really a shop, just a little cart parked in a lot that sold ice cream in the summer and closed up every October, boxed in by used cars. I got strawberry and Moira watched me eat it, sitting in the sandy grass. Chewing the sweet, soggy tip of the sugar cone, I asked her how she died.

"Someone pushed me," she said, her voice thin and wavering as always. "I fell and hit my head." Her hand touched the side of her head. I thought that it looked a little flattened, but I was probably imagining it.

"Did it hurt?"

Moira frowned, her face drooping. "I don't think so."

"Who pushed you?"

I imagined Matilda pushing that girl Hattie for calling her fat, Matilda kicking Joey between his legs because he grabbed her, Matilda waiting for our mom to come pick her up because she punched a white girl at recess.

Moira twisted her fingers through the laces of her shoes. "My sister," she said.

My ice cream was gone, leaving my hands cold and sticky. I stared at my own shoes, battered sneakers with peeling, glittery red plastic bits. For a few seconds I picked at them, pulling off pieces and dropping them in the grass. I wanted to ask Moira why her sister pushed her, whether she meant to kill her (some imaginaries were murdered). After a while, though, I got up, and she followed me home.

Matilda was out with friends. I showed Moira her room and talked about Klaus. I told Moira that I never liked him, didn't like how he made Matilda act. When she was younger she would use him as an excuse, telling Mom that he told her to do this, to say that. Whether he did or not, I hated him for it. He made her hard before she had to be.

We were still in Matilda's room when she came home. I

rolled off her bed and went to the top of the stairs, Moira following. Matilda was taking off her shoes, her T-shirt darkened with sweat. She looked up at us—at me.

"You better not have been in my room," she said. I shrugged. Moira moved back from the stairs, retreating almost to the wall. She distracted me, pulled my gaze from Matilda.

"What's wrong?" I asked.

Moira's eyes were wide, her face stuck in fear.

Matilda came up the stairs. As she passed, she gave me a shove. "Quit talking to people who aren't there," Matilda said. I stumbled, catching myself on the railing before I slipped down the stairs. Matilda didn't notice. She shut the door to her room with a snap.

When I looked at Moira, she was trembling. I walked over to her, tried to grasp her again. My hand slid away.

"What was your sister's name?"

I didn't really think about the question before it came out. Moira was still shaking, her faded dress jumping around her thin legs. "Ellie."

"Hey," I said, "that's my mom's name too!"

She just looked at me.

Moira stopped talking whenever we were at home. I took walks so she would speak to me, but I didn't ask her about her sister or her life. Sometimes she recognized places we went, but she never had much to say. She wasn't like Xin, who taught Radha how to speak Mandarin.

My mom just smiled and said it was good that I'd finally gotten an imaginary, and to have fun with her before I grew up and she went away.

I tried. I tried to have fun. But Moira was sad, and scared, and quiet. I missed Radha.

On the day Matilda broke Joey's nose, Mom came to pick her up and decided to get me too. We got into the car, ignoring the yells from Joey's mom about how she would sue our family and have Matilda thrown out of the school. Mom tried to reason with Matilda, telling her that violence wasn't the answer and she should always talk through her problems with people. Matilda snapped that Joey had no right to touch her and there was only one way to take things when boys didn't listen to your words.

Moira and I sat in the back. I was looking out the window, watching the houses go past. Every time I looked over at Moira, she was watching Mom.

"Was your sister older or younger than you?"

I was asking Moira, but the car jerked. Mom's hands gripped the wheel, her eyes piercing me through the rearview mirror. "What are you talking about, Jenna? I never had a sister."

"You did," Moira said.

I looked from Moira to Mom. "Did you?"

"Did I *what*, Jenna?"

I was going to ask if she did have a sister, after all. But looking at Moira, I began to see something in her eyes, something in her nose and mouth that reminded me of Matilda. And of Mom.

"Did you have a sister?" I said.

The car scraped to a stop. Mom turned around in her seat. Her face was twisted in anger like I'd never seen before. She was different, terrifying.

"Don't you *ever* suggest such a rude, ridiculous thing!" she said, spluttering and tripping over her anger. "Will I have to start watching you too? You and Matilda both?"

That set Matilda off. She uncrossed her arms, turning away from the window where she'd been sulking. "Joey deserved what he got! You wouldn't know what it's like, being Black in this damn school! You're an entitled—"

She didn't get any further, because Mom slapped her. Moira twitched beside me, and I shrank into my seat.

"I will not have my daughter speak to me like that—"

"You won't ever understand," Matilda interrupted. And before Mom could reply, Matilda got out and stalked away from the car. She was heading away from home. She must've been going to a friend's house.

Mom stared in shock at Matilda's empty seat.

"Confess," Moira said.

Mom looked back at us. She couldn't have heard Moira, but there was something off in her eyes. "It was an accident," she whispered, her voice cracking over the words. She wasn't looking at me anymore, her gaze on the seat beside me, the seat that held Moira.

"I didn't. . . it was just. . . I was a child!"

Through the windshield I watched Matilda jog across the street. She didn't look before crossing.

"*I* was a child," Moira said. I wondered if Mom heard her.

Matilda screamed. I looked out the window and saw her running to the other side of the road. A truck had come around the corner, speeding toward her. I could see her dashing in front of it, the headlights reflecting the sunlight and stinging my eyes. The truck braked, tires squealing as the driver tried to avoid Matilda. She just barely made it to the other side. I don't think she got hurt.

Mom turned, tears on her cheeks. We both saw the truck swerve across the lane toward where we were parked on the other side of the road. We watched it wobble, and fall, and skid toward us.

What happens to an imaginary when their person dies? Do they disappear, or find someone else? Can they move without someone to follow?

I remember the screeching, the crash, but I suppose I don't remember the exact way I died. From the moment the truck hit us until the time I appeared on the playground, there was nothing.

Some things had changed, though. The school was bigger, the kids different. I could see all of them; I could also see the imaginaries, their edges smooth and sharp. They looked less real now that I was one of them.

I didn't know which one was mine, which I was meant to follow. Standing alone on the side of the playground, I waited for someone to ask me my name.

"Moira and Ellie" started in the Montessori classroom I was working in, during nap time. Sitting beside a student as they drifted off to sleep, I wondered what the world might be like if children's imaginary friends were really ghosts. I scribbled a note to that effect, and wrote the full story during the second semester of my MFA program. This story is one of my favorites, and after a year of searching for a home, I'm so pleased it found its way into this anthology.

Marisca Pichette
Deerfield, MA
June 5, 2021

Marisca Pichette is a bisexual author of speculative fiction, nonfiction, and poetry. She earned her BA from Mount Holyoke College and MFA from Stonecoast. Her work has been published in *PseudoPod, Daily Science Fiction, Apparition Lit, Room, Channel,* and *The NoSleep Podcast,* among others. Her debut novel, *Broken,* is forthcoming in Spring 2022 with Heroic Books. A lover of moss and monsters, she lives in Western Massachusetts. She is on Twitter @MariscaPichette.

CRY ME A RIVER

STEPHANIE ELLIS

Jackie felt the drip on her arm and looked up. A network of lagging and foil-wrapped pipes wove their way across the ceiling. Leak or condensation, she wasn't quite sure, but she would report it after she'd fulfilled her output quota for the day; another hour, another hundred watts, precious energy being fed into the grid. She continued to pedal furiously on the stationary bike, disregarding the soreness, the blood which still seeped from her body, the tenderness of her breasts. The screen in front of her displayed the reason for her effort, caused her milk to leak in response, added to her distress.

Louise. One month old but two months early. Tubes ran in and out of her fragile body, monitors around the incubator beeped and fluctuated. This was not how she had imagined motherhood. No more than two years had passed from the time when it would've been flowers and congratulations, walks with the pram in the park, the coos and the fuss. A family unit; the glow of being a new mother. Not on her own, down in the dark. Not like this.

It wasn't even really a gym. It was officially a Generator

Unit, an addition to the bunker's power supply dreamt up by the council's scientists. It was one of the few remaining places in the complex capable of adding to the power grid, and the incubator was a greedy beast. Most were sceptical at how effective this really was, but when there were no alternatives, you could do nothing but hope for the best. You sat on the bike and pedalled. Especially when your baby was at risk. Everyone was expected to put in some time in the gym, but Jackie rarely saw anyone else in there and today she was on her own. The signs adorning the walls indicating how exercise was vital for mind and body had been crudely graffitied. New variations each day offered some small amusement to the gym's occupants.

Bunker. That, too, was a misnomer. The underground stronghold was more like a small city. It was here remnants of government had taken refuge, together with specially selected scientists, engineers, and health professionals. Only when the doors had closed did she discover how many places had been bought by big business. It had left the complex dangerously understaffed, full of dead-weight bureaucrats with no skills but the money and contacts to buy themselves a place. She had considered herself lucky when chosen, her husband a doctor, herself a nurse; now, she knew better.

An alarm brought her back to the present. Her output was dropping. She refocussed on the image of their—*her*—daughter. It was just the two of them now. Soon, she hoped, they would finally let her see her baby, hold her at last. Parted immediately at birth, Louise had been whisked away to the incubator which, at the time, was allowed full access to the bunker's electricity supply. Jackie, meanwhile, had been pushed back to work as soon as she could move, staff shortages and high casualty numbers following a disastrous foray above ground demanding her presence even though she was still stiff, sore, and leaking. The only consideration she was given was time to express her milk at regular intervals. Vital, they said, to strengthen her daughter's immune system, help her in her fight to live. Jackie *knew* that. They didn't have to tell her. Strange they would give her that time but not allow her near her daughter. A mother's touch. Skin to skin. Vital contact for a newborn.

Eventually the alarm went off again, but this time Jackie was able to slow down and stop. As she dismounted, she realised her arm tingled slightly. Whatever had dripped had left a small red mark. Her shower, however, eased the itch and she soon forgot about it.

In her uniform once more, Jackie made her way back into the wards, pausing at the shadowy bay window revealing the dimly lit baby unit beyond. Louise was in there, but Jackie was never allowed any closer. She pressed her face close to the glass, her hand against its cold surface. If only she could push her way in. The door was nearby but it was key-coded, and she had not been allowed the combination—for her own good. She worked with people who regularly went above ground, could be exposed to pollutants or the virus which had wiped out so many. She didn't want to pass that on to her baby, did she? Soon though, they told her. Soon, she would be able to hold her. They had been saying that for weeks.

"Jackie?"

Tamsin Sewell appeared at her side. Glamorous in pre-bunker life, she remained so in their underground world. Even the gym appeared to agree with her, not that they'd ever been there at the same time. She'd never thought they would be friends, but since both had babies in the same unit, were experiencing the same agonising wait for their child's improvement, they had bonded. The only difference being Tamsin was allowed in to see her child. Money still talked, even down here.

"Will you look in on Louise for me?" she asked.

Tamsin nodded. "I feel so guilty," she said. "I mean, they let me in, but not you. . . "

"It's the right thing," said Jackie, reluctantly. "You know what I could be exposed to. I can't risk it, even with the tests they give me."

She watched as Tamsin took the usual swab test required before entering the unit.

"But it's still hard, isn't it?" said Tamsin, as the green light flashed its welcome at her.

"I don't know how much longer I can bear it."

"Don't worry," said Tamsin. "I'm sure they'll let you in soon. Our babies are getting stronger."

Jackie smiled at her attempt to make her feel better. At least she could talk to Tamsin; she understood. For her, though, work was calling. Exhausted, and with a heavy heart, she turned and walked away.

Tamsin tapped in the combination and entered the ward. Headed over to the incubator holding her own little girl. The nurse lifted her out and Tamsin opened her blouse so her baby could feel her skin, took the bottle of milk to feed her hungry child. Ivan hadn't wanted her to breastfeed, hadn't wanted to see her body ruined. Her appearance was important to him. The archetypal trophy wife even in these straitened circumstances. Silently, she thanked Jackie, even though the woman knew nothing about her gift.

"She's getting stronger every day," said the nurse. "Won't be long before you'll be able to take this little one home. I'll come back in an hour."

Tamsin was left on her own. She cradled her daughter close, breathed in her baby smell, stroked the soft down of her cheek, sang her the lullabies her own mother had once sung to her. She looked across to the other incubator, empty and silent. The name tag lying there the only remnant of its occupant. She thought of Jackie, didn't realise she was crying until she felt a small drip on her arm.

The ward was relatively quiet for once, although it was still full enough to keep Jackie and the three other nurses—the only other nurses—busy. They should not all have been rostered at the same time, but there had been no choice and patients and rotas had blurred into one great mess. When she had first been told she was part of the medical team, there had been a list of at least forty nurses with varying specialisms. The reality had been half that, the places bought and disguised beneath fake qualifications until they were safely below ground. Numbers had dropped further as those who went above ground with the scavengers failed to return, whilst some of those who remained below became so demoralised they chose to take their own lives. Sometimes Jackie had considered joining their number. She had come closest when her husband had died, electrocuted by malfunctioning equipment, but Louise had kept her going.

"You should go and rest," said Deb. "You look done in. We can manage here."

"You've all done more than enough covering for me," said Jackie. "I should stay."

"No," said Deb, this time taking her arm and guiding her to the door. "You need to keep your strength up for Louise. Us three, we don't have anyone. You have your daughter. She needs you. Have you seen her yet?"

"They still won't let me in," said Jackie.

Deb frowned. "That really isn't right, you know. I mean, if

you need to take precautions, why can't you just use a mask and gloves like we used to? And they've got the testing as well."

Jackie shrugged, too tired to argue.

"Go and rest," repeated Deb. "Then tomorrow you should go and see her. Demand to see her. I'll come with you."

"Okay," said Jackie. "After I've done my morning stint in the gym. I'll come and find you."

She allowed herself to be pushed out of the ward and was soon asleep, fully clothed, on her bed. Her alarm went off at the usual time, 7 a.m. She had managed a full six hours sleep, a luxury these days. For once she felt she had the energy to confront anything. She breakfasted as quickly as possible and made her way to the gym. Two bikes were already occupied but their riders soon dismounted and she was left on her own. She swiped her ID card across the bike's tracker and the screen opposite came on so she could see Louise once more. Her arms ached to hold her. *Soon, sweetheart,* she murmured. *Soon.*

Jackie clambered onto the bike and started to cycle. A small red light in the corner of the room flashed, but she paid it no attention. Lights and alarms were always going off these days.

"Good morning, darling," said Tamsin, pouring out coffee for both of them. He kissed her on the cheek and flicked on the screen. Cameras showed Jackie in the gym and their little Jessica in her incubator. They ate in silence, quietly contemplating the scenes in front of them, only rousing themselves when the lights in their suite dimmed suddenly. A high-pitched squeal came from the baby unit, and Tamsin saw with horror that the lights there, too, were failing. Her husband didn't seem too worried.

"They're going to let Jess out in a couple of days," said Ivan. "All we need is power to keep the unit going that long, give her the best possible start. The energy generated in the gym this morning will give us that."

"She could probably survive without it," said Tamsin, thinking it would put an end to her encounters with Jackie. Her complicity in the woman's suffering was like acid eating away at her.

"I don't deal in 'probably,'" said Ivan. "Only certainties. The doc has said at least two days before they give her Approval, so we'll give Jessica two days."

A cry coming from Jackie's screen drew their attention to the woman. She was still cycling but rubbing her arm and looking up at the pipes. She looked as though she was about to stop, get off. . .

"No, no, no," muttered Ivan. "That will not do." He went over to his computer, tapped furiously at the keyboard. JPEGs of reality were flipped and distorted, sent to Jackie's monitor feed.

Jackie felt another drip; it stung just like the first one. She glanced up at the pipework and saw a small rivulet of liquid streaming along the pipe. Something had ruptured. Now she knew she had to call an engineer. Another drip. Another sting. This time she looked at her arm and noticed the angry weal forming where the liquid had made contact with flesh. It looked like a chemical burn. She continued to cycle, although at a slower pace; she could afford a minute to wash off whatever it was with the water from her drinking bottle. She'd just sluiced it away when a flashing light on her monitor drew her attention back to Louise. Alarms were going off and the lights were flickering. The unit was running out of power. Figures flashed up at the bottom of the screen, told her how much was needed—and needed now—to keep the incubator functioning, not just for storage. The levels were critical. If she stopped, Louise could. . .

It didn't bear thinking about. Jackie cast a glance up at the pipework, prayed it would hold and started to pedal faster. The baby unit continued to emit its warnings and Jackie felt another splash on her skin. More this time, fierce in its heat. She had no water left to wash it off.

Ivan poured himself another coffee, finished his bacon and eggs. His daughter's incubator had stabilised but she still needed a little more power to make sure the next two days ran smoothly. He tapped at the keyboard again, sent more warnings to Jackie's monitor, watched as her desperation grew and her pedalling became more frantic.

"It isn't right," said Tamsin softly as she watched the screen.

"No? I didn't hear you complain earlier," said Ivan. "Keep her alive at any cost, you said."

"I know, but. . . "

"But nothing. There was a choice to be made, the unit could only sustain one child. That woman's baby, or ours. Luckily, hers died."

Lucky? No Tamsin couldn't think that. At times she thought it had been just too convenient. When their babies had been born, when Ivan had told her of Louise's death, he had refused to look her in the eye. It was, after all, the answer to their prayers. The feeling, however, he had had something to do with it had eaten away at her, a corrosive suspicion which refused to leave her.

"Why couldn't she be told? We could have found someone to power the unit."

"Darling. Really? Only the strong are permitted to survive down here. Remember, the doctor said we could not waste resources on the weak, and that included Jessica—unless we found someone willing to work for her survival. And nobody else down here could give the time."

Tamsin thought of the other mothers in the bunker. How they had all looked away when she had asked for help, their own children came first. They could not expend the precious energy they needed themselves for another woman's child.

"I could've. . . "

"No. You need to keep your strength up. Think of the future."

The future. Ivan wanted a son. Wanted to build a reflection of his former empire down here. Changed circumstances had not changed his self-belief—or his greed. He considered the changed world offered new opportunities and he would be the one to grab them.

She nodded at the screen. "You could've. . . "

"*Me*? Now that is funny. I have a. . . certain position to maintain. If anyone saw me down there. . . well, I'd lose all respect."

She looked at Ivan. Overweight, even in these straitened times, he had done nothing since they had taken up their precious bunker place. She had caught the looks flashed their way, heard the whispers from those few who actually managed to keep the complex going. Tamsin couldn't blame them, even she despised herself, had come to loathe her husband. She moved closer to the screen, noticed something shifting in the ceiling.

"Didn't you oversee a maintenance audit on the pipes down there recently?"

She recalled seeing him looking at the bunker plans, examining the work schedule passed his way. Something else he manipulated. Aboveground, he'd been a fixer, that was how he'd made his money and a leopard doesn't change its spots. Belowground, he'd simply played the same old games, playing people off against each other with himself being the ultimate benefactor.

He looked annoyed and ignored her question.

She remembered though. Everybody was supposed to contribute to bunker life, do their fair share, and so teams and work rotas had been drawn up. But just like before, there were ways of getting out of it, or simply signing something off when in fact nothing had been done. All it needed was somebody to provide the appropriate signature of authority, and that had been her husband. It was how they both had avoided being caught up in the drudgery of work.

Jackie suddenly cried out as more liquid poured onto her arm from above. Her skin felt as if it was on fire. She looked up and saw the drip from the pipes had become a continual rush. . . but the monitor was still showing a power failure in her baby's cot.

She couldn't move to another bike, they were all wired up to feed different aspects of the complex. Nor would anyone allow the backup generator to be used for Louise. Times had become so difficult the edict had come down that only healthy babies would receive support, those who received Approval. Others would be left for nature to take its course. A difficult decision, the Director of the Complex had said, but one which they surely understood was necessary? Even

Tamsin's husband had been unable to get that rule changed. Jackie had to remain on her bike but, Christ, it bloody well hurt.

Another splash, and this time she tore her gaze away from the screen and looked at her arm, staring in horror as her skin started to bubble and dissolve. She screamed. She wanted to get away, but the screen showed Louise moving in apparent distress. The numbers on the monitors were dipping alarmingly. It meant she needed more oxygen, needed more nutrients in her body. All of this controlled by the machines her efforts were powering. To stop now risked her daughter going into cardiac arrest.

She continued to cycle, gritted her teeth as the burning continued, although the rate of spread appeared to have lessened. An all-too-brief respite, as she soon felt another drip, this time on her shoulder. The leak above was shifting, spreading backwards so she was more central beneath it. She screamed louder this time, pressed an emergency button to alert the engineers on duty. Another splash. The smell was sharp, bitter. Whatever was coming out of the pipes was acidic and it was eating into her with a fury no fire could match.

"Help!" She could barely get the word out, it hurt so much.

Jackie saw a figure pass the windows of the gym, but they failed to look in, did not appear to hear her.

"Help!" she screamed again. Her cycle rate had slowed considerably, but she still did not stop, the image of her struggling daughter forcing her to keep going despite her pain and distress.

Another quick look at her shoulder showed the flesh had gone, the acid devouring tissue and muscle below. She could feel its burning tentacles spreading inside her, being picked up by her bloodstream, transported to other parts of her body, eating at her from the inside out.

"Don't," she told herself. "Stop imagining things. It's bad but. . . you. . . can. . . keep going."

Then she glanced up and saw the crack in the pipe for the first time, knew it wouldn't be long before it ruptured completely. Still, she could not afford to stop. The incubator needed fifteen more minutes. Not long under normal circumstances.

She continued to sob, tears of pain and despair streaming down her face as the hopelessness of her situation dawned on her. She knew then she would never hold Louise.

"Please," she said, hoping someone might be watching the security cameras, might see her in the gym, might hear her. "Please, look after my baby. . . "

With a last great effort, she pushed herself harder, unable to shift herself away from the leaking pipe, feeling herself being washed away, her daughter disappearing in front of her. Acid mingled with her tears, burning rivers into her cheeks, a stream flensing skin, layer by layer, down to the very core of her.

Jackie's screams had their echo in Tamsin. She could not believe what she was seeing as the pipes continued their slow rupture above the woman, pouring their corrosive contents down onto her. And still, she pedaled as if her life depended on it. No, not her life, her daughter's. All because of an illusion created by Ivan, the woman was fighting for something that wasn't real. She continued to scream until Ivan grabbed her by the shoulders, slapped her hard.

"We could've stopped it," she said. "Sent someone in to help her."

"And risk our daughter?" asked Ivan. "When we're so close to getting her fit enough for Approval?"

Approval meant Jessica would at last be looked after properly, would become a priority in terms of care. Strong babies were the future. And those who could provide them had become the greatest currency. Tamsin's position had been made quite clear. Already, the doctors had her on a nutritional improvement plan to ensure her next child would be as healthy as possible. Her next child. There was to be no respite.

"You don't have to watch," said Ivan, moving to turn off the screen, his distaste at the scene evident. He'd always been like that, capable of ordering the most horrific acts of barbarism but not wanting to witness the consequences. It meant he could deny all responsibility. Nothing to do with him.

She stayed his hand, however, a defiance surprising them both. She unmuted the screen so Jackie's screams filled their apartment. "We both watch this," she said. "This is down to us. To you."

"And Jessica? How would you have had me save her? Would you have done it differently?"

Tamsin stared at the screen and shook her head. No, she could not have done it any other way. Her baby was everything to her, and she hated what she had become. They stood in silence, watched as the timer counted down, knew Jackie would keep going until that final minute. Not long now. The nurse had stopped screaming. Her mouth and part of her throat had been eaten away. Her body looked as though someone had hacked pieces out of her, but her legs still moved. It was as if the body was on autopilot. Jackie's face, too, had dissolved, eyelids gone, eyes almost but not quite, what remained still fixed on the image in front of her. The lie she had been fed. Thirty seconds and no let up. Ten. Nine.

Slowing now, almost gone but her ghost of a mouth curving up into a nightmare smile. A mother who would do anything for her child. Three. . . two. . . one.

Ivan turned the screen off. "It's done," he said. "Jessica's safe."

A tear splashed down Tamsin's cheek, and she felt it burn, become a river of acid.

"Cry Me a River" was born when I was on a cross-trainer at the gym. Above me were large pipes running round the space, which are apparently part of the air-conditioning system. I was ploughing on when I felt a drip on my arm. I thought nothing of it, then a while later another drip. I looked up and worked out it was from the pipes. That set me thinking, what if something more harmful than water dripped on someone below, but because of that person's circumstances they couldn't remove themselves, had to endure it, no matter what.

Stephanie Ellis
Hampshire, UK
June 5, 2021

Stephanie Ellis writes dark speculative prose and poetry and has been published in a variety of magazines and anthologies, including Off Limits Press' *Far From Home* and Silver Shamrock's *Midnight in the Pentagram,* and she will also feature in the upcoming *Were Tales* from Brigids Gate Press. Her poetry has been published in the *HWA Poetry Showcase Volumes VI and VII* as well as in the collections, *The Art of Dying* and *Dark is My Playground*; her dark nursery rhymes are to be found in *One, Two, I See You*. Longer work includes the folk horror novel, *The Five Turns of the Wheel* and the gothic novella, *Bottled,* both published by Silver Shamrock. Her new short story collection, *As the Wheel Turns,* will be published in June. She is co-editor of *Trembling With Fear,* HorrorTree.com's online magazine and also co-editor at the female-centric Black Angel Press, producing the *Daughters of Darkness* anthologies. She is an active member of the HWA and can be found at https://stephanieellis.org and on Twitter at @el_stevie.

THE OPENING OF THE MOUTH

CHRISTINA WILDER

I cut through the thread that's woven between your lips. Your mouth is stained a dark red, and a memory emerges: us curled on your bedroom floor, taking stolen sips from your mother's stash of wine as your parents slept. We laughed at each other's stained mouths, our girlish giggles betraying our adolescent need to feel like proper adults. You told me that I needed to have my nails done and decided to take on the job yourself, polishing, buffing, and painting as I concentrated on keeping my hand steady in your grip.

"You'd be so pretty if you just put in the effort," you told me, and blew on my fingertips. I nearly jolted at the sensation, but laughed it off, like I did with everything.

Girls like me aren't pretty, and we are well aware of our lack of beauty. I was never what you were, and instead was always your total opposite; a pale, short, wisp of a girl forever fading in the background. Lila's friend, what's-her-name, you know, that weird girl who's into spooky stuff. The one who follows Lila around like she's in love or something. I never cared what they called me, but I cared that you might hear. But none of that matters now.

I snip another thread and watch your lips part. If your mouth wasn't sewn shut, your jaw would hang open, as if you were about to take a deep breath. You'd hate that, with your careful attention to your appearance, everything matching—eyeshadow, nail polish, dress. Lipstick.

We never talked about how we were each other's first kiss. "It's just us," you said, and it was practice, so it didn't count. Still, when Ben Keller pressed his mouth against mine in his closet at his birthday party years later, all I could think was Lila, Lila, Lila. Your mouth was softer, your laugh sweeter, and you didn't tell the whole class that you got to third base with me afterward.

You barely even spoke to me after we kissed.

I'm careful not to move the sheet that covers you, not wanting to unearth the bruises and swollen skin that will never have a chance to heal. I imagine your skin still smelling like the sunscreen you applied religiously, even on the darkest days. In my mind, I'm applying your lipstick as you lay on your bed, and you smell of coconut rather than the chemicals congealing under your flesh.

Luckily, I can take my time, as I don't have to worry about interruptions. I've taken care of our parents, the funeral home staff, and anyone else who might disturb us. I've been preparing for something like this for some time now, and your death is only a temporary setback in our future together.

A hyacinth petal falls to the floor as I work, and I set the bouquet I brought for you higher up on your chest. Hyacinth, I once told you, bloomed from the spilled blood of a slain prince, made immortal by his lover Apollo. You only shrugged and said you were going to have them clipped onto your hair at prom. I wasn't going to go, but you insisted. We'd go together, you promised, but you spent most of the night with Craig Stevenson, who placed his hands under your ribcage as you danced, petals raining down from your hair as you twirled and laughed.

The next day I called you to tell you that I didn't want to be friends anymore. You showed up on my doorstep, hair filled with wilted petals, demanding to know what it was that I did want. We stood in the April rain on my front porch, both of us soaked to the bone as I stared at the smudged stain of lipstick on your mouth and remained silent.

I wanted to confess that I wanted to smell of coconut and hyacinth, and to feel your scent on my skin. I wanted to say that I'd cross through hell to have you, and that I'd burn through every holy relic to get there. I wanted to tell you, but I couldn't speak.

I'm ready to speak now, and I need to ask you if it was truly the rain and the curve of the road, like everyone told me. I want to know if you drove into that wall to punish me. I want to hear the words from your mouth.

This is my own birthday gift. I am a spring child, an earth sign, a handful of dust. Your sign was water, cleansing, rebirth, your birthday only weeks ago. An afternoon in mid-March, the earth shaking off the cold remnants of winter with the promise of sunshine, you in this same dress, pale yellow against your dark skin. I watched your smile, your laugh, my Lila, just as I watch your mouth now as it opens after I snip the final thread.

Now I can begin. I anoint your forehead with rainwater and speak words that I don't fully understand, but I feel every syllable, every push of tongue against teeth. My fingers press against your lips, your hands, your knees as I speak dead sounds and carefully place the tip of a ceremonial dagger at these same points, telling you to awaken, arise.

You remain still.

I speak the words again, and again, but nothing changes.

The blood of the sacrificed is still dark on the blade. Everything is as it should be. What more can I give?

The dagger grows heavy in my hand. I know what I must do.

In junior high, we climbed the trees outside your house, daring each other to go higher until I tumbled to the ground and fell onto my left arm. Later you swore you could hear my bones snap. I prided myself on not screaming, only moaning in pain as you ran to tell your parents.

I don't scream now as I cut into my skin, dragging the blade down and across to pull a piece of myself free. There's so much blood, and I imagine it's your blood spilling out of me, that I've become you in some way, and now we're bound to each other.

I place a bloody strip of skin to your mouth, past your lips and onto your tongue, then push your jaw closed and watch blood leak out down your jaw.

"Now you have all of me," I whisper, my vision hazy with pain.

There's nothing. Stillness. Nothing, until your jaw seems to clench, then move back and forth, grinding. Chewing. I tighten my grip on the dagger, but I release my hold on you and watch as your throat bobs with a soft click.

Your eyelids flutter and lift. My blood drips onto the floor and down the drain with the fluids that have kept you whole, kept you pretty. Your eyes, once dark and warm, are like pearls, staring at me with a blank gaze.

"Lila," I whisper, but the hyacinth girl is gone, and you are a broken image of her.

I cannot move, but you can, and you do. You place your hand on mine, a firm, frosted grip. Your eyes, pale and empty, look at the shaking blade in my hand, and you smile.

I fall, staring up at you as you watch me. You move slowly, bones cracking as you stand and grin at me, my blood dripping on my face as you crouch down, your teeth so close to my face, my eyes, my mouth. Your jaw widens as your tongue, red and shining, lolls outside your mouth. Lips red as wine, leaning down, capturing me in a deep, biting kiss as I finally begin to scream.

"The Opening of the Mouth" is influenced by imagery from "The Burial of the Dead," the first section of "The Waste Land" by T.S. Eliot. The title comes from the ritual performed in ancient Egypt to ensure survival in the afterlife. As a bisexual, I've felt longing that had to be hidden away, the fear of discovery haunting me until I came out in my early twenties. I wanted to write a story about this fear, and about how sorrow can lead to decisions that are rooted in pure emotion and devoid of logic, which can lead to horrific results.

Christina Wilder
Tacoma, WA
June 8, 2021

Christina Wilder was born in Santiago, Chile and grew up in New Jersey and Florida. Her writing has been featured in *Coffin Bell*, the #VSS365 flash fiction anthology, the *LOVE* anthology by Black Hare Press, and #FrightGirlAutumn. She lives in Tacoma, Washington with her husband Chris and cat Bellatrix. Her Twitter handle is @christinawilder, and she can be found on Instagram @christinamwilder.

TRADITIONAL WOMEN

DONNA LYNCH

On behalf of my sisters
the demons
the succubus
the legends
the wraiths
and the witches
We are old-fashioned girls
and just like you
we all have our jobs
we all have our purpose
But times have changed
and there are so many of you
with so many things to break
so many things to lose
Sometimes it's hard to decide
what will hurt worse

Back in the day
The choices were easy
it was your kids

or your crops
or your lungs
A simpler time
overflowing with tragedy
and ironic curses
We've always said
you can't appreciate what you have
if you don't know what it is to lose
But these days
it's subtle
and complicated
You feel things are mostly okay
until you close your eyes at night
and you see
so clearly
all the things you love
inching closer to the precipice
only needing one strong gust
a heavy sigh from one of us
or simply time
and everything slips in

But please
save your gratitude
Your serenity
your sanity
are sacrifices
we are willing to make
And it's just a job
like any other
keeping the old ways alive
lest we die with them
lest you forget the tradition
of being terrified.

"Traditional Women" addresses a recurring theme in my work: embracing, rather than combating, the way women have been demonized for centuries as a means of keeping balance and justice in the world. It's my way of attempting to normalize child-eating witches and vengeful ghosts who are just doing their jobs. People will never stop being monsters, so this satisfies my desire to level the playing field in fiction.

Donna Lynch
Bel Air, MD
June 4, 2021

Donna Lynch is a two-time Bram Stoker Award-nominated dark fiction poet and author, spoken word artist, and the co-founder—along with her husband, artist and musician Steven Archer—of the dark electronic rock band Ego Likeness (Metropolis Records). An active member of the Horror Writers Association and three-time contributor to the *HWA Poetry Showcase*, her published works include the novels *Isabel Burning* and *Red Horses*; the novella *Driving Through the Desert*; and the poetry collections *In My Mouth*, *Twenty-Six*, *Ladies & Other Vicious Creatures*, *The Book of Keys*, *Daughters of Lilith*, *Witches*, and the Ladies of Horror Fiction Award-winning *Choking Back the Devil* (Raw Dog Screaming Press). She is the founder of the Garbage Witch clothing brand, a part-time tour manager, an avid cross-country driver, and a geography fanatic. She and Steven live in Maryland.

CONVERSION

KATIE YOUNG

Looking back now, I wonder if it was chance that lead us to find Saint Augustine's, or whether something else was at play even then. It's hard to concentrate over the sound of the headboard hitting the wall repeatedly in the room above me. The bed legs screech over the scarred floorboards and set my teeth on edge. I haven't really slept for days. I wonder how long a person can survive without sleep.

We met at university during my second year. I was reading classics and David was studying anatomy. A mutual friend introduced us at a house party that got really messy. I wasn't interested at first. One of David's peers had smuggled a human hand out of the lab and was dipping the dead fingers into unsuspecting victims' drinks. I made to leave shortly after he used the disembodied extremity to lift up the hem of a girl's skirt. She screamed as the cold, waxy flesh brushed her thigh, and I shot David an icy stare to let him know I thought he was a dick by association.

As I headed for the door, I felt a tug at my coat sleeve. I turned to find David, all cow eyes and unruly curls, grinning sheepishly.

"You get desensitised," he said. "Gallows humour. It's how you deal with taking a knife to them. Doesn't make it right, though. I'm not making excuses. He's a twat."

I tried not to focus on the green flecks that lit up his brown irises.

"Why are you mates with him then?"

He shrugged. "I'm not. Not really. I'm David, by the way."

He extended a hand and I hesitated slightly before taking it, relieved to find it was warm and alive, if a little clammy.

"Julia," I said, with as much disinterest as I could affect.

"Can I walk you home, Julia?"

"I'm only around the corner."

"Then can I walk you around the corner?"

He looked so earnest, I almost laughed. I turned and he followed me out into the street.

I press the heels of my palms into my eyes and try to think past the stabbing ache in my temples. When I look up at the ceiling, blood—thick and dark as molasses—oozes through the dimpled plaster, but I blink a few times and it disappears. It's impossible to tell whether it's the sleep deprivation or the other thing causing these apparitions now. The thumping has stopped, and for a second everything is eerily quiet. But then I hear it, bleeding through from the bedroom, a soft rasping that builds slowly into a cacophony of dry, sibilant voices like a swarm of flies.

David and I became a thing. Once I got used to the smell of formaldehyde that clung to his skin, he started to creep under mine. He was pretty in a preppy sort of way, and kind, and competent. He had a fondness for bad puns and his body was compact and fluid, like he was really, genuinely comfortable inhabiting his form in a way that I found inexorably attractive. After graduation, we moved to London. I started an entry-level job at a marketing agency, and David bounced around a few pharmaceutical companies until he got bored and jacked it all in to become a personal trainer.

We lived in tiny, damp studios and one-bed flats for the first couple of years, paying everything we earnt in rent for Zone 1 kudos and walkable convenience. Then we moved slowly but surely farther away from the city centre, renewing our expectations and willingness to compromise every six months or so, gradually paying less and less for a modicum more space and longer commutes. I got promoted to junior account manager, and David established a loyal client base. After a few years of living in a maisonette with a tiny garden at the ass end of the District Line, we managed to save enough for a deposit to buy our own place. The estate agent called it a bijou family home. He said it was an excellent opportunity for a young couple to put their stamp on their place. What he meant was, it was going to take more money and spare weekends than we could possibly imagine to strip the neglected three-bed Edwardian terrace back to bare bones and start again.

It was shabby and the more we scratched the surface, the more problems we found, but it didn't matter because it was ours. We could sand floorboards and paint walls any colours we liked. We could hammer picture hooks into the plaster and replace the cracked plastic light switches with chic dimmers in a brushed pewter finish. Every new cushion or rug or throw felt like putting down another root. We started to think about the future—our future—starting a family, even.

I check my phone. No new messages. I try Father O'Neill again, but it goes straight to voicemail.

"Please," I whisper. "I understand now. I'm so sorry. Please come."

The buzzing and hissing fills the whole house. It sounds like a million malicious voices fighting through TV static. It fills the space behind my ribs, shakes my heart and lungs and pushes bile up my gullet into my mouth.

David proposed on Christmas Eve. We were staying with his parents in the Cotswolds. We'd had a nice, homecooked meal, a few glasses of Cava, and watched *It's a Wonderful Life* in front of the wood burner. When I couldn't keep my eyes open any longer, we said goodnight and retired to the guest room, where David fumbled in his pocket and pulled out a box containing a little diamond solitaire.

"I'm sorry," he said. "I was going to do it in front of the family at dinner, but I bottled it."

The next morning, we opened gifts in a blissful haze, waiting until we had the full attention of David's sister, her husband, and their kids before we told them the good news. David's mother welled up and his niece asked if she could be a bridesmaid. His sister looked at my ring and said,

"That's so pretty! Very... delicate."

I glanced at her engagement ring and realised the stone must have been at least a carat. I smiled, swallowing my resentment. It was Christmas, after all, and this was the happiest day of my life.

I give in when plumes of black smoke starts pouring under the door of the living room and the screaming begins. I take a big gulp of air, cover my nose and mouth with my sleeve, and drag myself up the narrow stairs on shaky legs. When I reach the bedroom, the roar of fire sounds within, and the handle is hot to the touch.

"For God's sake, Julia! Help me! Please!"

I pull my cuff down over my hand and slam it down, shouldering the door open at the same time. There are no flames. The noise and the smoke are gone. David sits bolt upright on the bed, shoulder popping as he pulls against the restraints. His hair is slicked to his head with sweat, his bloodshot eyes burn into me. I shudder and go to pull the door shut again, but in the heartbeat it takes me to spring into action, I see his face split into a terrible, animalistic grin, far wider and showing far more teeth than physically possible.

"Julia, Rupert works for Deutsche Bank. *That's* how come Alison got married in a fucking castle in Scotland!"

"I know that!" I said, keeping my voice light and even. "I'm not saying I want anything as grand as your sister had. But I just don't see why we can't set our sights a little higher."

"What's wrong with Enfield Registry Office?"

"I don't want to get married in bloody Enfield Registry Office!"

My cheeks flushed hot and tears of frustration needled behind my eyes.

"We have to cut our cloth, darling," David said, clearly tamping down his irritation.

"I know that, but I guess. . . I'd just always imagined my wedding photos a certain way. You know? Like a lovely old building, full of character."

"The registry office has loads of character. It's a big fancy building!"

"But it's just. . . very. . . town-hallish. And it's like a marriage factory. They just want you in and out as quickly as possible. There won't be time for many pictures."

"You're being ridiculous, Julia."

"David, we only get one chance at this. I want it to be perfect."

I sink to the ground outside the bedroom with the key clenched in my fist, gripping it like a totem. I'm not sure a locked door will offer much protection from my husband if he gets free of the cuffs. It's surely just a matter of time.

"Juuulia? Juuuliaaa?" A sing-song voice seeps through the wood. "Where is your friend, the priest? Has he forsaken you?" The laughter that follows sounds like nails down a chalkboard.

I check my phone. No messages. No missed calls. I get to my knees and peep through the keyhole just in time to see David's head cock to the side with a loud crack, and keep turning until his face is upside-down on his ruined neck. I scream until my throat is hoarse.

We stumbled across the church one weekend on a drive to see some friends who had moved to the Kent coast. The ancient stone building was nestled in the hills around a pretty little village, and as soon as I saw it, I knew that's where I wanted to get married.

I looked it up online the next day when we got home. David scoffed and said there was no way we could get married in a Catholic church.

"Why not?"

"We're not Catholics, Julia!"

"But we could be. Think about it, if we join the church, we can get married at Saint Augustine's, and down the line maybe our kids could go to a Catholic school. You know how hard it is to find decent schools around our way. This could kill a lot of birds with one stone."

"You're crazy."

"I'm going to call the church."

"You can't just become a Catholic, darling. You need references or something. You need to be confirmed. You weren't even baptised!"

My mind was already spinning. Forming a plan.

"Where there's a will, there's a way, David."

Father O'Neill was an amiable man in his early fifties with a ruddy complexion and a reassuring voice. He was the priest at Saint Augustine's, and he seemed thrilled to have two more potential sheep for his flock. I managed to bite back a veritable litany of curse words when he explained that it would take more than a year to fully convert to Catholicism. I'd done my research. While Saint Augustine's accepted parishioners from other dioceses, I knew there was little point trying to fake the documentation needed to approach the church about having our wedding there. They'd ask for letters and certificates. They would want to speak to our local priest or even the bishop, so even if I managed to forge the paperwork convincingly, eventually I'd come unstuck. The easiest way to get my dream wedding was to do it by the Good Book.

But it was an arduous process spanning a liturgical year. David agreed to attend Mass with me, and to meet with Father O'Neill, but he started to get cold feet when we officially started our formal education and became catechumens.

Our lives began to revolve around the church and the community surrounding it. We swapped weekends of lie-ins, boozy brunches, and clubbing with friends for fetes and coffee mornings and bible study. I viewed it as a grift. Part of me derived some twisted pleasure from pulling the wool over people's eyes; pretending to care about the roof repair fund and the harvest festival whilst secretly thinking about my dress, what kind of flowers I'd choose, and the perfect menu for the wedding breakfast.

For me it was a means to an end. I learnt to play my role with a fervour and aplomb that would've given Meryl Streep a run for her money. I thought about those photos, counted down the months and weeks until we'd be baptised, confirmed, and receive the Eucharist. I repeated *it's just a year, it's just a year,* over and over like a mantra and clung to the thought that, come spring, we'd be fully ensconced in the picturesque bosom of Saint Augustine's congregation.

But the deception weighed heavily on David. The existential questions we were required to ponder and pray on constantly were like water off a duck's back to me, but for him they seemed portentous. Now and then I'd catch a dark look in his eyes as Father O'Neill explained the difference between a venial and a mortal sin, or reiterated the importance of confession before receiving Holy Communion.

Sometimes, when I was getting ready for bed, I'd step out of the bathroom, into the hall, and hear the tail end of David's hushed voice muttering a hurried prayer.

There's an insistent knocking at the front door, punctuated with the occasional ding-dong of the doorbell. It's an incongruously cheerful noise in the midst of everything.

"Julia? David?" I think I recognise it as the bloke who lives opposite, although it could be a trick. The thing in the bed can throw its voice. "Answer the door or I'll have to call the police! Julia?"

My screaming must have been the final straw. I've been trying to keep everything contained. The day I saw David's eyes flash black, I crumbled a whole load of sleeping pills into his dinner and cuffed him to the bed as soon as they took effect. At first, the thing that used to be my husband stayed mostly quiet. It must have been getting used to the feel of flesh, testing its limitations and gathering its strength. It lay in the bed, watching, assessing, waiting. It tried out its vocal cords, producing a range of guttural, throaty moans and grunts before it learnt to use David's tongue to speak to me.

At first it used a language I couldn't decipher. It sounded old, and although I didn't understand the words, they sent shivers through me. After a couple of days, it used my husband's tongue and lips and teeth to spit filthy lies and cruel insults, and to threaten me in all manner of creative ways. It used his body as a macabre ventriloquist's dummy, his mouth inexplicably full of other voices. It even managed to recreate my mother's dying moments, a chillingly garbled string of nonsense made slow and clumsy by the morphine.

"The one thing you must always keep in your mind, and in your heart," said Father O'Neill, "is that your body and soul must be readied for the sacrament. It's easy to get complacent, but when you receive the Eucharist, you are taking the very body and blood of Christ into you. If you come to take Holy Communion with impure intent, are you any better than Judas, who took Jesus's bread and wine at the Last Supper with treachery in his mind, and was entered by Satan the moment he ate?"

I don't really remember much about our First Communion. The wine was sour and the wafer was dry and tasteless. I felt a pang of guilt when I looked up to see Father O'Neill's beatific expression, the pride in his eyes, but it soon passed when it dawned on me that we could finally start planning our big day.

Months of attending Mass and wedding preparation classes couldn't dull my excitement as I booked the photographer, tasted canapés and wines, shopped for my dress, and selected all the items for our online gift wish list. David seemed distracted. He worked long hours, often going to the gym early and staying late to work out around his client sessions. I assumed he wanted to look his best in his morning suit, but deep down, I suppose the first cold tendrils of doubt were starting to creep into my periphery and twine around my happiness. What if he was having second thoughts about getting married? What if he was banging one of his posh, yummy-mummy clients? What if I'd pushed him too hard and he'd really found faith? How ironic it would have been if —after everything—he left me for Jesus.

"OPEN UP! IT'S THE POLICE!"

There's a great crash at the front door, a moment of silence, then another. Wood splinters and metal shrieks as the frame gives way under the battering ram. Feet thunder on the stairs. I'm so tired. I can't focus on the features of the officers bursting onto the landing. I try to swallow, but there's no saliva to lick my chapped lips or moisten my throat. It clicks dryly, and when I try to say something, pain lights up my chest.

"Priest!" I croak. "We need a priest."

A female officer shouts at me to get to my feet, hoisting me up by my elbows. She pats me down and finds the key which is biting into the flesh of my palm. Someone else grabs my upper arms while she tries the key in the lock. It snicks open and there's a pregnant pause before a line of cops enter the bedroom.

"Jesus fucking Christ!" A man's voice.

Someone retches, and I turn to see the police standing around the bed. I blink and try to focus on the scene in front of me. The blood and puke on the walls. The deep grooves in the floorboards from the bed legs. Sheets saturated with sweat and piss.

David is lying in the filthy bed, his head at an impossible angle. His hands look like two red gloves, the skin cut around the wrists and peeled back where he's tried to pull them through the cuff bracelets. He's not moving. His skin is pale where it shows through the dirt.

"Psycho bitch," someone says in an awed voice, as I'm bundled to the floor and I let the darkness wash over me.

In the days after the wedding, when I tried to remember the details, it was like waking up in the midst of a beautiful dream and trying to hang on to the nebulous images as they fade into daylight. The more I chased the memories, the more they scattered and skittered just out of reach. I tried to tell myself it was the excitement, the pressure, the endless glasses of Champagne, and that once the photos came, I'd be able to relive every moment in glorious technicolor.

The photographer called a few weeks after we returned from our honeymoon in Barcelona to tell me there was an issue with the pictures, and that although she could find no satisfactory explanation for the issue, she'd be willing to deduct a good percentage from her final invoice as a gesture of goodwill.

I was at my desk in the office when the viewing files came through. David's face was blurry in every single shot. And there was something which could only be described as the shadow of a rope looped around his neck and stretching up into the air above him.

The moment I read the title What One Wouldn't Do *and started thinking about the lengths a person might go to in order to obtain or hold onto something precious, the lyrics from "Losing My Religion" by REM popped into my mind. I often find inspiration in music, and this beautiful song about obsession sparked a train of thought about sacred and profane forms of worship. When we discuss high stakes and ultimate sacrifice, we often speak of selling our souls, and I wanted to take that idea and explore the ways in which we sometimes fixate on and pursue things we erroneously believe to be important at the expense of the things that really are.*

I wrote "Conversion" in the old fishing village of Polperro during a stormy week in May, by an open fire in a little cottage perched atop a smugglers cave—the sort of surroundings a writer might well make a bargain with the devil for. All things felt possible there.

Katie Young
London, UK
June 5th, 2021

Katie Young is a writer of dark fiction. Her work appears in various anthologies including collections by Nyx Publishing, Ghost Orchid Press, and Fox Spirit Books, and her story, "Lavender Tea," was selected by Zoe Gilbert for inclusion in the *Mechanic Institute Review's Summer Folk Festival 2019.* She lives in North West London with her partner, an angry cat, and too many books.

THE WITCH OF FLORA PASS

SCOTT J. MOSES

4th Day of January, 1912

My name is Thomas Reardon, and I did not kill my wife.

I want to be absolutely sure the one recording this typed that correctly. Her hand is quick, and I must ensure that inattention to my words does not birth me a death sentence. Though death, if these two snickering BOI men are to be believed, is what I'll more than like be dealt. Some things can't be understood from the confines of our earthly senses, and while it may seem logical to condemn me for the deaths of my neighbors, John and Mabel Lawrence, having found me screaming in my home covered in their blood, I say again: I did not kill them. I can't make sense of it, despite having lived through the entirety of the day in question. Though, I *can* relay this: I loved my wife, Claretta Jeane Reardon—love her still, and though I did not kill her, I could not save her.

The events of October 27th, 1911 will haunt me till my dying day. I'm a man of thirty-seven years and have had the gift of powerless vigilance to watch those I love pass on without my say so, without the fortitude or means to do much about it.

But enough about that, enough about me. . . this is the true account of what happened that day at Flora Pass, along the Patapsco River, in a small town I'm sure's grown smaller given what transpired there. I will withhold its name from this record—lest curious souls travel to that desolate place.

"My wife, the murderer."

I rolled the phrase along my tongue, tossing it up and along the roof of my mouth, tasting its strangeness, and yet, peering through the dense pines at Claretta, my love, knee-deep in the Flora River, I knew it to be true. She ran her hands over the reeds as she went, the churning water rising to her calves below the hem of her gray dress.

I'll admit, I had suspicions Claretta was up to something, though I was blinded by love and perhaps still am, that most damnable of human conditions, and so here, even on the inevitable brink of my own destruction, I will not speak ill of her. She made life worth living for this poor Maryland boy and we had fifteen glorious years together. I know your intent is to make us out as the murdering couple, to sell more papers in Baltimore. This city, your organization—this account—are all corrupt. The things I've endured shouldn't be in a world ruled by a loving God, though if He exists, I assume the devil and his ilk must as well.

She'd taken the Lawrences' cart from their barn early on the day in question and stopped it at the river's edge. Though tempted, I will not paint myself as the sleuth detective, only that I knew Claretta well and that she was a driven woman, and with the loss of our son stoking the fires of her soul with hate, I think she. . . lapsed—though, perhaps I only say this in retrospect to what occurred in the weeks thereafter.

Our son, Matthew, a boy of eleven years, died from fever in the same room he was born. He suffered weeks before his passing, and we prayed to God for healing, to take one of us instead. But alas, God saw the trade unfit—we'd sinned much in this life, or so the reverend said—and took our boy, so full of life but for the scourge which afflicted him.

The weeks after Matthew's death near broke us, and we stayed holed up in our house on the outskirts of that unmentioned town for two weeks' time. A few members of our congregation dropped food and goods at our doorstep the days following the funeral. One couple had the audacity to sing hymns on our doorstep every second morning, *lest the devil get in*, an unwelcome ritual which ceased when I first cracked the door to dawn's light. How they scampered to their cart when confronted with the ones they had meant to comfort. Disgusted with the sight of me, Claretta behind me, though avoiding the light. She'd grown accustomed to the dark, and I believe it seeped into her, though whether by her own volition or by forced entry, I cannot rightly say. I think Claretta resented me for opening that door, for either inviting the world back in or freely stepping into an existence without Matthew, without our son.

I can't help but notice the typist clutches her cross, typing with one hand whereas two would be more useful. Where do I have to go? Am I late for something. . . ? Oh. . . a joke. Go on, then, laugh. Laugh at the man in handcuffs. Laugh at the man with nothing left to lose. Are you finished? Oh, continue? Interruptions will only further delay you from your own families. Those I believe you'll hold tighter upon my account's conclusion.

So, where was I? Ah. . . . We lay together in the sweat-soaked sheets where Matthew passed days prior, praying for compromise, for the illness crawling throughout the bedspread to seep into us as well, that we might be reunited with him. When Claretta and I woke the next morning unmolested, she turned to me, hair unkempt and matted to her face, something in her eyes gone, that spark fueling her joy, her laugh, her sweet kiss, lost in our son's creaking bed.

"You do nothing to return him. . . " she said, restless circles beneath her dark eyes.

"What am I to do?" I said, sitting up in bed. *"Raise the dead?"* The anger swelling in me. *"Have I not prayed with you these weeks? Matthew heeded God's call, walks with Him as we speak, as Reverend Norson attested."* My tears came then, and her dark eyes eviscerated me. *"I miss him, Claretta, I do. . . but it's out of our hands now. We must accept this, hell that it is, and remain strong. . . lest we break."*

She glared there in the half-darkness, said the last thing *she* ever said to me in the whole of our lives together.

"Where is God in this, Thomas? If He exists, he has forsaken us. You may be fine failing your son, but I am not. . . I will not."

From then on, Claretta would leave with the horse from the barn, who'd yet to starve thanks to our unruly neighbors, in the early mornings of that coming winter, going who knows where, and in my anger—I let her. Too full of pride for reconciliation, overflowing with resentment at the things she had said that night in Matthew's bed. I was blind with rage at her silence toward me. How she'd exchange words with the ether in bed there beside me in the dead of those nights, while I longed for her and her words. She would return with the setting sun most days, but as the weeks went, she reemerged later and later, coming home with night long upon the landscape, the moon high in the sky. The circles beneath her eyes grew dark with ash, or soot, and she would crawl into our bed cold, tracking soil through the house for me to clean the following morn'.

It continued like that for weeks, and— What do you mean *was she faithful?* Are you implying there was another. . . ? Do your superiors see through the one-way glass? How you torture an already tortured soul? Claretta was, changed. . . yes. Not the woman I'd known, not the woman I'd married. . . but *not* in another man's arms. . . perhaps, something else's. . . . I asked for this meeting, but I'll just as likely go back to my cell to avoid being interrupted and. . . oh, you'll be quiet now? You want to hear what happened after all? Well, okay then, and you're right. It *is* best to keep a dead man talking, the more answered questions, the less paperwork, no?

Eventually, as my wife wanted little to do with me, I coped the way men do: by throwing myself into my work. I couldn't help but feel I'd failed her, and so I would provide in the only way I knew. Practically. A home, a roof, stocked pantry, and funds to boast. The foreman asked me thrice before I convinced him to allow my return to the mill, just shy of two months after Matthew's death. *"What better way than work for one to occupy his mind?"* I'd said. *"In idle stillness, that's when my grief is loudest."*

On the way home from the mill with Mr. Lawrence—yes, *that* Mr. Lawrence—he mentioned something of a peculiar notion. He turned to me, as we rounded the bend near my semi-secluded abode. Said, *"Seen your wife headed out Flora Pass way while resettin' my traps yesterday."*

"What of it?" I replied. *"I've cast my line there many occasions, the fish are large, delicious."*

I admit my anger contributed to the blindness of my situation. In those days, I hardly saw Claretta, only felt her crawl into bed in the dead of those nights. I'm ashamed, but I was jealous of another looking on my wife in the sunlight, when I was too prideful to address her, lying next to me in the dark, conversing there with the nothing in our room grown cold.

I'd become used to my situation, if you can believe it. Grief works its way into your bones, boys. Amongst other things.

"Flora Pass," he said, looking through the thick pines. *"My grandda' told me stories. It's an evil there. . . "* He clutched the cross 'round his neck as I swatted a bloated fly from my face. *"Thomas,"* he said, cross still clutched. *"I suggest you speak with your wife, and avert your eyes from Flora Pass or any duration there. I set traps that way, sure...something draws animals there. . . something hungry, but I check them every other day, when the sun is full—bright. Never at night, hear?"*

I'd raised my hand as he dropped me home, and stepping onto my porch, I jerked at his shrieked gasp behind me. I whipped around to the pounding of horse's hooves on the soft earth. Glimpsing Mr. Lawrence's cart receding 'round the bend as if to escape violent rains. I'd thought him a fool, nothing more.

Mr. Lawrence quit the mill the next morning and did not arrive to procure me for the day's labors. I'd walked the mile to his house and beaten on his door for explanation, though he wouldn't answer. And so I walked into town, to the mill, seeing as Claretta had the horse, arriving hours late. The foreman must've forgotten me and my grief by then, as he'd no sympathy whatsoever when he fired me. And so, I bought a bottle of bourbon on my walk home. I thought of stopping by the Lawrences' again drunk, and full of hell from multiple fronts. Rage for my wife. Rage for him taking the one thing I had left. But I refrained.

When I arrived home, Claretta faced the rear wall of our main room, her back to me. She was still, her bare feet caked in mud, the tracks entering the house to where she stood. The mud at one time wet, now dry. Seemed she'd been there some time. She didn't acknowledge me, though this was commonplace, as we hadn't spoken in weeks by then.

I stumbled, catching myself on the table, which slid along

our hardwood floor. I'm still unsure if Claretta spoke to me or to the one in the wall. The one I'd yet to see, the one I knew nothing of. I retired to bed, reasoning I'd tell her about my unemployment in the morning, when I was sober. Oh, the lies we tell ourselves. . . . Before I fell into a drunken slumber, I heard our front door open, then close soon after.

You ask about my hand, why the fingers are removed, the cluster of uneven knuckles the only remnants. I already told you, though the redundancy of your asking must be for the sake of this record, and if that's the case, fine. My story remains unchanged: Matthew chewed them off, gnawed them down to the bone.

I must ask, is it standard procedure to mock those interrogated? At those whose stories are too surreal to believe? There are things beyond us. Things I've seen, *continue to see,* even in the dark of my cell. The typist is right to clutch her cross, just as Mr. Lawrence had, to— Am I not allowed to converse with her? Fine, then stop interrupting me. I came of my own accord, remember?

I awoke to Claretta slouched on top of me, her nails raking my bare thighs. I winced, but in my drunkenness neglected an explanation, welcoming the thought of intimacy with my wife. We had not been *together* since before Matthew's death. She smelled of the river. She groaned when I entered her, but remained still, utterly silent but for a low moan. Her moss-ridden hair tickling my chest with each thrust. I spoke her name when it was finished, lying spent beneath her still upright form.

She twitched, a croak in her throat, and leaned into me, whispering in my ear.

"You'd give anything for your boy's return, no. . . ?"

"I've missed you, love," I said, winded, breathless.

"No. . . " she said, and slumped from me to the floor. A path of muck and grime from the river trailing her through

the bedroom door. I was driven to thinking it all a dream then, or at least choosing to believe that the incredibly tall figure in the room's corner, observing me, was a figment of my drunken imagination. The way it hunched there. . . hands clasped, rubbing together as one kneads dough.

I'd watched them a season, all while conscious of the rifle by the cabinet adjacent from the bedroom door. My heart throbbed in my chest and ears, and as the front door slammed, my eyes lurched from it an instant. When I looked back to the corner, I. . . well, I was alone.

Eventually, I sat myself in the corner of our room, managing minutes of half-sleep, jolting awake to see the bed still upright and wedged against the door. The dresser still pulled before the room's window, stalwart as ever.

I awoke to a crash, something heavy flung through our front door—you and I now know it was the door itself, ripped from its hinges—and muffled as they were from my make-shift bunker, a woman's screams scampered up the walls. The sound of ten thousand swarming hornets crescendoed, only dying when the screams overtook them. Slow, heavy footfalls on the floor echoing amidst them.

Thud. . . thud. . . thud. . .

I sighted my rifle toward the mattress barring my room's door, sweating, muscles tensed as the cries turned to whimpers, and with a *thunk,* someone fell to the floor. I knew then what you'd confirmed upon my arrival here, that it was Mr. Lawrence's wife, Mabel, that— What? Well, would you? If you'd have torn down that mattress and opened the door, you're a better man than I'll ever be. See, I dared not open it. Something deep within me, something primal, didn't allow me to so much as budge from that corner. I'm a coward. I freely admit that.

Morning seeped through the window in angular slivers. The room was humid, sour even, despite being October.

Coward or no, I was compelled to check the house, to leave the room which felt more a cage with the sunlight's intrusion, and so rifle in hand, I did just that.

Blood was strewn along the walls, floor, the ceiling itself. I collapsed, clawing my open-mouthed face, trembling as my eyes took it all in through the gaps my fingers allowed. And after a one-sided conversation with God, I glimpsed strands of loose hair amidst the dried blood, stuck to the old planks, a trail of it leading out the front door. I remembered Matthew sitting there months earlier, whittling his wooden dolls, knowing that—

Is my story so unbelievable? Lo, even the typist chuckles with my words, emboldened by you *strong* detectives who snicker all the more loudly. It sounds crazy, and I know it's more plausible to condemn me the killer, though—I'm, what? Bleeding? Oh my, this is new. My eyes? What about them? Come now, no more interruptions. We're near the end, near the reason I've broken weeks of unmovable silence.

I picked myself up from that dingy floor, took up my rifle, and made for my old fishing spot, that place in the crevice of the mountain, the one Mr. Lawrence couldn't mention without invoking God. And as the wind stilled and the sun rose in a baby blue sky, I set out for Flora Pass, knowing in my marrow my love would be there.

I hid in a mess of brush within the pines as Claretta unloaded Mabel Lawrence from their cart. The one I'd ridden into town on many occasions. That's when Thomas came out of the woodwork, his clothes torn and crimson as if he'd been mauled by something starved, rifle trained on my love.

"Damned, witch," he said, arms shaking from the weight of his upright rifle. *"May you burn eternal for killing my wife. . . Mabel, my. . . "* He swayed there, before advancing on her and the river in an unsteady gait. Claretta groaned, craning her

ear to the wind as if for a voice to speak. Though, something did.

Two whispered words:

"Require him."

I wondered if Mr. Lawrence had hidden in his bedroom as well, as Claretta tore through his home, how she'd brought his wife to my house for the slaughter. Perhaps we men are all the same. Cowards when it is most necessary to live up to everything we're told we must be. How much stronger is woman than we. . . but I digress. . . see, it was Mr. Lawrence's own fault, clutching that cross on my doorstep, choosing allegiances that day, perhaps seeing in the window of my house, or atop the roof on all fours, the tall, lanky figure I had the night I lay with my wife.

Claretta raised her hand and Mr. Lawrence stilled before straightening. He then planted the butt of the rifle to the earth, knelt, fastened his chin over the barrel's end, and wept before pulling the trigger. His body jerked from the impact and fell limp, shriveled there on the smooth stones of the riverbank. My love dragged the corpses to the river's edge—a lioness pulling on a fresh kill—jerking, writhing. She stopped, tilting her head to the river again and I swear to God above—though He doesn't seem to care given all that has happened—Matthew, my boy, walked out of the river to meet her.

It was him, in the same clothes we'd buried him, trudging out from those murky waters back to us. My family was whole again. I lowered my rifle and breathed in the cool air, watching through teary eyes as Matthew lifted his hand to the river.

Claretta wiped the tears from her eyes, and without hesitation, walked into the river, pulling the Lawrences in after her. Matthew watched her disappear beneath the water.

I shrieked, covering my mouth for the sound already

gone from me, and dropping my rifle, I broke from cover, falling to my knees as my boy bridged the gap between us in too few steps, shimmering as he looked down on my frailness, his lips a tight line.

"Ma fought for me," he said in a voice that was and was not his own. *"What do you offer. . . poor, useless man. Your bride has told me much. . . but what are men. . . what are you but useless in this age of gluttonous abundance?"*

"Matthew!" I cried, erratic, my mind long-gone from me. *"Matthew, my boy. . . "*

He took my hand, kissed it, and whispered in the voice of an old woman, *"An offering."* Before the landscape melted away, I saw someone on the horizon, where the water touched the sky. Clothed in long blacks and browns. . . incredibly tall. . . standing hunched atop the river like Jesus in the parable. The weeds of the land strewn through her hair. The air permeated sulfur and fish rose to the river's surface, bobbing wide-eyed in the slow-moving current.

My hand crunched, and the pain shot through my arm as the blood came. Matthew cradled my fingers in his cupped hands, offering them to her across the river, turning from me as I writhed there, screaming.

My periphery blurred, my thoughts only pain, and as insanity scratched on the doors of my mind, Matthew saved me. Turned back to me then, his smile calming. His eyes, nose, and lips sliding down his face like melting wax.

"I leave you the others," he said, pointing to my remaining fingers. *"For the work which still needs doing."*

You found me in the Lawrences' home clutching my bloodied hand, sprawled atop their corpses, rounded me up without question, and brought me here. Letting me rot in that cell for as long as you have has given me time to think. Hurrah for the American justice system.

What's the matter? She seems to have stopped typing. . .

My apologies, but now it's I who can't help but smile. . . what's that? I couldn't hear you for the other man's screams.

I did not kill my wife, nor the Lawrences. . . though I did little to stop their demise. I've placed words throughout this account, words from my dreams, words which invoke her when said in a certain order, in a specific tone. And now that I am hers completely, I have no choice but to indoctrinate others. See, I am a man forever changed, and my shredded soul has all but left me. My wife and her mistress feast on it together, one strip at a time, while the son who is not my son looks on, drooling. My severed fingers adorning his neck.

I want to reiterate, for anyone left alive, that I did not kill my wife. For if you'd turn your head you'd see—she's here.

Smell the cool of the river?

See the fish belly-up in your mind's eye?

What's that? Your lips move but produce no sound. Though perhaps you can't speak, not with your jaw shorn, hanging there ajar, your bottom teeth a necklace of bone.

I shall make a record once I'm free of these cuffs. Free of these chains around my ankles, which drop almost as I say the words. As the glass cracks one line at a time, as it has for the entirety of our conversation, even now—again—there in the pane's corner—there on the sill's lower portion, *you*, the only ones left alive in this facility. Everyone beyond that glass in thrall to my wife and her mistress, their souls thrust on the banquet table my mouth waters for, yet may not take part in devouring. . . not yet.

And as Matthew crawls atop your wrecked body in the clothes he was buried, awaiting my completion of this account, I know he, *they*, are not finished with me. For I still have fingers to spend.

I could've told you of the flies sooner. How they crawl beneath my lids and the lids of my son—had you only asked. Though, you *were* occupied. She's dragged you all about the floor, pinned the typist high in the corner of the rightmost wall, unnaturally wedged there like a marionette, strings caught in malicious trees.

And here I was, thinking I was talking to a corpse. But no, your lip quivers, slumped there over your dead partner. The blood where Matthew stuck his hand in your side pooling around you and the one you laughed with. *Poetry*.

Yes, go on, reach for the cross the typist once clutched. I suspect you're an *only on holidays,* sort-of churchgoer, and well, I'm here to tell you God doesn't listen, doesn't exist, or doesn't care, and that your back-pocket faith can't save you. . . but the thing in Flora Pass? It's attentive. . . it listened. . . listens now.

We're all just clocks, you know? Tick-tocking things, things which stop. Our flesh and bones the hands on the wheel, turning, clicking. Be grateful for your fingers, though perhaps you *should* be afraid.

Perhaps they want more from you.

Perhaps you'll glimpse hell as I have.

This one was written here and there for about a year and was the first thing I attempted after finishing "What's In Your Name" (the most recent of the stories in my collection, Hunger Pangs). It fought me the entire way, as some stories do, but we eventually saw eye to eye. It's my attempt at ambiguity.

Scott J. Moses
Baltimore, MD
June 7, 2021

Scott J. Moses is the author of *Non-Practicing Cultist* (Demain Publishing) and *Hunger Pangs* (independently published). A member of the Horror Writers Association, his work has appeared in *Paranormal Contact* (Cemetery Gates Media), *Diabolica Americana* (Keith Anthony Baird), *Coffin Bell,* and elsewhere. You can find him on Twitter @scottj_moses or at www.scottjmoses.com.

BLOOD IS THICKER

ANGELA SYLVAINE

The crowd of beautiful people sipped champagne and nibbled salmon canapés, hardly glancing at the art they'd all supposedly come to admire. Diane gushed and fawned over them, hating herself for so desperately wanting the approval of these scavengers who were just waiting to pick her bones clean.

Her half of the white-walled gallery featured minuscule canvases delicately painted with graceful figures in muted hues by a finely haired brush. Viviane's half boasted large canvases screaming modernity, boldness of color, and an abundance of paint scraped and slopped. The two halves were an odd match, much like Viviane and Diane.

They were twins, but of the fraternal variety, merely siblings born one after the other. Viviane was thirteen minutes older and stood three inches taller. Her eyes sparkled a true green rather than a muted hazel, and her hair shone more auburn than brown. Viviane liked to joke that Diane had spoiled a bit during those extra minutes in their mother's womb, coming out bruised and soft like an overripe piece of fruit.

One attendee was far more interested in the art than anyone else, an influential voice that could single-handedly ensure an artist's success or failure. Mick Calibri should have been displeasing to the eyes with skin pocked and wrinkled. His scent should have been rank and sour to the nose, his voice should have sounded like the screeches of sewer vermin. Instead he was quite handsome, smelled of sharp pine and wood smoke, and spoke with a voice that could charm even the most modest girl out of her underwear.

He circled the room. "It's quite inorganic, I think. Forced," he said of Viviane's work. "Choked of emotion. A parody of anger."

"Your work is. . . bland and rather sanitized," he said to Diane, no passion in his voice. "Immature, a poor imitation of the Impressionist masters."

A flush crept up her cheeks and she dipped her chin to avoid his gaze.

Satisfied that his column in the *Times* would reduce the sisters to carrion, the crowd left their lipstick-stained glasses and crumpled napkins behind as they slipped back into the New York night. Diane had tried to tell her sister they were gallery owners, not artists ready for their own show. But Viviane was emphatic, confident in her own talent and insistent that Diane participate, if for no other reason than to make her look good in comparison.

Diane locked the doors, set the alarm, and trudged up the stairs at the back of the gallery that led to their loft apartment and studio. Owning a building in the city would have been an impossibility for a couple of starving artists, but their grandmother, Bee, was a shrewd businesswoman who'd foreseen the value of New York real estate and invested heavily.

When Diane entered the apartment, she found her sister pacing the floor between the mismatched cluster of armchairs that served as their living room and the long, gouged table that held their canvases, paints, and other tools.

"He's vile. Absolutely evil. A literal demon in a designer suit," Viviane said, her words punctuated by the creak of the worn wood beneath her feet.

A headache needled the base of Diane's skull, urged on by too much sugary champagne and not enough food. "I don't know, Vi. I mean, he's sort of right, about me at least."

"Have you heard his nickname? Mick 'the Dick.' Loves to get artists in the sack and then screw them again in his column."

Diane's face flushed at the memory of her night with Mick. She'd been dumb enough to believe he'd actually liked her, that he would call her again after their tryst.

"He has some hang up about women, you know that. We all suck, but every guy he reviews has potential that should be encouraged. I'm sick of mewling at the feet of pompous assholes and begging for scraps." Viviane marched over to the shelves against the wall beside the sofa and began rifling through the books. She grabbed one, tossed it onto the floor, grabbed another, threw it aside. "We're victims, you know? Sacrificial lambs for the patriarchy."

Diane followed, picking up each volume. "Careful, those are old." *And valuable,* she thought. Bee had dark tastes and had left behind books on Satanism, demonology, and the occult. If they didn't get another artist who actually sold some work into the gallery soon, they might have to hock some of the books to keep their lights on.

"Ha. Here it is." Viviane plopped down on the floor, a leather-bound tome in her lap.

Diane frowned at the sight of the inverted pentagram branded on the cover. "What are you reading?"

"Bee's journal. Haven't you ever looked at it?"

Of course she hadn't. Whispering of the dark and evil had

been Viviane and Bee's thing, a bond shared only between the two. "That stuff gives me the creeps," she lied. She'd always been curious.

The pages of the journal, covered in swirling, handwritten script and strange symbols, seemed to whisper as they brushed against one another. The air turned colder. Diane rubbed her hands down her arms, wishing they could afford to turn up the heat.

"Haven't you ever wondered how she accrued so much wealth? How she was so successful?" Viviane asked.

"Who?'

"Bee, idiot. She was only in her early twenties when Grandpa died, but she thrived as a single woman in the city when women had almost nothing."

"She probably rolled in her grave when Dad gave everything to the church." An act of atonement for his devil worshipping mother, he'd said. If their building hadn't been placed in a trust for the girls, it would be gone too.

"Bee knew the truth. That women have to be fierce predators or the Micks of the world will eat us alive."

"Exactly how much champagne did you drink?"

"I'm serious, Di. It's time we claim what we deserve." Viviane rose gracefully, like one of Degas's ballerinas. "Don't you want to get back at him for what he did to you?"

Diane flushed. "How did you. . . I mean, I'm not sure what you mean."

"Please. I know you slept with him too. He called you bland in the sack, you know. Laughed about the whole thing, like you're some kind of joke. Bee would have gutted him with her bare hands." Viviane extended the open journal.

Diane's empty stomach roiled with shame as she reached out a shaking hand to take the book, her ears filled with the imagined mocking laughter of Mick and Viviane as they lay in each other's arms. Diagrams featuring pentagrams and knives and human figures, adorned the book's page, but the scariest part was the heading at the top of the page in Bee's perfect script:

Human Sacrifice (Murder for Personal Gain and Profit)

"Don't be such a whiny baby. I'll do the hard part." Viviane looked at Diane with those eyes full of judgment.

The whole plan was crazy. Deals with the devil were the stuff of legends and clichéd rock 'n' roll songs, parables meant to teach people that nothing in life is free. They weren't real, no matter what Bee wrote in that old journal. It was just writing on a page.

"Bee would never have actually killed anyone." Diane bit her nail down to the quick, tasted iron. "And she would never want us to do something so. . . terrible."

"What's your big plan, huh? Selling stuff to make a few hundred bucks? That'll get us through a month, maybe. We can't even pay the property taxes on this place, and they'll eventually take it away too. Then we'll be homeless, out on the street."

There hadn't been much to say to that. So Viviane had planned and Diane had done nothing. Viviane would seduce "the Dick," invite him to the loft with the promise of an easy lay and ply him with drinks spiked with rat poison. All while Diane waited in her room, knowing that when it came down to it, her sister wasn't a murderer.

The waiting was harder than she'd thought it would be. Music blasted from the living room, thumping through the walls, loud enough to drown out screams. The hurt of Mick's rejection still stung, like a cut that wouldn't heal, and she hated herself for thinking of him, for wanting him. Why couldn't she be confident and strong, like Viviane?

She splashed more whiskey into her glass and took a slug, wishing it would offer her comfort but only receiving an enflamed throat and sour stomach. The lilt of Viviane's laugh rose over the music, drew Diane to the bedroom door. She knelt and peeked through the keyhole.

A flash of movement crossed her line of vision, then a moan sounded. She drew away and pressed her back to the wall. Had Viviane decided to screw him, after all? Diane clenched her teeth against the jealousy that twisted inside her, reminded herself that Mick had used her and thrown her away.

She tipped back her glass, drained the last drops.

A thump shook the wall and she tensed, holding her breath. The music stopped for a moment, a break between songs, and there was only silence. Then the beat started again, swelled to fill her ears. Every second gaped and stretched as she prayed that she was right, that her sister wasn't a killer.

The music stopped and there was a hard rap on her door. "You can come out now."

Rising on legs wobbly as a newborn colt, Diane tried to remember how much whiskey she'd had as she crept from her room wrapped in the comfort of her quilt. It was the one she and Bee had made together, sharing a love of detail and subtle patterns and hard work that Viviane had no desire to understand.

The loft was empty and quiet. The furniture stood just where it had been with lamps and vases upright, no sign of any fight. The walls, floors, and ceiling were clean, no hint of the blood splatter Diane had envisioned. A relieved giggle erupted from her throat.

Viviane appeared at her side clad in a strapless, skin-tight red satin dress, and brandishing a butcher knife. “Give me your hand.”

“What?” Diane asked, hardly able to complete the thought before the blade sliced across the meatiest part of her palm. “Ow! What the hell?” Pain singed, then floated away on a current of alcohol.

Blood welled and dripped into the bowl Viviane had waiting. She did the same thing with her own hand, opening a gash and catching the blood.

Diane clutched her hand to her chest, staining the quilt. Her gaze narrowed on the weird, off-white bowl that was marred with sutured cracks. “Wait, is that a freaking skull?”

“From Bee’s kit.”

She decided to try some other spell, Diane thought. *Something using our blood.* And that was okay, nowhere near as bad as actually killing someone. Maybe Viviane hadn’t slept with Mick, either had just given up on the plan entirely. Diane watched as her sister dipped a brush in the bowl and painted a large star surrounded by a circle directly onto their wooden floor. An inverted pentagram.

“That’s going to stain,” she said, entirely serious, and wondered if she might be going a bit crazy.

Viviane spent several minutes reading from the journal in a hushed voice as she painted more strange symbols around the circle. She grabbed the blow-dryer from their table of supplies, plugged it into an extension cord, and dried her creation.

Another giggle bubbled from Diane’s mouth.

“Come on, you grab his feet.” Viviane moved behind the kitchen island and looked down.

Diane’s vision blurred, righted itself, blurred again. “His feet?” She must have misheard, there was no one else there. “I don’t feel good. And my hand hurts.”

Rolling her eyes, Viviane muttered. “I guess I’ll just do it *all* myself." She disappeared for a moment then emerged from behind the island, dragging something. Someone.

The whiskey roiled in Diane's gut and she fell to her knees, vomiting up the contents of her stomach.

"Seriously?" Viviane said between grunted breaths as she lugged Mick's limp body across the floor. "You're cleaning that up."

"Well, you're cleaning up the blood," Diane mumbled, and for some reason that damn giggle wanted to make another appearance. Her sister had done it, she had actually killed someone. All for some stupid spell that wasn't going to work anyway.

A moan drew Diane's gaze to the inverted pentagram, where Mick now lay. His head lolled to the side.

"Shit." Viviane placed the skull bowl beside his head and flipped the music back on.

"He's not dead." The quilt slipped from her shoulders as she tried to stand, slipped in her own vomit, fell again.

Viviane stood over her victim, the knife clutched in her hand, her lips moving as she chanted words lost in the swell and thump of the beat. She descended on Mick, straddling him.

"Wait," Diane called, scrabbling across the floor. She had to do something, stop this before it was too late.

The silver of the knife flashed as her sister slashed it across Mick's throat. Blood sprayed across Viviane's face and neck, then gushed into the bowl she held close. "You've screwed your last artist, fucker."

Viviane did not clean up the blood. After doing everything else herself, she'd insisted that Diane be the one to do that. Sitting beside the bucket of soapy water clutching a sopping sponge, she supposed she was getting blood on her hands after all.

The whole nightmare seemed dim and hazy, though it was only the night before. Mick's body was gone, she wasn't sure where and she didn't plan on asking. She *had* asked about the Tupperware full of blood that sat next to the almond milk on the top shelf in the fridge. Her sister simply said that there were plenty of rituals that required human blood.

Diane wiped the sopping sponge across the floor again and again, turning the soapy water pink, but no matter how much she scrubbed the image of the pentagram remained, faint but permanent. As she sat slumped in the center of the symbol, she felt a warmth around her, a comforting embrace that reminded her of Bee.

She trailed her fingers through pools of blood-tinged water, creating her own symbols to combat those of her sister. Maybe Mick's life, his blood, didn't have to go to waste for the sake of some empty ritual.

Her clean up duty forgotten, Diane claimed the Tupperware from the fridge and placed it on the long, wooden table. Using her new ingredient, she blended paints in vibrant oranges, deep purples, dense black, and the most exquisite, vibrant red. The colors were so much bigger, louder than her normal muted choices, and the minute canvases she favored were woefully insufficient.

As if in a trance, Diane took one of Viviane's largest canvases and began to paint. She worked feverishly, frantically, not at all carefully, as the paint whispered in her ear. Possessed by a creative drive she'd never before experienced, she worked through the morning and early afternoon.

A voice pierced the bubble enclosing her, and she stumbled back from the canvas.

"What is this?" Viviane asked, her eyes fixed on the painting.

Diane lowered her brush and pushed her sweat-dampened hair from her forehead. She opened her parched lips to speak, but there were no words to answer that question. She stepped back to stand beside her sister and they both stared at the canvas, now complete.

From afar, it would appear to be abstract Impressionism, a mix of colors creating a sense of apprehension and unease. But up close the piece revealed to the viewer faint-twisted figures writhing within the paint, wailing and clawing from the darkest black-red shadows.

Diane had no plan, no intention to paint this vision, and in fact had no real memory of doing so. "The blood. I used the blood."

"You little bitch. I'm the one who did all the work, that blood was mine." Viviane gripped Diane's shoulders, shook her. "How could you waste it on some shit painting?"

Heat rose up Diane's chest and neck, flooded her cheeks. Anger singed her nerves, tensed in her coiled muscles, and she shoved her sister away. "It's not shit." And she knew it was true, down to her bones, she knew that this was the most beautiful piece she'd ever created.

Sprawled on the floor, Viviane resurrected Mick's hurtful words with a cruel sneer. "Oh, please. So you managed to make one single thing that isn't totally bland and boring."

Instead of wilting under her sister's judgement, Diane smiled at the clear jealousy on display. "His blood inspired me, I guess. I think he would have liked it."

"Whatever." Viviane stood and crossed her arms, angling a look at the now-cold bucket of water. "Stop screwing around and clean this up."

"You clean it up. I'm busy." Diane strode back toward the

table and her newly created paints. This time the oranges and yellows whispered to her, and red, always red.

Diane slept on the floor atop the pentagram wrapped in her quilt and took only the briefest breaks when her body forced her to. In six days, she had created an entire collection. That first painting was christened Torment, and those that followed it were Affliction, Misery, Agony, Torture, Anguish, Fury, Wrath, Passion, Adoration, and Devotion. Diane only stopped when all the paint was gone, all the blood now dried on canvas.

Viviane agreed they should show the paintings, but the malicious twist of her lips spoke of her true motivation. She was sure it would be a failure.

Diane didn't gush or fawn this time. She simply watched as the fashionable people succumbed to her work. The olive crostini went untouched as the assembled crowd stood enthralled and staring, their carefully controlled faces crumbling as her work wrenched pain, anger, sadness, and desire from deep within them.

"Shockingly raw," one patron said. "I want to look away, but simply can't."

"Gruesome in the most beautiful way," a critic, the one who had replaced Mick after his mysterious disappearance, replied.

"A bit derivative though, don't you think? Like a de Kooning with more color," Viviane interjected.

"Not at all. This is wholly original, I'd say, the emergence of a new talent."

"She's my sister, but this whole style, it's more my thing. I'm working on a new collection, myself, you know. I'd be happy to give you a private viewing. . . "

The critic turned his back on her.

Diane couldn't suppress the grin that tugged at her lips as Viviane muttered some excuse and slunk away to hide in the corner.

The night was an overwhelming success, with eight of the paintings selling for figures none of their previous artists had achieved. The critic from the *Times* raved about Diane's work, promising a column that would reveal her to the world as the next great artist to watch. The attendees finally, reluctantly, left the gallery, glancing behind them as they went, straining for one last glimpse.

Diane felt new, reborn. She'd transformed herself from spoiled fruit to a perfectly ripened plum. Filled with a confidence she'd never felt before, she knew one thing for certain. She needed more blood. There would have to be another sacrifice, but who? And was she strong enough to kill for her art?

Wrapped in her thoughts, she returned to the loft. She'd expected to be ambushed by Viviane, grilled about the remainder of the show, but the space was silent and dim, lit only by flickering candles placed throughout the room. Kicking off her shoes, she crossed the open expanse of the floor, stopping as her gaze caught on the pentagram, which was darker than before. No longer just a stain, it had been repainted with fresh blood.

A scream split the still night and she turned to see her sister lunging toward her, an empty bottle of champagne clutched in her hand and raised high. Diane didn't even have time to raise her hands and block the blow before the bottle crashed into her head and she sunk to the floor.

Pain singed her skull and lit up behind her eyes as darkness tried to pull her under. She fought to open her eyes, to talk, but the only sound to escape her lips was a pained moan. Hands gripped her ankles, dragged her body across the wood floor.

Diane had a bone-deep sense for the pentagram now, had communed with it over the past week, and felt the sting of its power as she was placed in the center.

She managed to crack open her eyes and was met with a monstrous vision. Viviane, hair wild as snakes and eyes wide and crazed, stood over her, still clutching the bottle.

"Why?" Diane croaked.

"It should be me, not you!" Viviane shrieked. "I'm the one Bee trusted with the books. I'm the one who made the sacrifice. You stole *my* blood, stole *my* power."

Tears leaked from Diane's eyes and streamed down her face. She felt the pentagram lap them up as they splashed to the floor.

Her sister straddled her, setting the bottle down and picking up a knife. Viviane grasped the knife in both hands and raised it over her head, the blade gleaming in the candlelight.

But the pentagram was Diane's to command, fed by her hours of sweat and obsession, and its touch infused her with strength and purpose. She reached out to grasp the champagne bottle and swung it, smashing into her sister's descending hands and sending the knife skittering away. She swung again, connecting with the side of Viviane's head.

Viviane slumped to the floor. Blood dribbled from her mouth in a slow stream, feeding the pentagram.

Diane rose, her breath coming in quick gasps, and grabbed several scraps of canvas from beneath the wooden table. She tied her sister's limp hands, then her feet.

"No, stop." Viviane's head lolled to the side as Diane returned her to the center of the pentagram.

The knife and skull bowl sat neatly to the side, as if patiently waiting, and Diane picked them up. This was her chance to prove herself, to truly claim her power. She knew exactly what to do.

"I don't want to die," Viviane managed, her eyes cracking open.

Diane giggled. "Oh, I'm not going to kill you." The knife flashed as she slashed it across her sister's cheek.

Applause thundered through the gallery, and Diane smiled as she angled a look at the ceiling, knowing Viviane would be able to hear it. The closet where she kept her sister shackled and gagged was just above them.

The show, Diane's fourth over the past year, was another success. Article after article recounted the story of the astonishing new talent who, consumed by grief after the disappearance of her beloved sister, had pushed herself to even darker and more intense extremes.

Diane's most recent exhibition brought those who looked at it to tears or sent them fleeing the sight. The *Times* critic called her work, "The most vivid of nightmares captured on canvas." And it was only the beginning. Diane had a steady blood supply, plenty to continue her work for years to come. She never cut Viviane very deep, just little slices each time she needed to restock her paint supply. After all, she wasn't a killer.

In the midst of the looming pandemic and continued challenges to women's rights, I decided to write an occult-inspired story with feminist undertones. Coincidence? Probably not. The main characters of "Blood is Thicker" formed quickly in my mind, my take on the trope of twin sisters. I've always been a lover of art and had recently discovered Vincent Castiglia, who paints using his own blood. From there, Diane and Viviane became starving artists and gallery owners in need of blood and ultimately corrupted by power.

Angela Sylvaine
Fort Collins, Colorado
June 6, 2021

Angela Sylvaine is a self-proclaimed cheerful goth who still believes in monsters. Her debut novella, *Chopping Spree*, an homage to 1980s slashers and mall culture, is available now. Her short fiction has appeared in multiple publications and anthologies, including *Places We Fear to Tread* and *Not All Monsters*. A North Dakota girl transplanted to Colorado, she lives with her sweetheart and three creepy cats on the front range of the Rockies. You can find her online at angelasylvaine.com.

TO SEE AN ANGEL

TOM REED

what have i done? it matters
not. i lie face down and naked
in this back alley these shadows
mocking me the knife
still in my hand

It was still in my hand.

i pull it to me, i hold
tight. the copper-aubergine scent
comes again and i remember
pieces of things

I crashed random words on my keyboard. The laptop did not complain. I sent out requests, I paid thousands over time.

Nothing, nothing. It wasn't to be had over the internet. I'd broken hearts for nothing. What fucking poetry was that? Who's to say anyone had hearts, anyway?

i scrape the blade on the dirty
asphalt i feel
something cold dripping
on my back

I tried drinking. Gin. Lots of gin, straight from the bottle. I felt so close, and I loved it, that herbal desire. If only it could tear the piece of me out that prevented me from seeing. I was never nearly as numb as I tried to be, the bottle hidden away from all eyes. I sat in the early morning hours in my car lying to everyone, including myself, as my head spun. I fell asleep to utter oblivions, severe lacks. I damaged my body on a regular basis, but somehow no one ever found out, and I wonder if I would have succeeded if anyone ever did.

i stand up, i realize
it is night, it is night.
pain shoots through my legs and
stomach the moon mocks
me and hides
behind storm clouds i
still grip a blade.
i think
i am
bleeding

I looked to recreate that moment with Elizabeth. She escaped this world years ago for mysterious reasons, and I hadn't known. She called to me in my dreams, blue lightning from my fingers reaching. And then I was in the car, alone, at night. She never came. That sense of abandonment. A green bottle of abandonment. Strong. If I could have felt that again, perhaps she would have come to me now. An angel.

E my styrene
E my yggdrasil
E my Ashwood tree
all dissolved into pink foam
pink foam floating like
a spirit

Maybe that is what I was chasing. Not an angel, but a ghost. . .

. . . a ghost. . .

I realized then it was behind me. Here was the abhorrent embodiment of my dread and loneliness, my fear of failure, my self-loathing. My vile anxiety. A creature of my own making. I felt its exhalations of soot and fire on my neck. Turning as quickly as I could, I stabbed my knife wildly at the dark blur. I tripped over my own feet—typical—and fell back to the filthy pavement, head sounding quite a fine crack on the curb. It was fast upon me. I no longer held the knife.

We looked into each other's eyes. It opened its stomach-mouth, and sucked me in.

i am darkness now, i feel
i am soot and fire
what are these wild things flying around me? they
scream ! like Cicadoidea, *their strange*
float, their strange
song within had i arms
i would reach out
but i don't and i don't and i don't and

The insides of the thing were larger than its outside. I was in a whole new universe of Hell. There was a constant rumbling and stink. The stink was its language, and everything else was its madlike hunger. A myriad of buzzing clouds drifted and swarmed. They danced mitosis dances. They performed swiftly crashing convergences. Two clouds surrounded me and stated their intentions in a gruesome whisper. The first wished to bite out the entirety of my desire. The second wished to torture me with it. They told me I had to choose.

oh but if only they knew
that i already do i
already do

I blinked slow and they were gone. The rumbling grew stronger. I bore witness to a giant spine bursting from the soft floor like a new tooth that pushes through a bawling child's gums. It uncurled itself, unfurled itself, it was born anew. The spine-tree reached to the darkness above, twisting. I felt it in my own back. I got up and climbed anyway. The spinous processes were dry, they felt as though they were the wooden rungs of an old ladder mired in cobwebs. I went up and up and up. The spine swayed slightly at great heights, I felt the creaking outside and inside of me. I did not let the pain nor panic of my hands stop me. Soon, I faded into the darkness above.

wake up

I broke open my eyes on the sharp shards of morning light. Dust in my mouth, I coughed. I uncovered myself from the chaos of old blankets and stumbled out of bed. A dream? I walked to the bathroom and looked at myself in the cracked mirror. I barely recognized myself. I was filthy, and my face was an ancient map of bloody scrapes and scratches. I turned the water on and waited ages until it was scalding. I drenched my hands in the deluge, they burnt, they stung. As what seemed like years of dirt washed away, I saw the splinters of bone in my palms. A dream?

"A dream?"

A whispering sound from behind me. I turned around and carefully pulled the shower curtain open. The pale girl, the open rib cage, the fungal bloom within. So many colors, and the bloody knife on the lip of the clawfoot tub, mine. I reached for it. I ran. Water poured onto the floor from the sink and the tub, undiscovered black waterfalls in the chancel of a kaleidoscopic jungle.

what is a dream anyway? she says
she's here now but i can't see
she tells me the story of how once
upon a time she ripped out her wings
she buried them

on a hill
in a forest
under a black waterfall
somewhere

and then she finds me
and then she opens up
her heart to me
pink foam flowing

and then she opens up
her ribcage to me
dark branches flowering
and hands me the knife

the black rivers
the symphony of crickets

she kissed me then
she tasted of gin and despair

I ran, I don't know for how long, nor how far. It began to rain. Dark cars with empty people within swept past. Something invisible pushed my side, and I fell, pavement-faced and clattering knife.

It was always the same. Ever since I was small, ever since I was innocent. The desperation of impossible desire, the falling. To see an angel—and for her to see me—it was everything.

*When I first learned of WOWD, the very first thought I had was the title of my piece. . . and what *would* I do? And what sort of angel am I looking for? What came to me after that answers nothing, and I still do not know at all.*

tom reed
Waltham, MA
June 6, 2021

tom reed is a poetwriterthing and sometimeseditorthing from Massachusetts, who wouldn't be the (strange) person he is today without the poetry community on Tumblr. He has a weakness for the sound of words, coffee, bizarre angels with tangled wiring, and the bright spot in the sky. tom can be found at amarthis.com.

MONSTERS CALLING HOME

CHERI KAMEI

People call us the Island at the Edge of the World because we are the last smudge of land unmoored from the continent, set adrift before the endless horizon. There have been many who have taken this truth for a challenge and set out for years on end, in every conceivable direction, but all anyone has found for their efforts is more of the same: salt and storm and the blue-green screams of the deep. No one has ever made it past the realms that belong to the Beasts who rule the seas. Those who return home alive only confirm the necessity of the price we must pay to safeguard our spit of rocky crag and stilted homes. We are the Island at the Edge of the World and we alone provide the last protection from the horrors of the deep.

This is what we have been told all our lives, we two Kaito girls: that it is our duty and privilege to provide tithings for not only the island's sake, but the wide world kept safe from behind our drop of land. It is why we are here, fighting rainfall and wind as massive stone sharks heave their solid boulder bodies against our dead father's boat. We are on the long journey to the Many-Headed Beast, who demands the personal delivery of this year's offerings.

"The helm!" Nagisa shouts.

The deck roils. The lashing rain is a wall of needles. I ignore her and keep heaving ashes over the sides of the ship.

The elders say the dead appease what monsters lie beneath. We save the burnt remains of those who have passed and load them like talismans onto any departing craft. "All those who obey the Many-Headed Beast know to respect the return journey of any soul, mortal or not," our head elder explained.

The stone sharks do not seem to agree.

"Forget the ashes." Nagisa slams into me. Soaked through, her hair lies plastered to her skin like an angry shadow, black and snarled. She pushes me back to the bridge and suddenly the wheel is in my hands.

A stone shark strikes against the railing on the port side. The entire boat rocks and creaks. It is a miracle the wood holds, that somehow Nagisa keeps her feet. As the lightning flashes, another raging bulk of gravel and teeth breaks the surface, wheeling back to attack. We cannot take another hit. Nagisa looks at the railing, then out to the sea. She rushes to the bow.

When I call her name, the slamming waves swallow it whole. The wheel stutters against my palms, protesting. I breathe raindrops into my lungs, helpless only to watch as Nagisa does what she always does: she breaks her promises.

Baring her teeth, my sister draws back and lets out the beastly shriek that lives at the base of both of our bellies, always.

The force nearly throws me back. Splinters sink into my clenched palms as I fight to hold the wheel. The storm stands no chance against her volley. Fierce and unafraid, Nagisa is the thunder singing sweet in the heavens. She is fang and foam and voice.

The water goes flying. So does the stone shark.

Inhuman, triumphant, Nagisa shouts down the stars.

Long has peace reigned between land and sea, but it hinges on our yearly offerings, given freely, to the Many-Headed Beast. Often the requests are unsurprising, if still cruel after so many years: a portion of our meager crops, a tree from the highest peak on the island, ships and jewels and swords. Other times, the unexpected cleaves us to the bone. I still remember the year we lost every firstborn on the island.

In response to our tears, the village elders told us of the dark years, of the nightmares beneath the shimmering sea's surface that would rise to devour cities whole, of the poisoned waters that starved the kingdoms even beyond the coastline, of the trails of blood left in the sand. The beasts of the deep knew no peace, had no taste for restraint, wanting all our world and never knowing or caring why. To stop such madness was worth every firstborn on the island and more. The deal drawn with the Many-Headed Beast saved far more lives.

Some years it is enough to send an unmanned craft forward into the waves, loaded with our sacrifice, surrounded by paper lanterns that disappear like stars winking out along the horizon. Other years the tithes must be taken directly into the deep. Then, it is always a Kaito who sets sail, for it was our ancestors who made the first exchange many years ago. It was a Kaito who dared to first travel into the realm of monsters, to meet the Many-Headed Beast and plead for mercy. It was a Kaito who was the first sacrifice, freely given.

Our father was the last volunteer in living memory. More than seventeen years ago, the summons came in the form of half a dozen severed heads that washed up onto our shore. As the elders interpreted the year's demands from their dreams and bone carvings, our father built a boat, small and light, to sail into the horizon. In the end, he took with him a tithing in the form of individual jars of congealed blood, collected from the veins of each villager, one drop a day for an entire year. He never returned.

In the year he was gone, his boat returned, empty and blood-stained. Our aunt drowned herself, one last plea and Kaito sacrifice to the indifferent seas. Our grandparents died with hope rotting their heavy hearts. It was only when our family tree had been felled that we washed ashore, my sister and I, wailing infants wrapped in seaweed and our father's cloak, red and well-recognized.

We are the last Kaitos left on the Island at the Edge of the World. This is our journey alone to make.

When the storm passes, Nagisa lies panting on the deck. "I'm fine," she says, waving a hand at me, placating. Her eyes are still golden green.

We'll never know what creature stole our father to its embrace, bore us and grew bored, but its blood runs like salt-water through our veins.

As the sea settles around us, I leave the wheel and help Nagisa to her feet, saying, "You idiot. You promised you wouldn't."

"No one's around to see." Sopping wet, she lets me right her and then pulls away from my hands. The deck rises and falls. The storm continues, determined as ever. Nagisa takes the wheel again and fixes her gaze on me. "We're not home anymore, so I didn't break any promises."

It would be more accurate to say that I made Nagisa promise, rather than meeting any mutual agreement on the point. I decided for the both of us that no one could find out what we discovered very early on. She always fought against such secrecy, though we'd both heard the rumors surrounding our birth and inauspicious arrival. We both grew up knowing that no islander holds love for the sea or the Beasts beyond. All the creatures of the deep are full of dangerous desires, or so every child is told. We observe its truth every year, sending up our futile payments, promising they are freely given for the sake of all those monsters no living islander has ever even seen.

My sister never cared about anyone looking our way and seeing something monstrous within. She ate sweets until she made herself sick; she stole whatever caught her eye at market; she crept to the sea at night and let out the screams that everyone talked about by daylight but never investigated come dark. She stared out at the horizon with all the longing I fought against. She can never help it: she is always full of want.

I say, "You should've helped me with the ashes. They would have left us alone."

Nagisa sneers. "They're stone sharks. All they care about is gem and blood, both of which are on this boat. They don't care about the dead."

"You promised."

I am just as full of want as she is, only I want to be *safe*.

Nagisa sighs. She steps back towards me and holds me close in a cold, wet hug. "I'm sorry," she says. "I was protecting us." Her grin is less beastly by the time we separate, but her eyes are still golden green.

The way is treacherous, but we knew it would be. I wake one morning to serpentine beings nudging curious snouts that nearly capsize the boat. Another night, a nest of mermaids brings our father's boat to a complete stop when they crowd close. For hours they try to tempt us overboard. When Nagisa leans over the side to let out a volley of sound, the mermaids only circle frantically, ecstatic, fins and tails splashing, a mass of slippery colors gnashing their white, white fangs in delight.

As we near the Many-Headed Beast's realm, his brethren rise from the water to watch our passage: goggle-eyed, glittering, some scaled and tentacled, others with lantern-like lights protruding from their heads or notched fins rough as rust. They all tower over our craft. They make no move to attack. Instead, they touch at our ship, a threat, a caress.

My sister's eyes glow golden green more often than not. She seems far more alive here than she ever did on the island, where she spent too much of her time sullen and surrounded by sand. "I hate it," she used to say. "I hate the digging and the fungus. I'm sick of the scent of the rockrose and the pine. Sick of waiting here." The sea and all its horrors called, tugging at the wild caught deep down in our bellies, but I was never waiting for anything more than our home in the forest or the sun through the trees on market day, the sight of our neighbors returning home on their boats.

We have shared everything, from the womb to the discovery of what we hide beneath our human skins, that never-ending shriek, that gnawing want like a shadow spreading. As Kaito girls, we must share even this journey past the edges of our world, though it brings us further from one another, every day. The truth of it lies uneasily between our beds: Neither of we sisters have told one another what we have brought to sacrifice to the Many-Headed Beast.

Deep in the cargo hold, we have collected an island's worth of sacrifices. It is unusual as beastly demands go. Perhaps this is why we have been asked to personally deliver this particular tithe to the Many-Headed Beast himself. This year, he requests, of all things, secrets freely given from every living soul on the Island at the Edge of the World.

Before we left, the village elder reminded us: it is not our place to ask what the Beasts will do with these secrets. It is not our place to question how they will know what each secret means to its owner, or what defines a secret, or even what counts as a secret for such a sacrifice. All we must remember is the recorded years when single villagers failed to pay their tithes or the times when clever young villagers thought to trick the Beasts with double-edged gifts. There were other islands, once, the elder reminded us. We are the last.

Where our journey ends, we haul our cargo up to the deck, armloads and handfuls, secret after secret: a cracked locket here, a stained envelope there, books and dried flower bundles, rings and bracelets, cloaks and a single ceramic dog, speckled and grey. Mostly there are bottles upon bottles of empty glass, corked up tight to hold fast furtive whispers. Together, my sister and I drop them into the sea.

Nagisa doesn't look at me when she asks, "Did you throw yours?" Her long hair is tied up. Her eyes are deep brown.

"No," I say. "You?" She shakes her head. She holds my hand. We share this moment, this likeness, and it is our last.

The Many-Headed Beast does not so much rise from the ocean as it seems the sea simply splits down the center to make room for its sheer mass. A torso could exist, miles and miles beneath; perhaps there are arms and legs. It doesn't seem to matter when there are that many eyes, all staring. Heads upon heads upon heads block out the sun.

I never knew how much the oceans could hold.

There are no niceties. The Many-Headed Beast speaks in its hundred million voices. They are a growl and a screech so loud that the world blurs and breaks between breaths. If the Beast asks why we have withheld its due right or whether it has sensed the saltwater in our blood, I could not say, overwhelmed by the wall of sound and breath from so many tongues, so many teeth.

I want, with all the might in my bones and blood, our home on our island and nothing more. The weight of sacrifices, given freely, feels like a single drop in the sea. The glass bottles bobbing in the foam are trifles. I would deliver boatloads of bottles, of secrets and firstborns, a hundred thousand times over.

The heads are all human. No one had ever warned us.

Perhaps I let go first, or perhaps my sister makes her decision. As I step back, she goes forward. Our linked hands separate.

Nagisa steps up to the railing, her whole body tilted forward as though for a kiss. The saltwater in her blood calls for so much more than I could ever have imagined. She takes a blade from her sheathe and draws the bright metal across her palm. Warm red drops into the waves, swallowed whole —given freely. She says her secret aloud: "I won't go back. I never planned to. I will stay here. . . where I'm supposed to be."

When she climbs up a rung on the railing, the wood creaks. *Stone sharks,* I think dimly, of that night so long ago. My sister lets loose the scream at the base of her belly. What was once so unearthly, rattling the clouds in the sky, is now high and thin, dying out against the Many-Headed Beast's unending body.

Dwarfed and desperate, the light in Nagisa's eyes is a golden green pinprick. She is just another creature of the deep with all its desires and demands.

The ocean churns against our father's boat. I do not know how to move, to breathe, beneath the weight of a hundred million gazes.

How many Beasts, I wonder, lumber beneath the surface, wanting, taking?

The Many-Headed Beast does not move. The world rushes back in a flash of breath and blur when Nagisa grabs for me and pulls. I am half over the railing before I catch myself on the splintered wood, flailing. "Stop it! Nagisa!" The boat groans beneath us.

"It wasn't enough," she hisses at me. "I can't go back. I won't." Her eyes are lit up, sickly gold, and she offers no apology as she fights to fling me into the sea, one last offering, freely given, from her heart.

"Wait," I plead. "I haven't given mine yet. He's waiting for mine too!"

A hundred million eyes drift indifferently in a hundred million directions. The Many-Headed Beast exhales and its breath becomes the sea breeze, pushing the tides out and out. Somewhere, on the other end, gentle waves lap along the soft sand of the Island at the Edge of the World. The village elders count the days we have been gone and pray that we succeed, all the while waking in the night, wondering if tomorrow will be the day the Beasts return, seeking vengeance, wanting too much.

I take a breath. I grasp my sister's bleeding hand in both of mine and squeeze. I look her in her beastly eyes and tell her my secret.

"I'm going home," I say. "I'm leaving here and going home and I'm going to make sure no one ever knows what we are." Nagisa's face twists, ready to argue. The railing wobbles beneath our weight. "They'll never know what *I* am," I say and do not apologize either.

I do not know who moves first. We claw at hair and draw back fists, scrape blood and tooth and nail and knuckle alike. My sister is silent. The wail I let out disappears across the water. Above us, around us, the Many-Headed Beast waits patiently for me to deliver my secret, paid in full.

In the end, all it takes is one last push. Our palms lie flat against each other's hearts. We shove off. The railing snaps. We share flight. The single scream my sister lets out is all too human.

She hits the water, taking my secret with her. The final tithe is paid.

People call us the Island at the Edge of the World because we are the last smudge of land unmoored from the continent, set adrift before the endless horizon. When I return home, I tell everyone only of the salt and storms and the blue-green screams of the deep. I tell them of the Beasts that rule the seas. I confirm the necessity of the price we must pay each year to safeguard our spit of rocky crag and stilted home. I return to a life among the dirt and fungi, the rockrose and pine. I feel a stillness in my soul that tells me I want no more than this.

Yet, sometimes, in the night, I wake myself screaming.

After all, there is a beastly shriek that lives in my belly, always. I spend my days dreading the signs that will mean one more journey out as the last Kaito, carrying more offerings, carrying more ashes. My dreams are filled with the impossibly large Many-Headed Beast, its hundred million gazes, its hidden body beneath the murk and the miles. Always, I am able to recognize just one head among the many, its golden-green gaze lancing through me like the sharp end of a spear. When I wake in the night, I crawl to the shoreline and stare into the black. I think about how it felt to want and to take and to destroy. When the sun rises, the saltwater in my veins recedes. It slides below again, beneath the surface, into the deep.

"Monsters Calling Home" was originally written for the 2020 New York City Midnight Short Story competition with the following prompt: action/adventure, a burial at sea, and a traitor. As someone raised on an island, a lot of my stories involve the ocean and my all-consuming fear and fascination for deep-sea gigantism. The Many-Headed Beast lumbered in from another story I could never quite finish; he made his own home here as a terrifying sea god and I'm pretty okay with that. As for the Kaito sisters, I believe all women go through life with an inhuman scream at the base of their bellies. Let's talk about that more.

Cheri Kamei
Honolulu, HI
June 7, 2021

Cheri Kamei is a basement goblin and a floral print disaster. Her short story, "Blood in the Thread," a queer retelling of the Crane Wife folktale, is available on *Tor.com*. She resides in Honolulu, Hawaii with her wife and all the plants she struggles to keep alive.

SEVEN SNAPSHOTS OF A BROKEN HEART

SHANE DOUGLAS KEENE

I.

She turns her back,
as if on to the next chore;
as if she just finished folding the laundry;
as if she hadn't just plunged a
five-inch blade repeatedly into the
flesh of lust and brutality;
as if she weren't dressed in
blood like lace lingerie,
standing sleekly naked and red
before a breath-clouded window,
smiling softly, humming a tuneless tune
as she watches children
make their way to wherever children
go in the frosty morning

II.

she holds her pale hand,
fluttery like a dove or a
flickering lamp,
across her barrenness,
trying to retain what
she no longer has,
her womb now
blessed only with
darkness and sorrow,
the scar on her
hollowed-out heart
unchallenged
even by that
on her skin,
mark of a scalpel
flash,
still livid,
throbbing red,
enraged

III.

his, she believes, are the
hands of a lover,
his eyes, those of the wolf,
she the fair flesh,
sweet-succulent-fallen
into his roaming gaze
and floating
the current
to its
source

the headwaters are
treacherous,
deadly, and soon enough
she drowns in him,
bequeathed to his
selection of belongings
for ever and ever till
death, damnation
severs the thread that
binds her to him

she worries the wolf
will scent her
silent cycle
and take umbrage, add
another fracture to
the soul he's
already shattered

IV.

the gift is looming large
within her soul,
belly too, and she's as near
happy as she'll ever
be, but she knows
the gift,
the glow,
of unconditional love,
and it's a boon to
her broken spirit
to know something
so ethereal, as yet nonexistent,
could be her Genesis anew,

her son;
Adam

V.

his God is violence,
and the child will never
set eyes on the
living, never have a
cherub face to turn to
the sun;
the only things
this angel will experience
are warmth, suffering, and
the silence of mortality;
innocence passed into
hands of rage,
and thereby into the
open arms of darkness;
a candle
extinguished
by the match that lit it

VI.

when the
brazen bleeding
is on pause she
vows, *never again,*
but in hospital, she
is all protector,
all denial

never him, no,

Doctor,
yes I'm certain
Officer,
it was a fall
traumatologist,
his are the
hands of love,
and off home she
goes, every picture
she sees on
every false front
is an ancient
billboard, tagged by
its own indecision

VII.

he's in the kitchen,
cutting green lime for
a blue cocktail,
knife sharp,
flashing with fluorescence
when she shuffles in
the door, more
zombie-wraith
than ever;
she hides the
widow she already
is deep inside

he looks up,
scowls,
she stands meekly
mild-mannered,

watching the glorious
gorgeous
blade—
slash, flash,
flash, slash—
in the vision of
eyes that will never
look rested
again;
he tosses the flashing
wonder he holds
on the countertop;
her tumultuous mind quiets
but her heart sees red;
for the first time in weeks,
she smiles,
but it isn't pretty

like plants in fertile soil,
or a child in a woman's womb,
something grows in the heart of
that silent place in her mind;
she sheds yesterday one
slow, scabrous garment
at a time;
her steady fingers wrap
around a handle, worn,
wooden, rivets beginning
to oxidize,
blade (*slash flash*) as
bright and
comfortable as
sunshine on an
unfamiliar day;

she wonders how her
soul would fare were it
homeless, without
her body;
she approaches the
wolf as it sleeps in
her den,
hears the soft
breath of slumber;
recognizes the
quiet that kills
him as the
bloody blade of
rage and revenge
rises and falls—
slashes, flashes—
red in the rising
morning

Originally, the first verse of this poem was the entire poem. I never liked it, felt the ambiguity and lack of motive made it too soft. And I always wondered, why did she do this. I saw this submission call and thought, I know what she would do, but why did she do it? So I had the answer, I just needed to pose the rest of the question.

Shane D. Keene
Portland, OR
May 30, 2021

Shane Douglas Keene is a poet, writer, and musician living in Portland, Oregon. He is a co-founder of inkheist.com and he wrote the companion poetry for Josh Malerman's serial novel project, *Carpenter's Farm* in 2020. He also has short fiction in Cemetery Gates's *Paranormal Contact* and has multiple works forthcoming. He is a neurodiverse queer and caregiver to his wife, a stroke victim, and he is a person who believes song can fix everything when sung loud enough.

BABY GIRL

J.V. GACHS

"No heartbeat."

Just two words. A simple incantation to destroy a world. The doctor speaks as I wipe off the ultrasound gel. I must pay close attention to my options. I have to understand everything she says. My brain goes too fast, unable to form a coherent thought. My knees shake as I stand up.

"There's no rush," she says, reading my mind, or maybe she's done this way too many times. "Go home. Call someone. Read this pamphlet. Rest over the weekend and come back on Monday."

Perinatal death. Now, what? The rounded, pastel-colored letters of the brochure curl around my chest like a python, leaving me breathless. The doctor points to a certain page.

"Look, this is the part you need to read, after the fifteenth week. There's everything I've told you, and if you have any further questions you can call this number here. It is an association that helps people going through this process. For now, you just have to pay attention to your fever. If it rises, come to the emergency room immediately, okay?"

I nod as I stand up to leave. I should call someone. My

mother. Eva. How does one start that conversation? How do I tell them you've died even before opening your eyes? The next thing I know, I'm home. My feet float. At the same time, I have never felt so heavy. I lie down on the couch and place my hands on my bulging belly. I pull them away startled to realize I'm caressing a heart that no longer beats.

"I am a coffin."

My stomach shrinks. My throat is knotted. I grab my cell phone to call the doctor, overwhelmed by the need to tear you out of me as soon as possible. To get rid of your body. Of your weight in my womb. It lasts an instant. Deep down, I want to keep you safe in here forever. Once I make my decision, whatever it may be, I will no longer be pregnant. I will no longer be your future mother, Paola. I contemplate our possibilities according to the brochure. An oxytocin-induced delivery when I see fit. Or wait. Expectant management. My body will realize what has happened soon. It will try to get rid of you on its own. Like a normal labor. Normal. Like such a thing exists. I also have to decide if I want to see you, spend some time with you. With your lifeless body. Your corpse. The repulsion toward the idea tinged with irrational hope. What if you cry when I hold you? What if my love makes that tiny heart start beating? In fiction, pure love, the real good kind, can achieve anything. Even that. No shock this time. I stroke my belly. Closing my eyes, I embrace the absurd idea of pretending nothing has changed. I hide the pamphlet under the couch cushions. Nothing that confirms the certainty of your untimely death is welcome here. Calling anyone seems impossible right now. I just want a gazpacho. Yes. That's what I want. Play some music and cook a gazpacho as if it were yesterday. As if the words "no heartbeat” had never been uttered. As if the most important decision these days still were which car seat to buy for you, Paola. Unravel those two words. Undo the spell.

When I was little, my grandmother always had a jar of fresh gazpacho in the fridge. When I moved on my own, she gave me a notebook with all her recipes in her round and childish handwriting. I know how to prepare this fresh tomato soup, but I always take out the notebook and place it on the table next to the vegetables. The pages are stamped with tomato and garlic flowers created by my fingerprints after chopping the ingredients. Following her instructions, I feel her watching over me. I start with the cucumber, the garlic, the green bell pepper. The smell of the vegetables lights up the kitchen. I cut the tomatoes while humming a copla, one my grandma loved. Yo me clavaré en los ojos, alfileres de cristal, pa' no verme cara a cara, contigo y con tu verdad. I'll stab crystal pins in my eyes, so I don’t have to face you nor your truth. My will is so strong that it’s capable of forcing your heart to jump start. Rage invades me at the thought of all those people who don't deserve the air they breathe, the space they waste. The annoying neighbor across the street that we can't get rid of. My wretched boss. The bastard who is your father because I was too drunk that day. Because I missed him and fell into his trap. Because he intended to make you an anchor to keep me by his side. I hated you for being his until you started to move inside of me. How many nights I spent biting my pillow wishing you weren’t here. That you weren’t at all. Now, God, wasn't it a bit too late to answer my prayers?

The knife cutting my finger brings me back to reality. My body is still mine. The pain reminds me I'm not a wooden coffin but human flesh. I instinctively stick my bloody finger in my mouth as I search for a Band-Aid in the bathroom. The metallic taste floods my senses. I stop in my tracks. A spark. A small shock. Your feet pounding against my body.

"Baby girl?"

Nothing. But I am sure as hell I have felt it. I run to the kitchen, grab the knife and slice open my palm with it. A clear and distinct thought is now burned into my mind. A certainty I cannot ignore. Blood comes to the calling of the blade. I overcome the disgust cupping my hand. I plunge my tongue into this tiny red sea and swallow in the throes of longing. I wait.

There you are.

Stretching. Untwisting your limbs inside me. I cry. I do. I allow myself to because these are not tears of sorrow. Because I feel you more than ever. How you are now, still in my womb, and how you will be. Green eyes, singing voice, and pale skin. A cascade of freckles from eyes to lips. Small hands. Light feet. You're ticklish. And very hungry. You're starving. Your voice flows through my veins. Whispering to me what needs to be done. The sacrifice to keep you here with me. One I'm willing to offer. I cover the wound on my hand with a bandage before throwing myself on the phone. I don't hesitate. I don't tremble. Immersed in the certainty of your voice, crazy as it may sound, I trust you, my child.

"I thought you didn't want anything to do with me," your father answers on the other side.

"I know. . . Efrén, look, you were right. Why don't we spend the weekend at La Caseta and talk about it?"

"So, good to know you've finally got it into that head that you can't do this alone. When I get off work I'll get my back-pack and go up there."

I hang up smiling. What a surprise the doctor is going to get on Monday. I make a list of what we'll need. The country house I inherited from my grandmother is an hour away from the city. Plenty of time to go to the supermarket, pharmacy, and hardware store before Efrén arrives. Lucky I didn't get rid of my grandmother's arsenal of pills. In winter, the village is always empty. The tourists won't come until spring. Just like you, Paola.

"I brought firewood," Efrén says with annoyance when I open the door, looking at the empty woodshed. "How come you always forget of something so important?"

"You're always on top of everything. Thank you."

He holds my wrist too tightly. He caresses my belly. My skin prickles. An unpleasant tingling settles at the end of my spine. He kisses me. You stir. I try to get away. He pulls us closer.

"Let's have dinner first," I manage to say, slipping away from his kisses. "Your baby girl is hungry."

We sit at the table and I place the wine flask in front of him. I chew slowly, listening to him talk about the plans he has made for us two, but without asking us. Slower and slower. Dragging out the words. His mouth dries up, he drinks more wine and you cry with hunger in my womb. Efrén falls to the floor dragging the tablecloth with him, spilling the wine and the roast. Breaking my grandmother's china.

Although painless thanks to the epidural, I do feel the tension, the pressure. The nurses talk to each other. They laugh. The sun comes in through the window of my private room. The doctor smiles. My mom, your grandma, is holding my hand, soaking my sweat. She's so joyful. Delighted. We both wish my father was alive to meet you. Such a perfect day for induced labor. My doctor has been so worried since she made that unforgivable mistake with the diagnosis. She wouldn't risk taking any chances and wanted to get you out as soon as it was safe for the both of us. I agree. She let me pick the date, though. March 21. My spring rosebud, my baby girl. After all we've been through, I'm so looking forward to seeing that little angel face.

Going from vegan to meat-eater wasn't all that pleasurable at first. It is certainly one of those acquired tastes, like beer or tobacco. That rotten fish they eat I-don't-remember-where. I might even miss it now that my pregnancy is over and I can go back to broccoli and hummus. I will never be grateful enough to my grandmother for forcing me to participate in the hog slaughters at home when I was a little girl. She believed it would toughen me up. It turned me into a strong advocate for vegetarianism instead, but it also ingrained in my mind in such a way that when necessity presented itself, I knew by heart every step of the process. Grandma's sturdy hands guided mine that night, placing the cauldron for the blood, cutting open the flesh to collect the entrails. She gave me the strength to take care of your needs, baby.

The matanza, when done at home instead of sending the hogs to the slaughterhouse, was a process in which the whole family participated. Almost like a party. Even the kids had their part, and were later offered some of the clean entrails as balloons to play for the day. Doing it alone was a challenge, but your incessant calling encouraged me, cheered me on and did not allow me to faint. While stirring the blood in the bucket so it would not curdle–which would ruin it for the blood sausage–your hunger was unbearable. The metallic smell, your screams drowned out in my mind, the cold of the cellar, my hands shaking. You're going to have a temper. That's a given. I had to reopen the cut on my hand to calm you down when walking back in the dark from the swamp after throwing Efren's car and cell phone in the cold water. How convenient your father was a scumbag. No one questioned his messages saying he was leaving. It wasn't out of character that he would flee to avoid paying me alimony.

It was the longest night of my life. It was worth it. I'd do it all over again to be here now, as I am, overwhelmed by the certainty that you will cry soon. We will go home and it will all have been nothing more than a nightmare from which we will finally wake up.

The slaughtered meat has to spend at least twelve hours just there in the freezing air of the cellar before being cut up. That time is not for leisure or rest. The guts have to be cleaned with hot water, vinegar and lemon. It is an arduous task, necessary to prepare the chorizo and the black pudding. Otherwise so much of the meat would go wasted. I sleeplessly roasted onions and pumpkin following grandma's black pudding recipe all night. Before I had a second of rest, it was already time for the quartering. Loins, belly, ribs, brains. . . I managed to get it all stored in grandma's big freezer before Monday came. I'll never forget the doctor's face. Her shame. She does not know our little secret. Your medicine. I will miss Saturdays batch cooking for the week in grandma's kitchen among the smell of roasted garlic, peppers, stewing meat, *chorizo* snacks, and sips of warm wine with cinnamon. Wouldn't it be great if we make a tradition out of that, Paola? Would you mind making some changes in the main ingredients, I wonder.

"I can already see her head," the doctor tells me with the biggest smile. It's not every day that you help deliver a baby you gave up for dead three months before.

Your body pushes through mine. My mom cries with joy. Your head is out of me and now come the shoulders. A deathly silence falls in the room.

"What's wrong?" I ask nervously, trying to sit up and see something. "What's wrong, Mom?" I cry, demanding an answer. She isn't holding my hand anymore.

Wasn't it enough? Wasn't my sacrifice sufficient for you to live? The doctor gives me a horrified look. My mom covers her face. You are no longer part of me. My body's empty. Your cry shatters the silence. You are alive. The nurses turn away from me. One of them runs out the door yelling. The doctor observes you, mute. Her hands tremble. She swallows. Lost for words.

Your high-pitched shrieks pierce my ear. She lifts your contorting body. I can finally see you.

There you are, my baby girl.

Over the years, I have realized that trying to imagine worse outcomes for the situations I find difficult to process is my way of coping with them. I was pretty young when I learned that I wouldn't have kids of my own. Women's infertility, perinatal death, and miscarriages all seem to be, still, taboo. Something to keep as a secret. As if it were something shameful. As if you were broken.

This short story sparked from the need to address that but also to picture situations potentially worse than not experiencing motherhood at all.

J.V. Gachs
Asturias, Spain
June 6, 2021

J.V. Gachs is a Spanish classicist, writer, and aspiring librarian currently working as a Latin teacher. After many years without writing fiction, she got back to it during the Spanish pandemic lockdown in 2020. Obsessed with sudden death, ghosts, and women villains, she always writes with a cat (or two) in her lap. Both Spanish and US magazines have published her short stories.

RED ROTARY PHONE

TIM MCGREGOR

"I did it," the caller says. "I took Jeremy."

"Oh yeah?" I'm the one who answers the phone. I'm always the one who answers these days. "Where'd you take him?"

"To a quarry," says the caller. Male, voice quivering. "I didn't mean to—you know—I just lost control. I'm sorry. So sorry. . . "

The caller breaks into tears, blubbering down the line.

I have no time for these people anymore. "Which quarry? How far from the abduction site was it? What time was this?"

"What?"

I hammer more questions, demanding specifics. He flounders and then hangs up.

Another crank. I don't even bother logging the calls anymore. The machine records them anyway.

There are two phone lines in our house. The regular residential number and the one that the police installed. A tipline about Jeremy's abduction. The tipline rings all week long and we have to answer it.

Jeremy was twelve when he was abducted. My kid

brother, three years younger. There was one witness at the time, Jeremy's friend, Derek. The two of them were on their bikes when a white van forced them off the road and the driver abducted my brother at gunpoint. Derek bolted into the cornfield and ran home.

Derek had a good memory, recalling a lot of detail to the police. A white van with rust on the wheel wells and out-of-state plates. The driver was white, six feet tall, middle-aged. A blue baseball cap, plaid hunting jacket. Dirty fingernails like a mechanic.

The police went into action, coordinating with police departments in nearby towns. It was all over the news at the time, everyone looking for Jeremy, for the white van. Every mechanic in the tri-county area was brought in and questioned.

And then there was the tipline. Calls from all over the country, at all hours of the day. The police followed up every call, but the search for Jeremy went nowhere and everything ground to a halt. Except the tipline. Even now, four years later, the calls keep coming.

It was a lot for a small police station in a rural town. They took the calls diligently for the first three years, fielding thousands of tips. None of it useful, none of it leading to anything. Then the calls got crazier and the police got tired of the hours it took to man the tipline. So they installed the line in our house.

The telephone is candy-apple red, like the Bat Phone. It sits on a side-table in the hall. An older rotary phone, not a push-button. There is a notepad and pen next to it. On the shelf below is the clunky machine that records every call.

My mom and dad ran to it every time it rang, but the calls just got weirder and more bizarre. And cruel. They hung up after each call with their eyes a little more hollowed out. Dad grew ashen, Mom began to flinch at every stray sound.

Within three months of the tipline being installed, the two of them became zombies. The callers just pummeled them both into numbness.

That's when I took over the task of answering the tipline. I understood then how they'd had the stuffing punched out of them. The phone calls are awful. Psychics call to say that Jeremy is dead, but they know where his body is buried. Others claim they saw my brother at a truck stop or the mall. Some, like the caller tonight, phone to say that they killed Jeremy. Sometimes they go into graphic detail about what they did to him. Some call just to cry.

Every call on the tipline has to be answered. I've become numb to it, like my parents, but I cope better. I've constructed a shield between me and every weirdo who feels compelled to dial the number on the milk carton.

A lot of people call to say that Jeremy is in Heaven now. He's an angel, sitting in a meadow at the feet of our Lord and Savior. A saint.

That's what Jeremy has become since he was taken; a saint. He wasn't, of course. He was just a kid, but no one mentions how he made a big display of farting or how he wet the bed until he was ten. Now he's an angel. He's more of a ghost, really, haunting every room in this house. He consumes everything, takes up all the oxygen. His room is a shrine that no one, except Mom, is allowed to enter. People still leave flowers on our porch. Sometimes it's a football or comic books. Gifts for when he comes home. That's what everyone is waiting for. Our lives have been put on pause since the day someone took Jeremy. All of us holding our breath and turning blue.

The truth is that Jeremy is gone and he's never coming home. I have to keep that to myself because everyone needs to keep going, to hold on.

Especially the callers. There it is again, the red phone ringing in the hallway.

It's astonishing the number of people who call to tell me that they killed my brother, but as awful as these are, they're not the worst. The really bad ones are the kind that's calling now.

"Jeremy's line." This is how I answer the phone.

"Katie? Is that you?"

Lots of people know my name. It's no big deal.

"Do you have information about Jeremy?" I don't bother hiding the apathy in my voice anymore. Some people hang up right away when they hear it.

"Katie, it's me. Jeremy."

You'd be surprised at how many of these we get. The voice on the other end is male, teenage-ish. Jeremy was abducted before his voice dropped. Even if it really was him, I wouldn't know his voice. I'm numb to these calls too.

"Where have you been, Jeremy? Everyone's worried about you."

"I don't know where I am. It's dark. It's always dark here."

"I see. But you got to a phone? Call 911. They'll trace the call and come find you."

"I can't," he says. "The phone only dials this number."

"Right. So, you're calling from Heaven?"

"I don't know what this place is. It's not Heaven. It's dark. And lonely."

It's usually at this point that the caller breaks into confession or tears, often both. I wait for the sobs, but they don't happen.

"Katie, can you tell Mom and Dad something for me?"

"Do you want to tell them yourself? I can go get them."

"No. They won't listen. But they might if it comes from you. Tell them to let it go. I'm not coming home. They need to move on."

This isn't how these calls usually go. I want to hang up now.

"You too, Katie," he says. "You have a life to live. I don't want you wasting it on something that will never happen. I'm sorry."

Now I'm angry. I'm angry because it hurts.

"Why do you people do this to us? What kind of sicko gets off on this?" I've been told over and over not to lose my temper with these callers, but even I have my limits. "Do you really think this is funny?"

"I'm sorry."

The line is quiet. I should hang up, but I don't.

"Hey," he says, "whatever happened to Snowball? Is she okay?"

"Who?"

"The cat. Remember she was limping around and acting weird?"

The barn cat. We called her Snowball because she was white. I'd forgotten all about her. She was limping and acting skittish. Jeremy was worried about her. That was just before he vanished.

"I don't know," I tell him. "She kind of got forgotten about in all the chaos."

"Too bad. I always liked Snowball. Remember how she used to sun herself on the hood of the truck? Dad had to honk the horn at her every morning."

Details. Little things only Jeremy or I would know. Now I really want to hang up.

"Did you just let Snowball die, Katie?"

"Stop it."

The voice sours, turning into a babyish singsong. "Wittle Snowball wuvs you, Katie. She's with me now. But she's sad you let her die."

Laughter erupts down the line. More than one person. I can picture them all huddled around the phone, giggling.

"Good job, asshole," I say. "You stayed on the line long enough to be traced—"

They hang up.

It takes me a minute to calm down. Mom comes into the kitchen, asks about the call. Just another crank, I tell her. She puts the kettle on, asks if I want tea. She's a lot better these days, now that she doesn't answer the tipline. Dad too.

Down the hall, the red phone starts ringing again.

"Red Rotary Phone" was inspired by the 1989 abduction of Jacob Wetterling of St. Joseph, Minnesota. National media coverage brought thousands of calls to not only the police tipline, but also the Wetterling home. So many, in fact, that the police installed a second tipline in their house. The parents answered every call, no matter how absurd or horrific, and passed these tips on to the police. The case went unsolved for 27 years. I learned about this a few years ago on a podcast and it has haunted me ever since.

Tim McGregor
Toronto, ON
June 6, 2021

Tim McGregor is the author of *Hearts Strange and Dreadful* from Off Limits Press and the paranormal series *The Spookshow*. Tim lives in Toronto with his wife and two children. His new novel, *Wasps in the Ice Cream*, will be out in spring 2022 from Silver Shamrock Publishing.

TAKE CONTROL

EMMA E. MURRAY

As Sara swung the door to the parking garage open, the roaring white noise of the storm and the chill in the air surrounded the two young girls. Her little sister, Kiara, shivered and rubbed her arms as she followed Sara around the corner to the ramp leading down to the third floor. Water cascaded down the sides of the structure, the few cars empty and waiting on a Wednesday afternoon, their dark windshields facing out toward the rain. Sara nearly had to shout to be heard above the din.

"You get to try first since it was your present, but don't hog it."

She set the large toy jeep on the concrete and reluctantly passed the remote to her sister's eager hands. Kiara's entire face beamed with pride as she tried the controls and watched the purple vehicle lurch forward then backward at her command.

"Be careful now," Sara warned, reaching out as if to take the controller, but Kiara twisted away. Her thumb orchestrated a sharp turn, almost flipping the toy car.

"I got it! I got it!" she shouted, furrowing her brow and

twisting farther away from her sister. Concentrating on the tiny joysticks, the tip of her tongue stuck out from her lips.

"Careful or you're gonna crash!" Sara shouted, and grabbed for the controller again.

"No, I've got it. See?"

Kiara guided the jeep in a perfect figure eight before bringing it back to stop at their feet. With a smirk and side-long glance before quickly bursting into giggles, the five-year-old handed the controller to her sister as if challenging her to prove the supposed superiority she pretended three years gave her.

"Now watch this," Sara said, right away pushing the joystick as hard as she could so that the little car skidded, then roared full throttle back down the ramp. Suddenly, she lost control and Kiara started screaming in her ear, making her mind glaze with panic. As her shaky hands attempted to steer, she over-corrected and the jeep dramatically flipped over and over again before landing on its wheels and careening around the corner, stopping out of view with a loud crash.

Both girls gasped as the color ran from their faces. Kiara started to whimper, her bottom lip jutting out and quivering as tears spilled down her cheeks.

"Don't cry. I bet it's not too bad. Let's go see," Sara said, trying to be brave for her little sister, but holding her breath as they made their way down the ramp, almost too afraid to look.

There it was: the purple paint scratched, wheels still whirring, and resting on its side next to the fresh dent along the door of a minivan.

"Momma's gonna kill us," Kiara whispered, eyes wide and fixed on the wreck.

"Naw, she'll never know," Sara answered as she picked up the jeep and righted it.

"But look, there's even a little purple on the van! Momma is gonna kill us for sure."

The kindergartner burst into tears, but her sister ignored her except for a cursory hush as she squatted next to the dented door and attempted to scratch away the few telltale purple flakes with the bitten nubs of her fingernails.

"There, look. There's no way anyone will know it was us now. You can stop crying."

"Momma told us we weren't allowed to play without her watching, and now she's gonna find out and take it away, and I've barely even gotten to play with it at all," the girl said, interrupting herself with sobs every couple words.

"I told you, she'll never know!" Sara shouted, but as soon as the words left her lips, she got a strange feeling and the air caught in her lungs and throat, ice cold. Her mouth dropped open a tiny bit as her eyes scanned the shadows and empty cars for the person she could feel watching them. Finally, she found him.

A pasty-skinned man with square, dark-rimmed glasses watched the girls from behind the wheel of a scuffed-up light blue, Mercedes. His face was almost expressionless, like a mannequin, but his dark eyes burned into Sara's and made her stomach squirm. The car sat dark and parked between two other unoccupied vehicles, six or so cars down the line. The man watched them, half hidden in shadow and barely blinking.

Kiara sensed her sister's unease and stopped crying, sniffling a little and looking around before also catching sight of the strange man. His gaze slowly shifted from the eldest girl to the younger one, and for a moment, they both stared back as if hypnotized.

Sara finally broke free and picked up the jeep, cradling it in her arms, then turned away so she wouldn't feel compelled to look any longer.

"Let's go up to the top and play."

Kiara whimpered again. "But that guy saw us hit the car. He's gonna tell on us."

"No, he won't. He's just some weirdo. Come on, let's go."

"I've never seen a guy like that before. He's staring at us."

"I know," Sara growled, hugging the car tightly to her chest with one arm while the other yanked her sister along. "He's freaking me out. Let's go."

"What's wrong with him?"

"Probably just drugs, like Momma always says."

"I wanna go home."

"No, not yet. Momma's gonna know we snuck out the second she hears that door, and you know you're gonna step on the creaky spot like always. Don't you want to play with your car just a little more before she takes it away?"

"Fine," Kiara said, biting her lip and bowing her head slightly as they walked.

The wind howled and blew chilly raindrops through the parking garage as they walked up the ramp, then the next, and the next until they reached the top of the building where the roof ended, opening up to the swirling gray sky. Only a few cars were left in the storm on the exposed roof, the rain mixing with small hail that bounced up from the concrete and made tinny noises as it collected on the hoods and windshields.

Sara set the toy car down as the girls huddled together near the top of the ramp, just far enough from the opening to stay dry. She drove it out onto the roof, splashing through a puddle, but then noticed Kiara's still teary eyes, and with a sigh, handed the controller back to her sister.

They laughed and cheered each other on, passing the controller back and forth as they took turns racing the jeep around the roof of the parking garage until that same uneasy feeling came over Sara and she compulsively turned around.

The car with the waxy, pale man had soundlessly creeped behind them at some point over the last ten minutes, parking in the middle of the lanes, facing them. The man was standing outside the driver side door, watching them. He was a little taller than average and his pallid face and the black frames of his glasses made the dark irises of his eyes even more prominent. He wore casual clothing, nothing unusual: jeans, a faded blue tee with a red and orange bird spread across the chest, and a black baseball cap, but there was something unnerving and strange to Sara about seeing an adult in such casual clothing in the middle of the day on a Wednesday. She tried to brush the thought away, but everything about the man caused a feeling of pulsing red alarm to flash through her mind.

Kiara instantly felt her sister stiffen. She turned around and gasped. She dropped the controller but quickly bent over and picked it up, looking to the man, then her sister, then back to the man again. She felt the sobs building inside her, but she kept them contained as she looked to Sara to cue their next move. The jeep sat idle behind them while hail and hard rain pummeled it.

"I saw what happened downstairs," the man said, his voice slow and sugary like sickening molasses, though loud enough to hear over the storm. He clicked his tongue and shook his head with displeasure.

"It was just an accident, mister. No big deal." Sara spoke in a nonchalant, calm voice, but inside her heart quaked in her chest.

"Ah, no big deal. No big deal? I bet the family who owns that van wouldn't think it was 'no big deal.'"

"Sure, they would. There was hardly a dent. Now would you please leave us—"

"Oh really? Do you know the family that drives that car?"

"No, sir," Kiara muttered, holding her hands together in

front of her, eyes downcast and face darkening. Sara nudged her with an elbow.

"No, we don't, but we will write them a sorry letter and leave it on the car. I'm sure they won't—"

"A sorry note? Heh, I'm sure your mom would want you to do more than that. Oh buddy, she's going to be mad at y'all."

"No, she won't," Sara snapped, but Kiara was already nodding and crying.

"You girls better come with me so we can all go tell her."

Kiara's cries intensified, becoming audible even above the crashing rain. A shiver ran down Sara's spine, and she felt like she was breathing deeper and faster than before, her eyes taking in every detail around her; and yet they all became jumbled in her frenzied thoughts.

"What do you mean? You don't know our mom. You need to leave us alone right now!" She spat the words out like venom, her upper lip rising a little as she finished.

"I do know your mom, and I'm also a police officer so I have a duty to report your accident. Even if it was a toy car, you still caused damage so there has to be a report. So now, come along."

An ancient instinct made Sara put her arm up against her sister and step back, forcing the sobbing girl a few paces back with her.

"You don't look like a cop, and you definitely don't know our mom. You need to go away right now or. . . or. . . I'll scream."

The man took two steps toward them, closing the distance she had created. He seemed calm, though he moved his lips together like he was hiding his agitation.

"I don't want you to start screaming because there's no reason for that. I'm a cop and I'm just here to help the poor owner of that van. But if you did scream, it wouldn't matter. .

. the rain'll drown it out. And if it doesn't, no one will hear you anyway, or they'd just think you're screaming while you're playing." He half smirked before his face smoothed back into an expressionless mask.

"Not if I scream for help," Sara said, but the man stood, just as relaxed and blank as ever.

Sara's heart pounded like a drum in her throat as she realized he was right. She pushed Kiara back another few steps with her until they felt the rain splattering on their hair and backs, almost out from under the overhang.

The pale man moved back toward his car, opened the door and bent over. The trunk clicked as the lock released. The man walked behind the car, opening the trunk just a little before slamming it closed again. He came back to the door and bent to reach inside, as if collecting something from the cupholder or passenger seat.

For just a second, Sara let herself believe he might leave, but he straightened again and returned his piercing gaze at the girls. She hated herself for not taking the opportunity to run for help. She tried to move her feet, but they felt heavy and dull. Kiara sobbed quietly by her side.

The man walked toward them again, stepping in front of his car, and Sara's pulse raced as the tire iron came into view from behind his leg, his left hand clutching the handle.

"Why do you have that?" she asked, but much too softly for him to hear over the rain. She didn't need him to answer.

Next to her, Kiara's cries stifled, and Sara looked over to see her sister's mouth gaping, bottom lip quivering, and her eyes opened so wide the white showed all around. Then her eyes snapped shut, looking small and tight in her face as her mouth opened in another howling wail.

She glanced back to the man who wielded the tire iron, a simple tool now posing an ominous threat she'd never thought of before. He bounced it gently in his hand, passed it between his palms, then bounced it again as if weighing it, his own eyes caressing the tool with an almost loving gaze.

Sara's stomach tightened and twisted. She breathed in quick, shallow breaths, feeling like she couldn't get enough air. Her vision blurred in and out as her mind swam, light-headed. Kiara's cries continued next to her, making it hard to think. Swallowing, trying to retain composure, Sara swayed on her unsteady legs and silently prayed for a miracle: take us away, anywhere but here.

"Shut up! Won't you shut her up?" the man's whispered shout hissed through the roar of the wind. He took a few jerking, almost lunging steps toward them and Sara scrambled to hush her sister, stroking her hair and begging her to quiet down.

Kiara continued to sob, but buried her face in her sister's sweatshirt, which muffled it enough to calm the man. Sara continued the rhythmic strokes down the back of her head, her fingers gently tracing the tight braids, not just to calm her sister but to give her something to focus on to ground her mind.

"You're not going to scream," the man said, taking another two steps closer, now only ten feet from the girls, "Or you'll get hurt. I wouldn't want that. Two pretty little girls like you. It'd be so sad if something happened to you."

Sara's eyes darted back and forth between the tire iron, held nonchalantly in the man's left hand, and his face, white and sticky like spoiled milk. The dark eyes glistened, and though his face still stayed soft and limp, revealing no expression, his eyes almost twinkled in their dreadful glee.

"You're not a cop," Sara said, and the man laughed without joy.

"Maybe you're right." His words slipped out smooth as quicksilver and took with them any last semblance of safety or reality.

Sara felt herself float away from her body. She looked down to watch herself from far above. An uncanny feeling of electricity pulsed through her.

"Someone will see you and you'll get in big trouble."

"There's no one. You and I both know it."

Sara's eyes darted to the car, at the gap between it and the wall, measuring and calculating, but the man watched her and knew what she was thinking. She shifted her weight, ready to grab Kiara's arm, ready to run.

"Before you do that," the man's voice startled and stalled her, "think for one second. Maybe you'll get away, but she won't."

Sara held back tears as she realized he was right. She didn't need more than half a second to imagine the dash around the car; her sister stumbling, falling, and being left behind. Kiara would cry as she left her, taking long strides down the ramps to the door, the hall, their apartment. She might make it, but Kiara never would.

"I want to go home," Kiara shrieked into her sweater.

"What do you want from us?" Sara's voice strained to ask through her tears.

"Just get in the car. Both of you. You'll be alright. It'll all be fine if you just do what I say."

The man took a step back toward the open car door, relaxed just enough, and Sara darted to the wall facing the passenger door. Her open palms pressed against the cool concrete, ready to push off and run. His eyes glanced at Kiara then back, the metal tool twitching in his now unsteady hand. Kiara stared at her sister, wide-eyed again, her cries softened from shock.

Moments and memories flashed through Sara's mind as her consciousness floated above the scene. She could see the moment her mom walked through the front door, bringing her baby sister home from the hospital: small, dusky, and swaddled in a pink blanket with little birds all over it. Then the time her mother showed her how to feed her new sister with the bottle and even how to rock her to sleep. Next, the fishing trip with their dad last summer, and she remembered Kiara accidentally knocking the entire lure box into the lake, her tears, how she'd taken the blame for her sister, and how that night Kiara had crawled into bed with her after their dad had gone to sleep, hugging her tightly and whispering "thank you" over and over again.

"You'd leave her?" the man asked, a hint of disbelief beneath the cruel steel tone.

"Listen! Just listen, okay?" The words tumbled out fast as Sara still watched herself as if from above, sinewy and strong. "I'll run. I can make it back and you know it. You'll get caught."

"You'd abandon your sister?" he sneered. He tried to hide it, but disgust and fear crept across his face.

"If I run, you're done. But if I don't—" Sara took a deep breath to steady herself. Her own fear coursed through her veins like boiling water. "But—but—what if I don't? If I get in there, you'll let her go."

"Why?" As he asked, he raised the tire iron and stepped toward the trembling five-year-old. She called out to her big sister in a voice raspy from crying.

"Because if you let her go, you won't get caught. She's just a little kid. She's scared. She won't even be able to remember you. Just let her go home. Just promise you'll leave her, and I'll get in." She swallowed hard again and watched herself in awe of her own bravery.

"How do you know I won't just push her in too? Maybe she needs more punishment than you." His eyes slid back to Kiara and she shuddered under his gaze.

"I don't know that, but I'm saying I'll go with you if you

leave her. Follow whatever you say. Just leave her. Please. I'll do whatever you want. Just promise."

The man shifted his weight from one foot to the other. His face stayed placid, but his eyes revealed a slight softening, a twinkle of pride.

"Fine."

As he spoke, Sara's body flooded with relief. Her arm reached out toward her stunned sister who was still murmuring about wanting to go home. From her viewpoint far above her physical body, she knew she was in charge of everything for just a moment, but it was long enough for what she needed to do.

"I'm going to be okay. Kiara, just go home. Okay? Promise you'll go home. Give Momma a hug from me. I'll be back. Don't worry about me." She forced a smile and hesitated, then added, "I love you."

"No, Sara! Don't go!" The little girl pleaded, but Sara opened the passenger door and slid inside. The man looked to the little girl, moved as if to approach her, but then his dark eyes went as pale as his face, his mouth fell open to gape like a fish, and his arms hung limply from slumped shoulders. Kiara gasped at his transformation, but the man just turned to walk back to the car door, stumbling like a zombie, and got in. Kiara watched as the blue car reversed and turned around, maneuvering in and out of a parking spot to face the right direction, then headed slowly down the ramp.

Kiara collapsed to the floor, sitting with her head thrown back, wailing at the ceiling. The wind changed directions just enough that rain now splattered across her face and body as the pangs of grief and fear flowed out of her. She couldn't stand up. She couldn't do anything but cry.

After a few minutes, the tears trailed off and she had nothing left inside her. Her adrenaline stores were emptied and she felt hollow and light as she stumbled to her feet like a baby who'd just learned to stand. She thought of the man's eyes and how strange they had looked for that moment. A gust of wind blew through the garage, chilling her through her clothes, and somehow it reminded her of Sara's breath on her ear when she whispered secrets. A deep pain in her gut told her she'd already wasted too much time. She walked down the first ramp, then the next, and quickened her pace as she got closer to home.

Just then, through the angled gap between levels, she saw the man again. He was walking quickly, tire iron still in hand, arms swinging in time with his hurried steps.

Her breath tucked itself deep into her lungs as she ducked behind a large red truck. His footsteps echoed through the garage as he headed up her ramp. Flattening herself, she struggled to slide under the truck, pulling in her hand and foot just as his feet appeared in her view from the undercarriage.

He didn't stop, and she didn't dare breathe more than in tiny, shallow flutters. She tried to follow his movement with her ears, but the rain and wind were too loud. She imagined him walking up each ramp, expecting to see her framed in the opening at the top level, and then his surprise when she wasn't there.

She counted in her head, not trying to measure how long it took him, but just to keep herself from screaming.

There he was, running back down the ramp. His feet pounded against the floor, and as he passed the truck, she could hear rage in his labored breathing.

She waited there, taking tiny sips of air and shaking as she expected him to come back and find her any second.

Minutes passed. After almost half an hour, she worked up the courage to creep back out.

She peeked from behind the truck, and when she saw he was not there waiting for her, she took a deep breath and sprinted down the final ramp, bursting through the door into the hallway of apartments on the third floor, and leaping past the seven doors before she made it to her own.

Throwing open the door and slamming it behind her, her shaking hands pulled each lock closed, and she found a deeper layer of tears, beginning to cry again. Sobs gushed out of her, arms outstretched in front of her, mouth pulled wide with her two baby teeth missing, as she ran into the room and straight into her mother's arms.

"Honey, what's wrong? Hold on," her mother said, pulling her daughter into her lap and then turning her attention briefly to the conference call on her computer. "Sorry guys, I've gotta go. You should have enough to get going. I'll send you the rest of the details later."

Ending the call, she gave her full attention to her daughter, and the gravity of the situation settled in the air around them.

"Baby, tell me what's wrong. Where's Sara? Did I hear the door?"

The story babbled out of Kiara all at once, like turning on a faucet. How they'd snuck out to play, the toy car crash, the light blue car and the sickly white man, the rain, the fear, and how Sara left with him to save her. By the time she had finished that part, she was crying so hard she couldn't bring herself to relive the further fear when she saw him again.

Her mother listened carefully, staying calm despite the tears collecting in the rims of her eyes, and had Kiara repeat the details about the man and his car again as she dialed 911. Halfway through her description of the emergency to the operator, she couldn't hold it in anymore and burst into sobs of her own, making it difficult to understand her and causing the woman on the line to ask her to repeat herself again and again.

"He took my daughter! Dammit, don't you understand? He took her! She's in danger! You need to get here right away!" The mother's words were full of pain, and she pulled Kiara deeper onto her lap, close to her chest.

The girl clutched at her mother's shirt with one hand while she sucked the thumb of the other, something she hadn't done in years. She had thought she'd feel safe with her mom, but the anxiety and emptiness persisted. Her eyes looked through the office doorway, through the living room, back to the locked front door. She couldn't tear them away.

She tried to think of Sara, but something kept every memory of her sister pushed down, not letting her access even a glimpse of her face. She sighed and cuddled deeper into her mother's arms.

Her eyes stayed glued to the door as her mother's words morphed into indecipherable screams of absolute grief. There was a siren outside the building, but it sounded like it was just passing by. Her entire world shrank to the size of the front door. She imagined the handle turning and felt she couldn't look away, couldn't even blink, or it'd be true.

We've all heard stories about mothers who lift cars off of their trapped children, or victims of violence who miraculously pull themselves to safety despite their injuries, but what if there are other unknown, quieter instances where extraordinary abilities are temporarily acquired by a person because of their resolve or sacrifice? I was contemplating this while parking my car during a rainstorm when I was suddenly struck with the idea for this story of ultimate love and sacrifice between two sisters, and how there can be flashes of wonder found even in the darkest circumstances.

Emma E. Murray
Austin, TX
June 1, 2021

Emma E. Murray is a writer whose novels and short stories explore the dark side of humanity. She spends her days taking care of her daughter and her nights writing. You can find her at EmmaEMurray.com and on Twitter @EMurrayAuthor.

ELLA MINNOW

NICK YOUNKER

I sometimes forgot who I was, who I lost, and why I do it. Twenty-one years ago, my six-year-old daughter was taken from me at Conley Port in South Boston while I was doing a drop and snag for William Tomlin's operation out of Des Moines. It was summer. Julia started kindergarten early and was out for break, readying for her first year in Grammar School.

Julia spent summer nights on the road so I wouldn't get to missing her, and her me. She cried at night when I was gone. I spent two weeks on the road and nine days home during the fall and winter, when she was in morning classes. Her mom dressed her in long shirts or dresses to cover up a large birthmark at the base of her back, shaped like Africa.

We were close, and since her mother's name was Julie, I called her Ju-Ju, my little Ju-Ju. She was happy, we went everywhere together. I told myself the kid would see the nation before she hit school. We camped at rest stops in the back cab and she enjoyed the roadside diners. Ju asked waitresses for a penny to collect from every city. They never disappointed her.

Julie and I had settled in Polk City two years before Ju came along, less than a half-hour north of downtown Des Moines. I drove commercial OTR while Ju was a baby and Julie started school, working toward a degree in marketing. The plan was to get Julie through so I could cut down to part-time and be Ju's primary. We made a decent living, had some savings and spent summer vacations in our backyard on Saylorville Lake in community cabins. Ju and I sat on the dock and practiced her vocabulary, sang the Alphabet Song over and over. Ju modified it.

AB, D-C,
EF-G,
Ella Minnow, Ella Minnow,
E-E-E!

Ju-Ju had a great childhood until it was gone, she was gone. Julie stuck around for two years until the grief was too much. Our divorce was quiet and she remarried soon after, moved to Highland Park outside Chicago and gave birth to twins who're now in college. She never pursued work, a stay-at-home mother. I last spoke to her eleven years ago and she asked me not to contact her again. It wasn't her coldness, nor my unwilling nature to give up on Ju-Ju.

She'd put Julia out of her mind. She chose to live forward, and good for her. It was unnecessary for both of us to suffer.

Polk City remained my home, the same home. Ju-Ju needed to come home to her family, me. My rationale was irrational. Throw a grenade through the window, I'm staying. Ju's room unchanged, undusted. Her clothes—unwashed. Her bed—unmade. The scent on her pillow faded, I can still smell her in my mind's nose. I can still hear her in my mind's ear. I see her toothless smile in my mind's eye. . . *AB, DC – Ella Minnow, Ella Minnow.*

My road gigs run through Mike Fisher Logistics now.

William Tomlin moved his operation to the Northeast, in Portland. We were close in our early years. He'd dated Julie before me, we became friends after I married her. I was of a handful of people that knew William was his middle name. Jobe William Tomlin. His parents called him J.T., his friends called him Will and his employees called him William.

He may not have been able to handle me after Ju's vanishing. I blamed him, I blamed everyone. It was my own fault. A drop and snag anywhere but Conley Port would've been safe, and that wasn't true. Ju and I'd done it a dozen times on the Eastern seaports. She stayed in the truck, doors locked, keys in my pocket. I thought I had it secure, I thought she'd be safe. Ju must've had to potty. She always had to go. We pulled over so often I considered a five-gallon bucket for the back cab. I didn't mind, though. I cared less for Tomlin's schedule than my daughter's needs. Tomlin didn't fuss.

I continued to search for her, drove part-time to all the major ports. Just enough money to get by, more than enough time to prowl the prowlers. The lurkers, the stalkers of families with small children. I was certain Ju was still alive, taken by a sex trafficking op and not a lone wolf. Someone, somewhere knew something. Someone, somewhere. . . had to pay.

The darkness never left me. I was deep in it and organized fifteen years ago. Ju and I were not alone. People like me were all over and some moved to Saylorville, where I set up The Fowler Investment Group as a front for my Midwestern operation. Those who moved worked part-time OTR with Fisher and branched out to the gigs we were looking into.

I eventually got some contacts with the FBI and they were sympathetic to our cause, even allocating dark funds to us in exchange for help identifying potential victims of international sex trafficking ops they had their eyes on. We could get closer to it than them. We had unsullied backgrounds for dark undercover operations. They knew it.

What the Fibbys paid us fell under their budget as cleaning and utility services, off the record and no trace of confidential informant funds. My contact, I'll call him Dave, told me we were allocated $3 million for furnishing Wit-Sec houses with furniture and appliances, etc. We hired and filed tax nexus in various states to stay off the security clearance protocols. All to cover Fibby Dave and his internals who believed in our cause. Our people stopped driving to focus on the payloads.

This all came later.

It took us two years to gain any real traction, long before Silk Road sank. No matter how bad it was, Silk Road was more dangerous for the criminal entrepreneurs. People like me made sure they never slept with two closed eyes. We were always there, always watching, always waiting. Patience and time were all we had, nothing left to live for. My crew, men and women, had no other purpose in life, with the rare occasion of parents finding their lost child. Rare, as in twice. The parents stayed connected and helped at times, but I never pushed nor expected them to blow up their second life.

It was Year Three when our op first made the kind of progress we'd hoped for. Deep down, we knew our children were dead. We told ourselves we did it to save other children. That wasn't true either. Saving kids was an afterthought, a bonus. We were in it for the payoff, the revenge, the bill. We were owed a debt from an unknown monster, and if it wouldn't pay, every monster we found would. One way or another, we collect, we tear the skin off monsters, then bury their fibrous living muscles on a bed of loose soil and lye. I could think of no better way to end them. We waited to fill graves until their life was hair-thin, knowing they'd never be found, and maybe, with any luck, have hell to look forward to.

People don't think of these things until they've had the air sucked out of their lungs, no refills. Maybe I was a monster too. I caused them more pain than any human could endure. I kept them alive. I attached an IV to keep their heart strong, their lungs clear, then removed their skin, slowly, cautiously. Only one man died before I had his suit off. Lucky him. Just another dead monster that checked out before tipping the waitress.

Cookie, I called him, had a medical background and extensive training with cadavers from Emory. He practiced cosmetic surgery in Nashville before he joined us. Anyone can guess why. He trained me to remove the entire suit fully intact. We displayed the suit for the monster before we buried it. It was Tokie, I called her, that started pouring soy sauce on its legs, arms, and genitals. A painful burn caused many to faint. We also had female monsters, more common than most think. They ran their litters and the cameras that ultimately led us to them.

It'd be easy to think we busted the front door down and caught monsters in the act, but we were never so lucky. We found video footage that got us who we wanted. Once I or another mole were close enough, we retrieved tapes, found footage, of monsters doing monster things to young children. I'll spare the public details I wish I could spare myself. If I was to hunt monsters, I had to watch the entire performance.

Monsters made the videos on analogs, VHS, to avoid digital tracing, and most tapes were sales pitches for an hour with a kid. It was a multi-billion-dollar criminal industry across the globe. Skinning monsters was a way to the top. I wanted the shiny gold brass to pay the bill.

Very few kids made it through the first tape, but I never found one of Ju. Their tiny bodies gave out under the grueling pressure of internal trauma caused by large hairy men in cowboy hats and gimp suits, the tapes would be repurposed for snuff collectors at $20K a pop. Gimp suits only cover portions of the body, parts they thought could identify them. In our op, we learned to make alternative identifications that wouldn't hold up in a court of law. We learned how to ID and find monsters, even the ones behind cameras.

We burned locations by paying special attention to the little things. Mirrors usually got us the filmmakers. Slap, rip, slash, skin, peel. If we couldn't ID the monster, we'd establish a time or a location. A mute newscast in the background with a time or date in the lower-third ticker. We had technology to reverse a mirror image and recreate the details we needed to know. We learned how to identify regional and international accents. We isolated channels of audio to hear low-volume radio broadcasts and found its location, usually by local advertisers, other times hearing the station's call letters, required by FCC law to identify at the top of every hour. Some basements used cement blocks, local manufacturers that marked their product. Forget about train whistles. They were everywhere.

For nearly a decade I'd been after a whale. The filmmaker that spoke English with a Russian accent. I'd named her Mishka. She initially had us fooled. If I'd brought her to public justice, the change in accent alone would establish *Pre-Meditation with Intent* for anything she was charged with. Only one time did her painted face appear on a discarded mirror. That's not what I used to identify her. It was her hand, a small tattoo on the web of her right hand, between the thumb and index finger. A Christian cross with a hook at the bottom, or an upside-down Devil cross if seeing it from her point of view.

Anyone could have a cross, but that hook at the bottom narrowed the search. Other filmmakers had the hook cross, but her hook had a meth-needle scar in the belly and a misshapen mole below the arch. She was daring us to find her.

I'd known about her for eleven years. It was only the past eight she became my obsession. A recovered tape put me on her permanently, what she did, the direction she gave her gimp on a boy no more than four years old. It was the first VHS I found where she'd directed the sodomization of a tiny boy. It seemed personal to her. The kid didn't survive. She walked the camera closer to him and put a small hand mirror under his nose while he lay in a bed, a puddle of his own blood and tissue. No fog on the mirror. No life. That's what $20K customers wanted to see. That was their payoff. That was eight years ago.

I'd zoomed in on the cleanest shot of her hand and used our equipment and software to render the clearest view, then printed fifty images, some for Fibby Dave and his team, the rest for us and our expanding crew. She was at the top of our Ten Most Wanted List.

In the last eight years, Cookie, Tokie and I had torn the skin off twenty-six monsters and buried them in various parts of the country. All graves were twelve-feet deep and we relocated poison ivy over them to discourage wandering souls. Even though we identified at least three men at the top-brass, it was their filmmakers we sent gift-wrapped packages to. We wanted them to know we were out there. We wanted them to fear us. We sent them the suits. Nothing painted a picture that loud. No person or monster could look at those suits and not hear the screams, feel the pain.

Fourteen hours ago it all came together. A drug-trafficking warrant Dave and the Fibbys served in Buffalo produced no fruit. Dave was on a secondary team, on scene for support only. He worked a different division with no current activity. The Fibbys were fooled into thinking the loot was there, even the perps thought they'd sandbagged the op. But they had no idea my Dave was on the scene armed with a picture I sent him burned into memory.

Dave put the cuffs on all three men and a young woman, a woman whose hand was an exact match for Mishka. I don't know for sure what happened, but I imagine he asked for her name and she spat on him and told him to arrest her or let her go, in a low R-drop Boston accent. He knew he had to take her without the drug agents knowing, so his team planted a small bag of methamphetamine under the toilet tank and everyone got hauled in until they could establish a suspect. Dave had her eliminated and released. He took the cuffs off and said he had to take her back to her last known residence, then put her in the car and his rogue unit put the cuffs back on, gagged her, bagged her vision, and took her to a safehouse in Rochester.

That's when I got the call. We were low on Fibby funds, so chartering a direct flight was out. Cookie, Tokie, and I hopped in the transport van and turned a fourteen-hour drive into eleven. The safehouse was an outpost for field agents working the border trafficking cases and had a complete mobile op set up in the basement of the country home, with an interrogation room that could be open or closed to spectators. The house had been vacant since the Buffalo mess and all agents were at Quantico trying to justify the Rochester Field Office. It was just Cookie, Tokie, and I along with Fibby Dave and three of his unnamed agents.

They shook my hand and left the room, wishing me happy birthday as they walked out the door. We only knew of each other, never met. Only Dave knew me and now he knows Cookie and Tokie. This was the first and last time Dave and I would ever be candid.

"You know what I do. You know how I do it. Only stay if you want to see. Otherwise, let us work alone."

Dave nosed around to Cookie and Tokie, whose faces said *All Business,* then looked back at me.

"I'll be in Buffalo. Sanitize when you're done."

I gave him the nod and entered the interrogation room with a box of pictures. Some pics were kid survivors, some were the monster suits, one was the boy and a picture of Mishka's hand. I had a picture of Ju-Ju, but Mishka couldn't have been more than two days old when Ju was taken. I always bring Ju, just in case. Hope's a dangerous weapon they use against me.

I locked the door behind me and closed the blinds to the observation window. I heard Cookie try to open it and shake the door knob, then he stopped and made no other noise. It's an intimidation tactic we'd used before, a way to shake up a monster before one of us got started. It told Mishka the interrogation was blacked out and no one was coming to Mirandize her. It said *torture.* The ceiling-mounted camera had already been unplugged and pointed down. Dave knew. He'd never witnessed, but he knew.

Mishka was not impressed. She had no facial reaction to any of our tactics. I started taping photos of survivor kids on the wall. I taped one of the boy and one of her hand under it. The interrogations worked faster when I said as little as possible, sometimes nothing at all. They knew what we wanted and it wasn't necessary.

"It's a fine day for an exorcism, ain't it, Fath'a?"

I didn't look at her, nor was I fooled by the New England

accent. She probably thought we only knew her with a Russian accent, never shown her naked face on camera.

Elmer's glue is where I started, it's where I always started. Ju had buckets of it before she left me, maybe two dozen bottles for her home crafts. I was down to her second to last bottle by the time I got to Mishka.

I splat it on my hand and smudge it around while mostly viscous. The trick is to let it dry some, not so much it didn't stick. It helped the slap make effective contact against a monster's face. It helped form the first rips in its skin. I could usually get twenty slaps in before the glue had fully congealed and I had to tear its dead skin off and reapply more for another round, assuming there'd be another round.

Maximum force with Mishka. She took nine slaps without reacting before she started audible gasps. The glue lasted another seven slaps before it needed changing. There were no rips yet, only redness. Mishka was lucky and unlucky. I'd spend all night on her if I had to.

I applied the second coat of glue and restarted the slaps without saying a word. Ten more and she was wearing down. Me too. Three more and the rips started. My job hits paydirt. The rips usually started on the back cheek or the temple, depending on the weakest pores. Mishka's started with both.

Once I hit the payload, I slowed down, let her feel it. She took over fifty slaps with the back of her left face opened up. Blood poured down her neck and from parts unknown under her scalp. I rip the third coat of glue off then point to photos of kids presumed alive. Mishka, hung over her chair, lifted her face and chirped at me.

"Don't you sc'eam, gay'l. I'll kill ya' folks in tha' sleep."

She weakened and let her head slump sideways.

"Don't you tell, p'incess."

She was clearly on the edge of faint. I cracked ammonia salts below her nose, she lifted to attention. I smacked her with a new coat of glue twenty more times and half her left face detached from her muscles. Her actions were delirious. Her head swayed with no direction, rolled around on her shoulders, her neck a rope on this ball and chain.

I pointed forcefully at the kids I thought were alive. She couldn't focus or respond. I wasn't gonna get any info out of her. It was time for Cookie.

He saw me open the blinds and turn the mic on. The suit cutting was cosmetic art, his area. I stepped out, he stepped in with precision cutting tools. The cuts had to be on target and clean for complete removal. In the beginning, it took him an hour to make all the cuts. Now, just forty-five minutes. His suit skills were improving.

Tokie and I watched and listened from the other side of the glass. He laid her out on a portable surgery table, stainless steel with rusted edges. Mishka tried to mask her screams with psychotic laughter, but we weren't impressed. Just another dead monster to us. It took him forty minutes and he would need our help to detach skin from muscles. Tokie entered, I got a call from Dave. I told them to keep her quiet until I was done.

Dave was on site at another residence in Buffalo. They squeezed their mules and got a location.

"Dave?"

"Listen, Mac. I don't know how to put this. . . "

"Just say it, quickly."

"We found Julia's tape."

My brain lost cabin pressure. I sat before I could collapse.

"Did she die on tape?"

"She survived."

I initiated the pause. I needed to roll it around, the pain gearing up like an F-5.

Mishka started in again, blubbering at first, then making the best threats she could. I heard her on the mic.

"Jobe'll get ya!"

The paydirt took me by surprise. Only a handful of people would respond to "Jobe," and only me in The Fowler Group. I had no reason to mention him before. Cookie and Tokie were in the dark.

"I'll be back in Pawtland this time tomo'wah. . . "

Portland. Jobe Tomlin. For fuck's sake, William Jobe Tomlin! The shiny top-brass who branded his kids with a hook cross. It wasn't a hook cross, it was two overlapping letters: t and J.

I told Dave I'd call him back and hung up. Ju-Ju was alive, I knew it in my bones. I pulled her picture out of my box and burst through the door. Cookie and Tokie stood back, unsurprised and ready to follow my lead. I held the picture in front of her face. Those eyes could still see if I wiped the blood away, a couple eye drops.

Mishka heaved as her vision cleared.

"This girl." I showed her Ju. "You give me her location, you live!"

Her brows furrowed, her face lost strength. Mishka was no longer an uncooperating witness, nor reasonable.

"What do you know of he'r, huh? What's she to ya?"

I lifted her chin with my thumb. All business.

"You give me my daughter, I give you your life."

Cookie and Tokie were stunned. They knew I was on to something. They suspected the call. Mishka howled, uneasy, losing her mind. She cried a laughing tear and choked, an emotion. She laid her head sideways on the table and sang, gently.

"*A-B,*
D-C,
E-F,
G,
Ella Minnow,

Ella,
Minnow,
E-E-E. . . "

She sucked the air out of the room and I steadied myself on the side of her table. I gently rolled her naked, brutally battered body filled with past scars and suit wounds, until I could see a bright red Africa on her lower back.

After twenty-one years, I hurt my Ju-Ju for the last time.

My sweet little Julia.

I spend a lot of time reading genre bastards, stories that don't belong. Is it horror, thriller, suspense, drama, mystery? They're the Omega to something, that's all. Ella Minnow doesn't belong to anything, but it's what we fantasize about when we loose precious cargo. It's how far we'll go for justice. It's the road to hell paved with explosive justice. It's the suicide confession a vigilante leaves before he pumps a hot load in his veins. I had to see this story through. All the injustices I've seen, the pain and suffering good people endure, their path to the dark side. It had to be told.

Nick Younker
Newburgh, IN
June 7, 2021

Nick Younker spent twenty years working in local and national media. After transitioning from television to online journalism, he now pursues work solely in dark fiction and satire. With the exception of his debut novel, Nick focuses his work on short stories and novellas drafted in grunge narrative style. His dominant influences are Palahniuk, Spanbauer, Hempel, Larsson, Blatty, Chabon, Blackwood,

Bukowski, and Gabriella Coleman. Lyrical influences include Cobain, Vedder, Springsteen, Jett, Hetfield, Hendrix, Morrison, and Roky Erickson. He's spent most of his life in Southern Indiana, excluding four years in Atlanta working for Turner Broadcast Networks. You can catch up with him on Twitter @NYounker.

MAZE-MINDED

JENNIFER CROW

We stitch ourselves
into the labyrinth,
walls tapestried
with silk cocoons
and torn webs
where our knives
carve a way
for nightmares
to cross into flesh.

Here stone swallows
blood, mortaring
itself with clots of gore
thick with the scent
of rusted metal
and death. We thread
our needles on twisted
cords of gut primed
by curses and doubts.
Tie a knot in the future

and draw it tight,
make a net, a nest
where our newborn
nightmares can curdle
into fierce and hungry demons.

Like many of my poems and stories, "Maze-Minded" has its roots in some of my favorite myths and folktales, but I wrote it as a mother, angry at recent events in the world and wishing for a way to harness that rage and turn it back on those who deserve it. The mothers of monsters free their children by any means necessary, nurturing them with magical craft and fierce wisdom before unleashing them to wreak havoc.

Jennifer Crow
West Falls, NY
June 3, 2021

Shy and nocturnal, Jennifer Crow has rarely been photographed in the wild, but it's rumored she lives near a waterfall in western New York. You can find her work in a number of print and electronic venues, including *Analog Science Fiction, Uncanny Magazine,* and *The Wondrous Real.* Readers who'd like to know more about her work can catch up with her on Twitter (@writerjencrow), where she can be found any time she's trying to avoid working on her new poetry collection.

I MARRIED A DEAD MAN

JOANNA KOCH

The rules change down at the docks after dark. That's where I'd find him, where daytime people masquerade, donning their desires inside-out so the raw truth shows. You can spot your own kind, try on a new mask for size and throw it into the ocean if it doesn't fit right. Things go on that don't stand up to logic and light, things that need to happen so the daytime world can keep on kidding itself that it's all merry and bright. He liked it there, where the deals are made, sacrifices taken for granted and thrown away. You know better, we all do; but you still gamble, get a bad hand, lose everything, and keep coming back to do it again. Compulsion trumps etiquette nine times out of ten.

I'd find him by the water's edge. One of a dozen dives crammed between alleyways, smelling of fish. Clapboard signs with not-so-subtle hints: *Entrance in Back*. A new one each night during that summer in 1984 and being underage and looking every year of it gave me an advantage with certain types of men. Yeah, he was that type.

A tattooed giant in the doorway eyed my buzz cut and

combat boots, and then settled on my breasts while sloppy couples stumbled past. "Go home, little boy," he said.

After I bummed a cigarette, I let him fill his eyes and one massive, greedy hand for a few minutes.

"Enough, man." I pushed past him, the price of admission paid.

Grim sailors drowned in scotch. Muses of elaborate gender nodded in post-coital stupor over tepid, drained carafes. The sound of water spilled through the open windows, as careless as the clientele. Water lapped the dock like the long tongue of a parched animal tasting the pier's rotten wood and fresh sting of salt. Barnacles spied from below sea level, a horde of swollen eyes.

A woman who was either fourteen or forty-five leaned on my table. I didn't know how to order a real drink and she didn't ask for ID. "How about I bring you a Coors? It's on tap." She tagged me as a fish out of water. I was grateful for the assist.

I fidgeted alone, feeling like fresh, young meat blinked on a neon sign over my head. I sipped my watery drink. I stood my watery ground. I waited for the waves to shift. An hour swelled up and ebbed by. I pissed the time away and had another beer. I dreamed about what would happen when the man I'd been dreaming about showed up.

Sometimes, the worst thing about dreaming is when dreams come true. There's nothing left to dream about. Your hope gets used up and your heart floats and fills like an empty bottle with no message left inside. If you ask me, it's better just to dream.

It's like that jazz-singer-slash-bartender at the club said last night while he mixed my old-fashioned and sank sweet black cherries down into the bottom of the glass. They drifted like blood clots in amber. He said, "Some people have *all* the magic." He swirled the "all" around in his mouth with the same rhythm he used to stir my drink and gave me what you might call a meaningful glance.

It's all an act, like what I do on stage when I dress as a woman and do the act. At least, that's what I'll tell you in the daytime, especially if you're the one buying drinks.

At night I'll tell you we're all acting, all the time. My bartender understands this, and I'll explain it to you straight: smart people wake up one day and realize it's easy to get what you want if you're willing to cross certain lines. You figure out where those lines are. You mark them, and tamper with them, and your luck changes. Everything changes. Your dreams come true. Soon you begin to wonder why you thought about dreaming them in the first place. Once you get everything you want, you forget what the hell you wanted it for.

I didn't know that in 1984. I sent out my hope like a naked beacon of desire in the darkest night. I fell in love and fought so hard, even when the wrong vessel approached. I didn't understand that lighthouses are meant to warn ships of dangerous coastlines and hazardous reefs, or that I was sending out the wrong signal. To this day, warm beer on a hot night still disgusts me. It tastes like infantile rage.

Thunder gathered outside the dive on the docks as I waited, mocking my puny internal squall. The deluge burst through the sagging clouds and sent all the wharf rats running for cover. The small bar swelled full, and there he was in the flesh: the doomed vessel, the answer to my warning light.

He'd slipped in with the huddled crowd. Valise in hand, he smacked a rain-spattered fedora against his slender dancer's thigh. He was well-dressed, of course. A man of his age and position had an image to maintain. He smoothed his trousers and hitched his tie.

The bar was packed. He smirked in my general direction

and I volleyed for his eye. He didn't know me, but he came over like I'd planned. He took the only seat left, the seat I'd saved in shameless, stubborn hope. He took the seat across from me.

A succinct nod of greeting acknowledged and dismissed me in one elegant move. When the woman who was fourteen or forty-five brought over his scotch, I forked out cash quick before he reached for his wallet. He knew a gift when it fell in his lap. He didn't need the free ride, but I knew he'd never resist. He wasn't exactly a generous guy.

He drained one glass and ordered another. I paid a second time. He graced me with a curious, meager sneer. I guess he thought it passed for a smile.

With a third drink his stern gaze softened. Liquor made him muddy. He ignored me while I waited like the patient tides. He tipped his small chin over his glass to nod at a stranger. A young seaman at the crowded bar, obliquely alone despite a tall, handsome frame. His fathomless brown eyes ebbed and flowed from me to the man who summoned him. I guess he saw the family resemblance between us.

I put my money on the table and turned away as he approached. I wasn't here to pry.

The seaman's voice surged from the same depths as his dark eyes. "Hello, sir. I am Emmanuel." I snorted. His mother must have been Catholic. "Good evening, friend." He held out his right hand to me. He leaned down and pressed his left on the dark-stained table.

The wood grain swirled around the hand like it was a natural habitat, roughhewn wood supporting a sea-battered muscle. The fungoid-like tendrils of my father's pale white fingers laced through Emmanuel's left hand as I firmly grasped the right. I felt ropy sinew speaking to me in a language of Spanish stringed instruments and complicated sailor's knots.

I was in over my head. Emmanuel's grip said he'd make sure I didn't drown.

With his free hand, the hand that was still human and not some sort of parasitic growth, my father seized his drink and sent every liquid ounce of poison down his open throat. The glass crashed on the table when he finished. Ice chittered and cracked as glass beats wood, wood beats flesh, and flesh beats nothing, but is a thing forever beaten in the end.

Rock, paper, scissors: wood, glass, flesh. Crushing an ice cube between two molars and slurring around the chunks, my father addressed Emmanuel. "Whaddaya say we blow this popsicle stand and find someplace more civilized?"

Emmanuel moved behind me to pull out my chair. No one had ever done that before. My neck felt hot. I was ready to say stop when my father stood up, toppling, and Emmanuel rushed to catch him. Their arms interlocked.

The door facing the street opened. Light streamed in. Behind the couple, headlights flashed, framing their profiles face to face. My father's pale skin glowed like a geisha from a war-era postcard. His features seemed made of cut glass. The precision of their severe cut softened in Emmanuel's grasp. The larger man loomed with the heft of a predator, completing the pulp movie poster tableau.

The headlights swerved around a corner and the door slammed shut. Without the dramatic lighting, they were just two queers clutching in the dark. I grabbed my father's valise and fedora. Emmanuel winked at me. I followed them out.

The rainstorm didn't relieve the air of its intolerable humidity. It added a metallic smell to the waterfront fragrance of aquatic rot and deteriorating planks. Having cleared, the night sky flaunted her stars without shame. She didn't know or didn't care that her cloak of diamonds was wasted on the squalid world below, a world filled with creatures who pulled their bodies out of the sea and hauled their flesh to shore on meaty paddles, gambling they could swallow enough air to turn their swim bladders into lungs and defy her sister the ocean's hold. Ahead of me, the men leaned on each other with their heads bowed, foreheads touching. Their secret incantations were hidden from me by the sound of the waves.

Moonlight sparkling on dark water is supposed to be romantic. It's supposed to make you swoon and imagine the world is full of magic and beauty that only you and your true love can share. It's not supposed to make you think about the lurid disembodied forces that might be gazing into your world from another plane or try to entice you with murmured promises. It's got no business telling you to think of all the things you'd do if the barrier between you and that other plane somehow got broken down.

As we walked, the sea transformed into a beast with a thousand eyes. Bright and hungry, her stars stalked me, poised to devour all my love and life and secrets if I gave her the chance. Like other foolish dreamers before me, I gambled with the promises I glimpsed in her carnivorous eyes. You'll say I was young, a fish out of water, and that I don't deserve to pay such a high price for getting in over my head. You'll say I deserve a pardon because I didn't know better. But the sea doesn't care about that. We all have to pay. It doesn't matter to her how or when she sucks you in as long as she gets you in the end.

I thought I knew a thing or two about beating the odds and making it onto dry land, and I did. I made it out of that place, that family, that nowhere life, at least for a while, at least for now. Growing older, I feel her watching me closer and biding her time. I hit the bottom of another watered-down glass and suspect it won't be long until she ends the dream and decides she wants me back.

Behind the man of my dreams and his latest catch, I followed in tow, ready to be abandoned on the ocean's shore. I was alone on the moon. The water murmured suggestions. I listened.

The lovers ahead of me embraced. Stars danced on the surface of the sea. I saw my chance to leave. I knew getting out now was the right thing to do. I stayed.

If I were writing a mystery novel instead of laying bare the facts, I'd tell you I hunted my father down to kill him. I'd tell you that at the start, because that way there'd be more suspense. Maybe I'd let it slip that I grabbed his valise to better balance the weight of the revolver stashed in my book bag. I'd describe how nervous I felt handling the gun at first, how I had to practice for weeks and coach myself to calm down and hold it steady. How I went deaf for a day and a half because I was too dumb to wear earplugs. How I learned to aim with both eyes open wide.

But this isn't a mystery novel and I'm not a writer, and even though I had a gun, I didn't use it. I'm not a killer, not exactly. I'm just a kid who wanted to know why their father did what he did.

He wrote about it in a private letter to one of his friends, not as a plot for one of his crime stories. It's not hearsay or fiction. My father got married as a joke.

He had a kid as a joke and left as a joke. He never came back.

I guess a joke's a joke. Either you get it or you don't. I tracked him down to find out what the joke was. I guess I wanted to get in on the fun.

I asked the question a few hours later. "It was fun, wasn't it?

We had room three thirty-three at the Charley Noble Hotel. Emmanuel said I was a shellback after it was over, that

I'd crossed the equator. He didn't realize I'd crossed a bigger line than that. I asked my father the question while Emmanuel showered, when I had the man alone.

I told him who I was and what I was going to do. He didn't even bother to look at me or demonstrate fear. Shower water spit onto the cold tile in the next room. The door hung open. Steam moistened the air. The hotel room was infused with the fecal aroma imbedded in the well-worn mattress. My father lay across the disheveled covers, becalmed.

"The weight," he said, as if offering an explanation. His fingertips hovered above his chest. "The perfect weight of a man's arm across your body. A man's arm, with its heft and its hair and its callousness. The smell of him, opening up another world." He inhaled and pulled the silk pastel robe closer to his throat. Eyes closed, he smoothed his wig tenderly, and toyed with a soft curl.

The secrets of the valise adorned him, his makeup and powder all applied with more finesse than I had yet to master. The sacraments of his transformation smeared the pillow covers and bedsheets. He was more ethereal and beautiful than I'll ever be.

He came out of his reverie and lit a cigarette. He didn't offer one to me.

"You're not mine, you know. I never touched that woman. Sorry, kid." He smoked like a movie star, languid except for the filthy set dressing. "I mean, what did you want with your pop, anyway? A trust fund or something? Fat chance in this world. You're better off without the guy, whoever he was."

I shoved the window up so I could hear the sea and taste the salt. There had to be something more for me here than the smell of cigarettes and shit.

The ocean wanted to talk to me that night, even if my father didn't. She wanted to tell me stories older than the senseless affairs of men and women, prettier than the cruelty heaped on the starry creatures stuck between their grunting bodies. She wanted to answer questions I didn't know how to ask. She knew my secrets, and she told me a few of her own. Her eyes sparkled. Her tongue tasted the shore. She came and went in foaming waves, flirting with me. She had a lot to say. If I listened too long, I'd turn into a pillar of salt.

Emmanuel broke the spell and pulled me back from the window ledge. I didn't hear the shower stop over the sound of the ocean screaming her ancient desires and deadly commands, sinking her mighty jaw into the tender lip of the battered shore. I was halfway out the window on the third floor. Emmanuel put his arms around my waist so I didn't fly away.

"Careful, little one." He guided me away from the window, treated me like an animal that had been spooked. I looked up at him and shuddered with recognition. The ocean that was calling me infected his dark brown eyes.

I understood then that my father was a drowned man. The sea would take him, but not tonight. It would take him slowly, through the swell of a hundred merchant seamen's violent erotic beatings and the currents of hard liquor poured down his open throat. The ocean would fill him. I needed only to follow and bear witness.

He wanted that.

Black water would fill him, sinking into his veins like a cherry-flavored blood clot swollen in amber. He'd welcome it when the time came, but not tonight. He wasn't ready. He wasn't sorry. He had thirty years to go before he'd realize I spared his life so he could suffer alone with homophobia and the stench of a gangrenous leg. Thirty years before he'd drink himself to death trapped in a wheelchair and watching his mother die. I'd read his books. I knew his weakness. I knew how to use it against him.

But not tonight. He needed a few decades to get ready for remorse.

I'm patient. I know how to wait. It's one of the skills I acquired listening to the ocean, swallowing her salt, and wailing with her in ecstasy on that black ancestral shore. Stars like broken glass still litter her edges where nothing solid can tread. Like the brooding tides, I can come and go.

I threw the gun in the dumpster behind Wendell's Oyster House. I should have pawned it, but I was young and stupid.

My father died in 1968 when I was two years old. He didn't know who I was. He didn't remember me as the kid from the hotel and the bar. There must have been a lot of kids. But he knew who I was and that I was with him when he died.

I saw the terror in his eyes.

My mom will tell you I was at a birthday party that day and I was wearing a light blue sweater because it was a cool afternoon. She'll give you all the details and swear up and down it's true. She's probably got pictures. But these are the facts: I was with him when he died. He saw me in the lukewarm scotch spilling from his cracked tumbler, the one with the bad edge he drank from even though it kept cutting his lip. He saw me in the cigarette burns on the sheets reflected in his empty eyes. He tasted me in the last black drop of poison that seeped down his throat to render the gift of an aneurism and halt his empty heart. I was in the ocean, waiting for him, where I've always been, where he longed to be.

I took him, and filled him, and he welcomed me.

Joke's on him, for pretending to be the tough guy. Or on me for performing womanhood well enough to cultivate his dissolution through incestuous alchemy. When in the depths our bodies fill with fish, our tender flesh waterlogged, our soft tissues torn by bloat, we'll be together in a foreign, starry place. Watched by sea and sky, we'll be more than a woman or a man together, more beautiful than both of us alone. We'll be on another plane, where the sea keeps her promises and everlasting darkness feels like a fair enough price to pay for the remains of his bitter and tainted love. First we'll dream, then we'll die.

That's all he ever wanted.

I waited, and when the time was right I came for him across the ocean and across time. I'm here in the melting ice in the bottom of the glass that looks like a cracked skull. I'm in the poison that ousts the water in my temporal body and gives me the shakes early in the day. I'm in the amber water that smells like wood.

He sniffs, and approves, and takes the last sip unto death. I knew my father wanted me. I knew it all along.

"I Married A Dead Man" is my love letter to Cornell Woolrich. I stole the title because most love is stolen, and he wasn't putting it to good use, anyway. He wasted it on a book with too much plot. (The introduction as a stand-alone is glorious.) Woolrich at his best didn't give a fuck about plot. His crime novels point to the ineffable, as if he knew something he shouldn't about deeper, chthonic mysteries. He drank a lot, and I understand that, though not as well as my embittered protagonist. Having read Woolrich's biography, I can only confirm no record exists of what goes on when we're alone with our desires.

Joanna Koch
The House of Wolves, MA
June 3, 2021

Joanna Koch writes literary horror and surrealist trash. A Shirley Jackson Award finalist and author of *The Wingspan of Severed Hands* and *The Couvade,* their short fiction appears in *Year's Best Hardcore Horror, Not All Monsters,* and others. Find Koch at horrorsong.blog and on Twitter @horrorsong.

I HAVE BECOME A GRAVEYARD

LEX VRANICK

I carry them with me, these past-tense people.
But I can't ever seem to keep them in the past.
They were here once, and aren't they still? In
photo frames and movie reels and old notes,
in ratty paperback books and thrift-store clothes,
in songs and memories and the curve of the
moon, the way the sunlight bleeds red in the
morning. Mourning. it sounds like release.
beginning. Good Mourning. taste it on your
tongue. Feel the way grief settles in your bones.
It hurts. an ache, no soothing balm. we are
scar tissue and memories. and matter cannot
be created or destroyed, and maybe that
means we come back in the soil or the sand
or the stars, or that we never really leave.

I am here. I have always been here.
You have always been with me.
I will stay with you, too. I will

crack open these ribs, I will slit
my heart down the center, I will
let you crawl inside. come in, come in

come home. I will be your home.
I have become a graveyard. I will
tell the world about you, wear
epitaphs on my skin, white scars.

The pain? The pain. Life is pain.
And everything else, too. What's
a little pain? Among ghosts—

"I Have Become a Graveyard" started as a much smaller piece, intended to tie the loose ends of a long string of other poems about the same sorts of things: grief, death, history. But I felt a need to pull at the thread of the past-tense. I've always been the girl who pokes at ghosts. I love old houses, used books, vintage photographs. I love knowing that someone was here before me, and that someone will be here when I'm gone. That's what this piece boils down to. Connectivity. Continuity. The thread between the ghosts around us, and the one inside us.

Lex Vranick
Sarasota, FL
June 3, 2021

Lex Vranick is a poet and dark fiction writer from Long Island, New York. She currently lives in Florida with her dog, Ozzy, and an over-abundance of houseplants. Lex holds a B.A. from Excelsior College and is a J.D. candidate at Florida State University. Her work has been published by *Eerie River Publishing, Kissing Dynamite Poetry,* and *Fahrenheit Press,* among others. Lex can be found across the internet at @lexvranick.

THE LAST WORD

LAUREL HIGHTOWER

Alec sat in the medium's sun-filled waiting room, looking out the French doors to the woman's expansive back yard. She worked out of her home, which was in a pricier neighborhood than he was used to, and the place was furnished with elegance, even if it wasn't to his taste. Everything was so bright, so cheerful. The ambiance was all wrong–this was supposed to be a meeting place between the living and the dead.

He didn't know whether her obvious wealth should be encouraging or a red flag. It could mean she was good at her job, that she had many repeat customers and referrals. He'd heard good things from his own sources, but he didn't know anyone personally who'd been to see Linda Fairhouse. The money could also mean she was a successful shyster, a con artist who employed all kinds of tricks to ensnare her customers, preying on people at their most vulnerable. He'd run into plenty of those in the course of his investigations. He sniffed and sat straighter. If Ms. Fairhouse was a liar, she was about to be very sorry. Alec knew what he was doing and could spot a fake a mile away. He was the wrong guy to mess with.

"Mr. Delincourt?" came a voice from the staircase. She sounded brighter, louder, and more bubbly than he'd been expecting.

He frowned and stood, watching a tall blonde in a well-made, comfortable-looking black and white suit descend the steps. Her smile was wide, her lipstick a vibrant pink, and her gait as she approached him was rushed, as though she couldn't wait to arrive. His frown deepened. He was used to a certain gravity in sessions like these.

She held out a hand, the nails painted pink to match her lips. "I'm so sorry to keep you waiting."

He gave her a brief shake and returned to his seat. "Communing with the spirit world?" he asked. Even he could hear the sneer in his tone, and made a note to back off.

Her smile grew wider, her eyelids crinkling in a way that showed she did it often. "I was on the phone with my sister in Texas, actually. She's hard to get ahold of, and we're trying to get the holidays sorted."

Alec flinched at her mention of holidays. He'd forgotten how close they were, looming in a forgotten corner of his psyche, waiting to bring pain. Holidays were for people with family, not for the grief-stricken. He'd have thought she'd be sensitive to something like that.

She settled herself in the chair across from the one he'd chosen and crossed her legs. "So. Are you a skeptic, then? Here to prove I'm a fraud?" It was said without malice, her eyes still twinkling.

He sat up, his foot shooting forward and kicking over the bag beside his chair. The glass bottle within landed with a clunk against the tile floor, but didn't break, and he assured himself nothing could be seen through the opaque fabric of the bag.

Linda eyed it with interest, but refrained from asking.

Alec cleared his throat. "As a matter of fact, I'm not. I'm a believer. I've been visiting mediums for years now, and I've seen and heard things I can't explain."

She nodded. "And you've also seen con artists, yes? People taking advantage?"

He pursed his lips. "An unfortunately widespread occurrence. I'm adept at spotting the difference."

"Of course. But that's not why you're here. You have someone you wish to contact, yes?"

Hope and eagerness unraveled the knot of distrust at the core of him, and he leaned back in his chair. "Yes, I do."

She smiled and waited. So did he.

"Ah," she said after a minute or so. "You're not going to tell me who I'm looking for."

He shook his head, kept smiling. "I find I get better results if I don't. It's a bit of a control, you know?"

She leaned back and steepled her fingers over her chest. "Yes, I can see why that would be, from your point of view. From mine, however, you're asking me to open myself completely to the spirit world, without any guidance at all."

He raised an eyebrow. "Is that a problem? I thought that's what you did."

"Not without limits, I don't. If I just open the door and ask who wants to come through, it's far too big a liability. It could be anyone, or anything."

"Can't you just ask if there's anyone here to see me?"

"And if he doesn't answer?" she asked, her lips a straight line.

"I don't think I said it was a he, did I?" he said in a mild tone.

"No, but it's written all over you. You want to talk to your father."

A thrill went through him, standing the hairs at the back

of his neck on end. Maybe she was one of the good ones. "Does that mean he's here? Did he tell you that?"

She lifted a shoulder. "At this stage, I don't know who told me. I haven't issued an invitation yet, so it could have been him, or someone else close to you. Maybe I even picked it up from you directly. No way to tell for sure until the pathway's opened."

He straightened his spine and rested his hands on his knees. "All right, let's open the pathway, then."

Her gaze narrowed. "As I've said, I'm not going to do that without a connection to seek. A lot of the success of my sessions comes from the willingness of the seeker."

"I'm more than willing, Ms. Fairhouse. I've traveled a long way to be here today. To make contact. I'm as open as they come." He smiled.

She shook her long hair behind her shoulders. "We'll see." She closed her eyes, and the smile returned. "Is Alec's father here today?" she asked in a bright, over loud voice. "Do you have a message for him?"

Alec's palms were sweating, anticipation warring with irritation. She'd done no kind of preparation, no attempt to bring herself into a trance state. Trances weren't universal for mediums, he knew that, but still, the tone of this whole session was wrong.

She opened her eyes. "I have someone here with a 'K' name. Kevin, or Kyle, maybe?"

Close, thought Alec. His father's name was Kim, but he gave her no outward sign.

She plowed on. "He's an older gentleman, but not, I think, old enough to be your father. Perhaps an uncle?"

His heart rate quickened, the pendulum swinging back toward hope. His father had died young, in his early fifties, when Alec had been fourteen. Still, he didn't respond, waiting for irrefutable proof.

"Do you have a message for Alec?" she asked, and there was a trace of laughter in her voice.

Alec bristled, his mood deflating. "I'm sorry, is there something funny to you about this?"

The smile never left her face. "No, it's not that. It's just, every time I open a door in one of these sessions, there's so much joy. It's infectious. Can't you feel it?"

He wanted to. He wanted to reach for that joy and hold it close, the way he had after his father had first spoken to him from the beyond. It had seemed unassailable, the things the medium had told him, and the relief of finally making contact after all those long years without his father had made him giddy. But it hadn't lasted. It never did—there was always a tickle of doubt that crept in and stole that joy. Maybe today would be different.

She didn't wait for an answer, but turned her head to gaze at something he couldn't see. "He does have a message for you, but he says you won't listen."

He sputtered. "What? That's not true, of course I'll listen —that's why I'm here." For the first time since he'd been fourteen, Alec felt the bite of his father's disapproval. Shame made him feel small, but anger made him bigger. "That's you saying that."

She shook her head but didn't look at him, her brow furrowed. "He says he's given it to you many times."

"No, no, he hasn't. I've been waiting for it, but every time it's something different, something that doesn't help. He's never been able to get through to say what he really needs to say." Part of him still believed this was her doing, a way to con more money out of him, maybe set him up for multiple expensive sessions, but he still felt the need to convince his father, in case his spirit was truly there.

She turned her gaze back to him. "That's not what he's

saying, but try anyway. Ask your question, he might give you a different answer than he gave me."

He licked his lips, his mind divided. Did he ask for proof, as he'd intended, or for the meat of what he wanted? The itching need for proof won out.

"Ask him what's in the bag," he said.

All at once the room was colder, darker, the cheerful sunlight pouring in through the French doors dimmed by cloud cover.

She was frowning at him. "The spirit world doesn't like trick questions."

"Please," he said. "It's not a trick question, I just need to know it's him. Tell him it's his favorite. It's what I had on my twenty-first birthday." Alec's father had been gone seven years by then, but Alec had bought a bottle of his father's favorite port wine, from a specific region in Portugal he'd visited during his Navy days. He'd toasted his father, and that was the night he first felt a spiritual connection to the other side. His father had been with him, had shared the moment, he was sure of it.

They both waited in tense silence, then her shoulders sagged. "Malbec, twenty year."

Tears came to Alec's eyes, and it was all he could do not to hug her. Dad was here, really here in this room. Now he could finally know, and he had proof it was his father speaking and not some charlatan.

"Dad, it's you. It's really you."

Linda closed her eyes, lips pursed. "He's very tired now. He looks—defeated. He's going."

Alec stood, his chair scooting back across the tile floor. "No, no he can't go, I need to ask him, I need the message."

She slumped in her chair. "He's gone. I'm sorry."

"No," he said with a rush of rage, his chest tightening, blood pressure getting uncomfortably high. He made no attempt to rein it in. "Don't you pull this shit on me. If it's more money you want, fine, I'll pay it, but don't try pushing this off for another session. He's here now, and I know it's him, so I have to know."

She shook her head. "I'm surprised he answered as much as he did. He was so drained, so faded compared to the spirits I usually speak to. How long has he been gone?"

Only half hearing her words, Alec dug for his wallet, pulled out a hundred-dollar bill and threw it on her lap. "Are you listening to me? Call him back. Just one question, and then I'm done."

She stared down at the money like it was a spider in her lap. She brushed it off into the floor and stood, her eyes bereft of the joy they had held. "You insult me, and you insult your father. He said he'd already answered your questions, that he'd given you the message, many times. He was right, you won't listen, and he's tired of being tied here. It was long past time for him to go."

Panic clutched Alec's heart. "What does that mean, where's he going? He's already dead, where is there to go?"

She shrugged. "The next place. I don't know, no one ever comes back to tell me. If it helps, I believe it's a place of great peace."

He stepped closer, wanting to shake her, but kept his hands clenched at his sides. "He can't be gone, not like that. Not forever. I still need to know."

She looked down at his hands. "What is it you need to know so badly you've kept him here all these years? What's so important you've denied your father his rest?"

Alec stepped away from her, dropped into his chair. "I need to know how. Not just me, but my mother and my sisters—we all need to know how. We can't move on until we do. If he wants peace, then we need it first."

"How he died?" she asked in a tone far more gentle than any he had used with her.

"Yes," he said, wiping a sleeve across his eyes. "He. . . I came home one day from football practice, and he was there, lying on the floor in the kitchen. There was blood, but they thought it was from his nose, where he hit the floor. He just, dropped dead one day when I was a kid. And I need to know what happened."

She crouched before him, put a hand on his shoulder. "Whatever it was, he holds no malice for you, no blame. He wants what's best for you. That's why he's answered your questions all these years. You wanted proof, and he gave it to you, so you could move on. But you haven't, so he had to. That was his message, do you understand that? To accept the proof and move on."

She was wrong. Alec knew it in his soul—she was a faithless fraud, feeding him lies about his father. Worse, making actual contact then cutting it off before he got what he needed. This time, he did grab her shoulders.

"Get him back. Do whatever the hell you need to do, but get him back."

She tried to stand, but her held her down. She looked up at him, fear shadowing her eyes. "Please. Don't do this."

"Don't look at me like that—I'm not dangerous. I'm the good guy, and I'm asking you nicely to get my father back."

She trembled beneath his hands, which made him more angry. His fingers tightened on her shoulders, but before he could try convincing her again, the light behind her grew too bright to look at. The sun must have reached the right place to come blazing in through the French doors, and yet there was the suggestion of movement behind her, and a strange rustling sound.

She took advantage of his distraction to wrench herself from his grasp, and the sun went behind a cloud. There was nothing behind her beyond a tasteful sideboard with a pair of ornate, silver candle sticks.

"Mr. Delincourt, you need to leave. This session is closed." There was steel and finality in her voice, the way there had been so often in his father's.

"Please," he said, hands dangling at his side. "I'll pay whatever you want."

She passed a hand across her eyes, and to him she looked older than she had when she'd descended the stairs. "I'm too tired. It's not safe this way—you need to trust what I'm telling you."

When he didn't move, she took a step closer to him. "You *do* have his message. It's you who needs to figure it out—he's done all he can, and so have I."

Alec shook his head, his hands clenching into fists. "He *never* gave me the damn message. You wouldn't believe how many of your type I've been to, and if he *does* make contact, all he does is confirm things about himself, things I already know."

"And how do you feel when you've spoken to him? When you know beyond a shadow of a doubt it was your father's hand reaching for you through the darkness?"

He lifted one shoulder. "Good? At first, anyway. I feel reassured that there's something after this life, and that I'll get to see him again. Then doubt sets in, and I'm back to square one."

Her bright pink lips twisted to one side. "Don't you see, that's exactly—"

He didn't let her finish. He hadn't planned to push her, didn't remember making a conscious decision to thrust both hands out and knock her off balance. As the breath whooshed out of her chest and she tumbled to the floor, he didn't process that he was the one who'd done it, surprise slowing his reaction time. Otherwise he might have caught her, stopped what happened next.

Her head connected first, smacking into the tile floor, her eyelids fluttering but never quite opening. Crimson bloomed beneath her blonde hair, but it didn't reach far, so Alec thought it might not be that bad. He would have knelt, helped her to her feet, called an ambulance if she'd needed one. He knew he would have done all these things, but the vista that opened before him wiped his mind clean of memory or intention.

It was a pathway, open in this woman's living room. Rocky and steep, it narrowed the farther up it climbed toward a dark horizon where lightning flashes gave glimpses of strange creatures. He leaned to peer around it, to see if it was a projection of some kind, an illusion. But the staircase was gone, the rest of the house swallowed by what lay before him.

"Dad," Alec said in a breathless whisper.

Linda had opened an actual, literal pathway to the dead. He glanced down and saw that her eyes were still rolled back, her lips moving, but she wasn't conscious or anything like. Awe at her abilities dawned—it hadn't taken any time for her to get in touch with the other side because she was *always* in communication with the dead. He understood without knowing how that for her, the effort was in keeping the pathway closed, and he'd done the one thing that would grant him access. He took it as a sign.

The path was deserted except for a small, dim shape moving in the distance, far beyond the place where Alec stood. It was impossible to ascertain any detail this far away, but Alec knew it was his father. There was no other way for this to play out.

"Dad," he shouted, and set his feet upon the rocky path.

"Dad!" he called again, and his heart rose as the dim figure stopped, turned to look back.

"Dad," Alec said again, to himself this time as tears constricted his throat. This was the closest he'd been to his father since the casket was closed at the end of a service he didn't remember. He did recall being a fourteen-year-old boy and seeing the lid come down, hiding his father from him forever, and the pain of that goodbye had never fully left. This was it—after all this time, he would finally get the answers he needed.

He stumbled, caught himself and looked up. His father turned his back and began ascending again. Panic spurred him on. "Dad," he called. "Wait for me, please."

Fog gathered at Alec's feet, cold and damp. The path narrowed, a steep dropoff to his right, but he couldn't see his next step. Fear held him in place – he couldn't have gotten this close just to fail now. This was his reward, the payoff for years of keeping the faith, of continuing the search.

But the figure grew ever smaller, and no matter how Alec shouted, he never turned around again. He felt the panic of loss, of missed opportunities and childhood regret. He was afraid, but he couldn't wait any longer, and he began to climb.

He looked back once, but Linda Fairhouse's cheerful living room was gone. "Linda?" he shouted. "Ms. Fairhouse, can you hear me?" There was no response, and Alec pictured the way her eyelids had fluttered, the blood that seeped into her long hair. His stomach dropped and he felt cold. He was stuck here, on the other side. There was no going back now, no safety net to return to and start again.

Behind him, where reality should have been, was a dim, snaking walkway hidden from sight by more of the roiling fog only a few steps beyond. Squinting into the mist, Alec thought there were more figures ascending, but they didn't look human, and dread gripped his heart. He didn't want to be here when they arrived.

He turned his back and began to hurry, scrambling up the rocky pass. Stones and debris slid beneath his feet, and twice he barely caught himself in time. His hands were abraded, his legs aching, and his father was lost to sight.

"Dad," he cried, rounding an outcropping that gave little room for maneuvering. He placed his foot wrong, and it took him precious seconds to process there was nothing beneath the sole of his shoe. He'd already transferred his weight, his left leg rising, and there was nothing to hold him the mountainside.

Alec dropped over without a sound, the descent faster that he could have believed. The wind screamed in his ears, his stomach dropped and he flailed for purchase somewhere, anywhere. There was nothing in the featureless gray, no way to tell how far the ground was. He screamed but the sound was swallowed, like he was falling through cotton batting. He squeezed his eyes shut, clenched his teeth, and waited for impact, for the feel of his skull breaking open like a jack-o-lantern in November, but it never came. Instead he fell, his descent endless, no beginning he could remember. Nothing to hold on to, not even himself as his memories were stripped away. All but the memory of the right question, as the wrong ones fled, but now there was no one to ask. Falling forever, unable to see the hands that reached to stop his fall into the void.

"The psychic lady gonna be okay?" asked a neighbor walking her Pomeranian to the man who lived next door. She'd seen the ambulance pull away, but there was still an array of strobing lights in front of 2400 Mountainview.

He nodded, leaning against his silent lawnmower. "B'lieve so. Scared me at first, her lyin' so still in there, and all that blood, but she was breathing fine."

Pomeranian lady looked at him with new respect. "You were the one that found her?" she said in an awed voice.

The man wiped sweat from the back of his neck. "Yeah. I was mowin' out back, could see through the glass she was just lyin' there, her and the other fella. Called 911 then came to see what I could do."

She frowned. "Who was with her?"

"A client, I reckon. I don't know what happened in there, but he's dead as a doornail."

She clutched a hand to her chest. "Dead? What killed him?"

He shook his head. "Don't rightly know, and I don't think those paramedics did, either. He was facedown on the tile, blood everywhere, but they said it looked like he'd just busted his nose in the fall. No sign of what did him in."

She cast an uneasy glance at the house. "Maybe the doctors will find something."

He nodded. "Sure hope so. Here he is, at a psychic lady's house, and he just drops dead, no explanation. Can you imagine what that'd do to his family, never knowing what he was doing there, or what happened?"

"A shame," she said, before following the pull of her dog's leash. She felt chilled by the stranger's fate, but by the time she got home, he'd faded from her memory, as though he'd never been.

There's sometimes a fine line between staying connected to those who've passed, and becoming obsessed. I watched a show exploring afterlife experiences, and there was a man who'd been to see multiple mediums over the course of decades, always seeking contact with his father. Everyone's grief is personal, but it didn't seem that his search was making him happy, and it got me thinking about the effect that kind of fixation could have on a person's life.

Laurel Hightower
Lexington, KY
June 8, 2021

Laurel Hightower grew up in Kentucky, attending college in California and Tennessee before returning home to horse country, where she lives with her husband, son, and a rescue pitbull. She works as a paralegal in a mid-size firm, wrangling litigators by day and writing at night. A bourbon and beer girl, she's a fan of horror movies and true-life ghost stories. She is the author of *Whispers in the Dark* and *Crossroads*, co-edited the charity anthology *We Are Wolves*, and her short fiction has appeared in several anthologies.

SILVER DOLLAR EYES

ERIC RAGLIN

The name "Tuva" cut through the static. A girl's voice: high-pitched, lilting, and far too young to be dead.

In the dim glow of my penlight, I watched the tour group's reactions. The young daughter backed away from the spirit box. The mom squeezed the girl's shoulder, an attempt to comfort that instead made the girl wince. The dad donned a neutral face, but his toe-tapping gave away his nerves. It was only the teenage son who seemed genuinely unafraid. The boy stared down at his phone, its light disrupting the ambience. But I'd dealt with kids like him before and knew how to get their attention.

"Tuva," I said. "Use the energy from his phone to manifest yourself."

The boy frowned at me and stuffed his phone in his pocket. I grinned, rolling my wheelchair back toward the wall of my living room.

"Let's make space for her," I said. "She normally appears by the coffee table. Tuva, can you do that for us?"

The mom took cover behind my purple armchair, and the girl hid behind her. The dad stood between the living room and kitchen, hands pressed into the door frame as if it were threatening to close in on him. Even in the dim light, he looked sweaty. I glanced at the boy.

"If you feel cold, it's because she's right next to you," I said.

He brushed his arm as if swiping away an insect and squirmed backward. I resisted the urge to laugh.

"Here," I said, rolling forward and placing my penlight on the carpet. "Use this, Tuva."

All of us watched the glowing light—the family for the first time and me for the hundredth. I knew what would happen, what always happened.

A flicker.

A gasp from everyone but me.

Darkness.

Then, a voice bubbled into existence, a child's cry both liquid and piercing.

"Tuva!" it said.

Scarcely taller than the coffee table, the spirit's form coalesced like a column of smoke. The fabric of her T-shirt rippled slowly as if caught in a celestial wind, and her eyes shone like silver dollars.

Everyone in the tour group screamed and bolted out of the room. The boy hurdled over the armchair to avoid passing through the spirit. And despite being the last to leave, he didn't close the front door behind him.

Only after they were gone did Tuva dissipate—an invisible resident once more.

The family wasn't coming back, but it didn't matter. I'd gotten their money, and they'd gotten more than they bargained for. Few would believe their account of what happened, but those who heard it would come to me, just in case.

"Good job, girl," I said, fingering the wad of twenties in

my pocket. Cash was always my preference. Pleasantly tactile and harder to tax.

I turned out the penlight, cloaking the room in darkness. Seconds later, headlights spilled through the curtains, briefly illuminating the room before the family's car screeched away.

In the corner of the room, the floor creaked under the weight of nothing.

"Tuva."

Her voice was faint, defeated. She sounded like that more often lately.

"What?" I asked. "You want your cut? Not sure how much good cash will do you in the—you know, wherever you are."

"Tuva," she said again.

Always and forever: "Tuva."

A year before that tour, I was working a construction job when an I-beam slipped and my legs met an early death. I sometimes joke that my house gained half a ghost that night. Sure, my legs still pumped blood, but they were dead in the practical sense—Tuva's new spectral companions. I imagined my ghost gams propping themselves up by the fireplace, pacing the kitchen while cookies baked, and doing morning hamstring stretches.

These imaginings were strangely calming, but they didn't change the fact that I'd be in a wheelchair until the day I died. No amount of physical therapy could get so much as a toe twitching. Not only that, I was out of a job. I'd never been one to have nightmares, but suddenly I was plagued with ones about overdrafted bank accounts, foreclosure notices, and nights spent homeless in the bitter Colorado winter. I often woke up shaking with no one to comfort me. No one but Tuva, that is. Not that a little dead girl who spoke only one word and slammed cupboards could do much for me. We'd occupied the same house for three years but hadn't really bonded. Hell, I'd only mentioned her existence to a few people—none of the guys at work, of course. They wouldn't have believed me. Mostly I told matches on Grindr. "My house is haunted" turned out to be a great pickup line. Too bad most men ghosted me—no pun intended—when they saw my wheelchair.

Tuva couldn't save my love life, but she became my cash cow when nowhere would hire a man on wheels after fifty-plus job applications. I posted the first ghost hunt ad just as the leaves started to crisp and the thought of Halloween began entering people's minds. Tour groups came in droves, and like that, my money problem vanished.

But no good thing lasts forever. My legs hadn't. My construction job hadn't. My friendships with former coworkers hadn't. Why the hell would this be any different?

I was four months into running ghost hunts when Tuva suddenly went dormant: no shouting her own name, no apparating beside the coffee table, no pushing books off the nightstand. Nothing. Having lived with her so long, I could feel her presence in the room that night, but the tour guests —seven members of the US Olympic ski team—didn't seem to notice. After two hours of exploring the first floor and basement without any paranormal activity, the athletes grumbled on their way out the door. One of them—a guy whose coat probably cost more than my entire wardrobe—was bold enough to ask for a refund. I coughed up the cash, knowing it'd cause more trouble if I didn't, though I sure could've used the money. The blood clots in my legs needed some expensive medical attention.

Seven tours passed without any paranormal activity. I realized that if Tuva wasn't going to play her part, I'd have to make up for it with engaging storytelling. Perhaps guests would still leave disappointed at the lack of supernatural spectacle, but a well-crafted tale would satisfy them enough that they wouldn't ask for their money back. I did some internet research on the history of my house, seeing what I could dig up about the girl and her death. After hours of sifting through digitized land records and newspaper archives, I stumbled upon an obituary for Ingrid Birke, a five-year-old child who'd died of cancer a decade ago. I would have kept scrolling had the accompanying picture not looked exactly like Tuva. Skimming the obituary, a sentence caught my attention: "Ingrid is survived by her mother Laura and her sister Tuva." *Tuva*. Immediately, I opened a new browser tab and searched up "Tuva Birke from Denver, Colorado." Google Images displayed a woman in her twenties with close-cropped blonde hair and clear-frame glasses.

A voice cried out behind me, louder than I'd ever heard it before. Tuva's. No, *Ingrid's*. I'd been calling the spirit her sister's name the whole time.

"Tuva!" she said, and her ethereal form rippled like a disrupted reflection in a pond.

She repeated the word louder and with greater intensity again and again until my ears rang. I turned off the computer, the real Tuva's image banished to black. But Ingrid didn't stop. She'd seen her sister and couldn't unsee her.

I didn't sleep that night, haunted by both the dead and the living.

Tuva Birke wasn't hard to find. Turned out she worked as a real estate attorney in Denver. I called the firm to be sure and was met with a "she's busy at the moment—may I ask who's calling?" I should've left a message, but. . . well, I couldn't. I wasn't sure why.

Ingrid's activity had become stronger than ever, as if her dormancy had been a way of saving up paranormal energy for later. She came out during the daytime now, and that wound up being the perfect marketing opportunity. My "Daylight Frights" ghost hunt proved popular with locals and tourists alike.

I remember one 2 p.m. tour especially well. Among the group of ten was some asshole who wore sunglasses on the back of his head and smirked more often than he smiled. We were ten minutes into the tour when Ingrid knocked over a chair in the dining room and appeared beside it, practically opaque. The man went wide-eyed and swatted Ingrid's form. The other guests gasped. Ingrid yelped and vanished.

"Holy shit!" the man said, inspecting the room for hidden strings or hologram projectors. "How'd you pull that off?"

"Don't touch her," I said, my jaw tense.

"What? Oh right, don't want to mess up the special effects."

The other guests bit their lips and stared at their feet. I took a deep breath. The man's accusation of fraud didn't bother me as much as the way he'd manhandled Ingrid. Truth be told, he hadn't been the first. How many times had I scolded guests for touching Ingrid, throwing things at her, or calling her names like "creepy little freak" and "ghost bitch"? Bile rose as I considered how Ingrid must feel, but I swallowed it, steeling myself for the rest of the tour.

That night, I got into bed without bothering to undress. The day had brought in six tours, forty guests, and eight hundred dollars in cash—a hell of a better paycheck than bricklaying ever provided. I'd be able to afford my thrombectomy soon. But that little peace of mind and my physical exhaustion weren't enough to put me to sleep. I stayed awake thinking about Ingrid. How much longer would she have to put up with people like that backward sunglasses man? How much longer would she have to put up with me?

I paid for the thrombectomy two months later. The bill wiped out everything I'd saved, but being broke was better than dying of a blood clot. Still, I had a mortgage to pay, so I started booking tours the second I was released from the hospital.

That was when Ingrid went dormant again. I could barely feel her presence this time. It wasn't like she was easing her way into the afterlife but rather like she was vanishing from existence entirely. The tour guests started grumbling and demanding refunds once more. My storytelling couldn't make up for an absence of the promised spectacle. All it took was a few scathing online reviews to drop me from thirty tours a week to just five. My mortgage bill loomed over my dwindling bank account like the shadow of a mountain.

Desperate and drunk, I pulled up Tuva's picture on my computer again. When Ingrid failed to appear as she had before, I called out to her.

"Look, Ingrid, it's your sister," I said. "See? It's really her. Come back now, please. Please."

A small depression appeared on my mattress, but otherwise Ingrid stayed invisible. She knew what I was doing. Hell, I knew too—but what other choice did I have? I sat there pleading with my product.

Ingrid's dormancy outlasted my bank account. Soon, all I had to my name were a bottle of bottom-shelf whiskey, a FINAL WARNING bank notice, and a blood clot back for round two. I pictured myself sleeping in a cardboard box, nestled between a stinking dumpster and a growing snow drift. Whether the cold or blood clots would kill me first was anyone's guess.

I drank. Drank and said some ugly things—not to the bank manager, but to Ingrid.

"I'll kill your sister," I told her one night, whiskey hot in my gut. "I'll slit her throat if you don't show up for the tours."

Ingrid gave no response. She must've known I didn't mean it, or if I did mean it, that I couldn't make good on the threat. With two bum legs, I could get myself dressed just fine, but murder was a stretch.

Still, my barrage of threats continued until I passed out with a half-empty bottle in hand.

I awoke the next morning drenched in piss and spilled booze. My phone showed a missed call from the bank, but there was no need to listen to the voicemail. I groaned and rolled over, the late-morning light boring into the back of my skull. When I blinked to clear my eyes, Ingrid was standing beside my bed. Given my threats, revenge seemed as likely a reason as any for her return.

"I'm sorry," I said, squirming toward the far end of my double bed. "Please don't hurt me."

I couldn't read Ingrid's silver dollar eyes. Perhaps she was judging me, as well she should. Or maybe the dead left judgment to their gods.

Ingrid and I stared at each other for a long time. When she didn't move in for the kill, I realized this could be the moment my luck turned around—the moment that proved I wasn't a scammer. I reached for my phone. As I pulled open the camera app, I imagined the post I'd write online: *After a dramatic absence, the terrifying ghost girl is BACK! Book your tour TODAY!*

But when I lifted my phone to capture her, Ingrid vanished. I'd only ever see her one more time.

The repo men knocked on my door for ten minutes. I didn't have to look through the peephole to know it was them; the bank made it abundantly clear who to expect that February morning. I pressed the pillow over my eyes and tried to sleep through the knocking. No way was I going to make it easy for those bastards. They'd have to pull me out of bed and toss me in the icy streets themselves. I'd make sure they knew to throw my wheelchair out too.

The knocking got louder, and the man behind the door spat a threat that I couldn't make out with the pillow around my ears. The noise wasn't helping my hangover.

"Scare him off, Ingrid," I said. "You've scared plenty of people before. Don't want to get rusty."

I lifted the pillow to see if she'd made an appearance. Nothing. A groan escaped me.

"All right, your choice." The repo man's voice was clear now without the pillow blocking it. "Cops are coming."

"Fuck you, man," I said, though I'm not sure he heard me.

Acid rose in my gut, and I pulled myself to the side of the bed. Hot, watery vomit splattered the wood floor. I'd let the repo man take care of that too.

Again, I glanced around for Ingrid, hoping she could save me as she had long ago, but she was still nowhere to be found.

"Fuck you, too, Ingrid," I said. "This is your goddamn fault for not—"

I couldn't finish the sentence. The words tasted even

worse than the vomit—like a ball of shame, thick and fermented. I swallowed it. Tears came up in its place. I bit my knuckle to stifle a sob. As much as I wanted the repo men to take pity and stop the process, I couldn't bear to let them hear me like this. But I could hear them loud and clear.

"These fucking leeches," one said to the other. "Always making our job difficult."

I cleared the tears from my eyes and inhaled what felt like a dragon's breath. My mind wandered to the pistol in my nightstand drawer. I didn't know whether to use it on myself or the repo men. I opened the drawer, grabbed the gun, and clutched it like a prayer.

That was when Ingrid appeared in front of my bed, her form no longer translucent and rippling. She was as opaque as any living person. The only clue hinting otherwise was her voice, still half-underwater.

"Tuva," she said.

I stared at her, biting my lip until it bled, then gradually released my grip on the gun.

Red and blue lights danced in the window. The cops were here, and they had no problem with making a show out of this repossession.

I remembered that Tuva was a real estate attorney. It wasn't clear whether she defended tenants or landlords, but my chest fluttered at the possibility that she might be able to help me. And Ingrid too.

I let out a long-held breath and nodded.

"Okay," I said. "Tuva."

Ingrid's facial expression stayed neutral. Perhaps she didn't believe me. And why would she?

But I put down the gun, looked up Tuva's work number, and dialed it, hoping beyond hope that she was working today.

The cops and repo men agreed to wait for Tuva. One repo man had the gall to ask if he could wait inside, but I blocked the door with my wheelchair. I watched the men through the window, searching for any hint of shame on their faces, but mostly they looked half-frostbitten—an acceptable compromise.

When Tuva's car pulled up, it didn't look how I expected. I associated lawyers with money, but Tuva drove a sedan old enough to be a beater but not old enough to be vintage. Stepping out, she hesitated when she saw the house she'd lived in up until Ingrid died.

I told Tuva about the foreclosure over the phone, but never said anything about Ingrid. Didn't even mention that I knew their mutual connection to the house. Tuva's impatient tone changed as soon as I mentioned my address. She paused for a long moment, then said she'd be right over to help.

"Little late for a lawyer, isn't it?" one of the cops said as Tuva approached.

Tuva didn't reply or even make eye contact. She looked at the house as if it were a mausoleum.

I opened the front door, rolling toward the wall so Tuva could come in. She hesitated at the entrance—a portal to pain. It was a portal for me, too, but the pain existed on the opposite side.

"Thank you for coming," I said.

"Yes," Tuva replied, her voice as distant as her eyes.

I closed the front door, concerned that Ingrid might suddenly appear and turn this private reunion into a public affair. That moment didn't belong to the repo men and cops. It didn't even belong to me, really.

I cleared my throat, which still tasted like stomach acid.

Sunlight glinted through the windows and magnified my hangover headache. I needed water and Tuva needed space.

"I'm thirsty," I said. "Can I get you anything too?"

"Sure," she said, trancelike as she scanned the living room. "Water."

I wheeled into the kitchen.

"Tuva!"

The word I'd heard a thousand times before took on new strength, no longer sounding like a voice from the bottom of the sea. Tuva gasped and fell to the floor behind me. I didn't turn around. This conversation belonged to the long-separate sisters, not to me. I rolled toward the faucet, grabbed two glasses, and filled them up. But the sisters' conversation cut through the hiss of water. I sat there listening, even as the cups overflowed, cold water spilling down my fingers.

"I thought we'd have more time," Tuva sobbed. "It's why I didn't drop out when you got sick. I thought if I could make it through the semester, we'd have all summer together and. . . and maybe you'd get better and we could. . . could climb Pikes Peak together. We always said we'd—"

"Tuva," Ingrid whispered.

In the reflection of the water glass, I watched Tuva lean in close. Ingrid whispered something in her ear too quiet for me to register. Perhaps it was a message, a secret, a confession. I feared Ingrid was telling her sister every horrible thing I'd said and done to her. All the humiliation I'd put her through with each tour. Maybe if Tuva knew the truth, she'd refuse to help stop the foreclosure. Not that I believed much could be done. And not that the foreclosure was the only reason I'd asked her here.

I sat at the running faucet with my eyes closed, trying not to think about how different my life might be an hour from now. I focused on the black space between thoughts like the emptiness between stars, hoping I was far enough away to escape their gravity.

I don't know how long I stayed like that, but a hand on my shoulder jolted me back into the present. Tuva stood beside me, gray rivulets of mascara running down her cheeks.

"Thank you," she said.

"Don't," I replied, not out of modesty but out of genuine discomfort.

A knock on the front door, persistent and booming.

"Are we done here?" the cop asked. "A last-minute lawyer isn't going to change anything. You had your day in court and the court made its decision."

Holding back tears, I turned to Tuva.

"He's right, isn't he?" I said.

Blushing and blinking rapidly, Tuva looked away.

"Just tell it to me straight," I said.

She opened her mouth and said nothing for a long moment. Then, in barely a whisper: "I'll give you a ride to the shelter."

It would've felt good to confess the horrible things I'd done, but Tuva was harboring her own guilt. From her point of view, she'd given false hope that my house could be saved and now she owed me. Not that I agreed.

"I've got lawyer friends with housing connections," she said, dirty slush splashing the underside of her car.

I watched my home disappear in the rearview. The cops had done their job of getting me to leave, and now it was only the repo men going in and out of the house. Already, a careless pile of furniture formed on the curb. It'd probably be shipped to the dump before the end of the day.

"You won't have to stay in the shelter long, I promise," Tuva added. "I'd let you stay with me, but—"

"Please, no," I said. "You don't have to explain."

Tuva nodded and turned at the stoplight. My house was no longer in view. For all I knew, that'd be the last time I saw it.

Shivering, Tuva turned on the heater. Lukewarm, vinegar-smelling air poured from the vents. I stared out the window, watching the residential buildings give way to commercial ones and then vacant, fenced-up lots. We'd arrive at the shelter soon.

"Thank you," Tuva said, and again, I bristled at her gratitude. "I never thought I'd see Ingrid after—"

She sniffled, not just from the cold. After collecting herself, it looked like she'd continue with the thank-yous, but I couldn't let her.

"I ran ghost tours for a while," I said. "Ingrid made me a lot of money. When she stopped showing up, I. . . well, I didn't treat her very well. I knew she wanted you. But how could I give her up when. . . "

I gestured at my legs. Here I was justifying my cruelty in the middle of a confession. I resisted the urge to punch the glove compartment.

But Tuva only swallowed and nodded. Her car slowed to a stop at the shelter. Groups of women and children huddled together outside, waiting for the doors to open for lunch. There was also a man like me, wheelchair-bound and a couple decades my senior. Puffy black patches of frostbite lined his nose.

"We'll be in touch," Tuva said, parking the car. "You won't be here long."

She got out first, opening my door and getting my wheelchair ready. I stared at her, desperate to read her eyes though they never met mine.

My wheelchair rattled in a gust of frigid wind, and I pulled myself into it from the car. Tuva grunted as she hauled me out of the snow and onto the shoveled but slushy sidewalk. As soon as she got me in place, she returned to her car, wordless, her head hung low. She pulled away, becoming a blue speck on the gray horizon.

I sat in my wheelchair and listened to the people around me. An old man mumbled to himself, a toddler cried to his mother, and a shelter volunteer peeked her head out to ask that we "please form an orderly line."

Winter wind cut through my bones, colder than I'd ever felt before. Colder than Ingrid. I hoped the girl had found peace: her connection to me severed, her closure with Tuva obtained, and her consciousness purged into nothingness. I was no longer her villain, but I wanted to follow her. Right into the bliss of oblivion.

This story is based on a local haunted museum. I remember going there and thinking, "Wow, the owners know so much about this ghost haunting the place. She seems miserable. Why don't they help her pass over?" That's when it clicked for me. The ghost was their product. They had a financial incentive to keep her trapped in the museum, so to speak. The seed of "Silver Dollar Eyes" came from this experience.

Eric Raglin
Lincoln, NE
June 5, 2021

Eric Raglin (he/him) is a Nebraskan speculative fiction writer, horror literature teacher, and podcaster for Cursed Morsels. He frequently writes about queer issues, the terrors of capitalism, and body horror. His work has been published in *Novel Noctule, Dread Stone Press,* and *Hyphen Punk*. His debut short story collection is *Nightmare Yearnings*. He is the co-editor of *ProleSCARYet: Tales of Horror and Class Warfare*. Find him at ericraglin.com or on Twitter @ericraglin1992.

ALL THE MISERY THAT WAITS FOR US AT THE END OF THE DAY

ERIC LAROCCA

There was something distinctly excessive—something perhaps overstated to certain residents of the small town of Henley's Edge—about the way in which Mr. Oliver Botibol prepared for nighttime as if he were hosting a gala or a cotillion ball. The only difference was this particular event had a guest list of merely two—Mr. Botibol and his husband, Bernard. Any trespassers brazen enough to intrude upon their privacy would suffer grisly fates or perhaps even worse—live to survive their encounter with Mr. Botibol and his husband after dark.

Although many in town speculated why Mr. Botibol and his husband were seldom seen after twilight, most conceded that whatever they were hiding—whatever remained locked behind wrought iron gates and steel-barred windows—was better left undisturbed. That was precisely why Mr. Botibol chose to settle in such a quiet Connecticut town like Henley's Edge—everyone kept to themselves and most never seemed to gripe of the extreme modifications he had made to his home. Modifications that were sure to keep outsiders away and the inhabitants of the house mere prisoners.

That was exactly what Mr. Botibol and his husband were —prisoners.

Of course, he would never tell. Only the full moon knew of their secrets, their indiscretions, their most shameful and wanton perversions.

It was late in the afternoon on the third snowy Thursday in January when Mr. Botibol's meticulously calculated pre-evening rituals came to a sudden halt, the house lights flickering and dimming until they were completely out. The only sound – the dim noise of wind beating snow and ice against the side of the house, as if it were an insult from nature, as if it were a condemnation from God, himself, of Mr. Botibol's heedlessness.

"This can't be," he shouted to his husband in the adjoining room as he watched television. "It can't be."

Mr. Botibol hastened down the cellar steps and came upon the only room in the house where he felt most safe from himself—the bunker. After all, not only did the full moon know their most reprehensible secrets, but the bunker acknowledged their nightly confessions without comment, without judgment—a small concrete chamber they had installed recently. No larger than a jail cell and just about as comfortable.

He could scarcely count the number of nights he and Bernard would file inside, chain themselves to the walls, and merely wait for misery to find them—for their nightly curse to claim their souls and make monstrous puppets of them. Then, as if rousing from a terrible dream—their bodies still aching from the agony of transformation like an insect when it molts—they'd unshackle themselves and bid farewell to their prison chamber until night called upon them to change once more.

It was just as he feared—the panic room's electrical lock would not budge from its place. He silently cursed himself for not making the trek to town and acquiring enough gas for the generator. Even if he made the journey now, the generator was small and most likely wouldn't last through the night.

It was then his mind began to race. He invented horrific scenarios—thoughts of him barreling through the front door and scampering down the driveway, leaping over the wrought iron gate and sprinting down the lane as he searched for his first victim. Then, he thought of something worse—both he and Bernard caught in a skirmish, two feral beasts clawing at one another until they both expired.

Mr. Botibol knew full well it was considered a sin to kill a member of his own pack. But something told him he might not be as mindful of such an offense when nighttime finally arrived. After all, when the moon was full and as bloodless as dry bone, he wanted nothing more than to feed, to gorge endlessly until his very excrement ran red. It frightened him to think that Bernard may well be his next meal. It disturbed him even more to consider seeing Bernard's remains bobbing inside a toilet bowl in the morning, knowing full well he had put him there.

Racing back upstairs, Mr. Botibol was greeted by his husband in the kitchen.

"The bunker?" Bernard asked, concerned.

"It won't lock," Mr. Botibol said, swiping his cell phone from the counter and Googling locksmiths in the area. "The generator's out of gas too."

Bernard began to pace, covering his mouth as if some futile challenge to keep the beast stirring inside him at rest. "What will we do?"

Locating the name of a nearby locksmith, Mr. Botibol pressed "Call" and held the phone to his ear as he waited.

"Millner Lock Repair," the woman's voice said on the other end of the line. "How may I help you?"

"Yes, I need a lock repaired in my house," Mr. Botibol said, his voice threatening to tremble. "It's an emergency."

"Well, sir, our next available date is next Tuesday," the woman explained. "Would you like me to schedule you an appointment for then?"

"No. I'm afraid that won't do at all," Mr. Botibol said, gritting his teeth. "I need a locksmith to come to my house today. It's a serious emergency. A matter of safety, you see?"

"I'm sorry, but all of our contractors have left for the day because of the storm," the woman said. "I'd be happy to arrange an appointment for you for Tuesday."

"Tuesday won't do me any good today. I need this lock replaced as soon as possible. I'll be happy to pay double. There must be some contractor – someone available to come out today."

There was a long pause on the other end of the line, the faint sound of clicking on a computer keyboard. Then the woman released a deep sigh as if knowing full well she had been defeated.

"There's a contractor we don't typically use, but he's usually on standby in case we need him," the woman explained. "I can see if he's available to come out today."

Mr. Botibol softened slightly. "That'd be very good of you," he said. "Please let me know as soon as you can."

After he hung up, Mr. Botibol's eyes darted to Bernard who was standing in the kitchen doorway with eyes glued to him. A soft, gentle expression lingered on his husband's face —the mournful expression of a feral creature that wanted more than anything to be tamed, to be saved, to be killed if he couldn't be protected from himself.

Without saying anything, Mr. Botibol answered him with a look that seemed to say, "I know." He, too, wished for peace, wished for a sign that they wouldn't hurt one another.

After all, he'd sooner chew silver and vomit blood than hurt one of his own kind.

After several hours, a small black car passed through the front gate Mr. Botibol had manually opened and glided farther up the driveway where it finally parked.

Watching the short, paunchy little man climb out of his vehicle as a gust of snow battered him, Mr. Botibol couldn't help but feel a semblance of pity for the poor creature. If only he had known the true extent of the kind of house he was entering. Of course, the poor man probably had some vague idea with the spiked fence guarding the property and the steel bars fixed on every window. Regardless, he seemed incapable of registering the vicious kinds of monsters that awaited him inside.

"He's not going to finish in time," Bernard whispered, his tone weighted with dread.

Mr. Botibol sensed his stomach curl. Although he would never admit it to Bernard, there was the horrible possibility that he was right. There was every likelihood that the locksmith would not repair the door in time and that his and his husband's hideous transformation would begin under the mercy of the full moon. There was the prospect that both Mr. Botibol and Bernard—mouths foaming and breath growling like car engines—would turn on the poor locksmith and rip him apart until pieces of him were scattered from one end of the house to the other. Finally, there was the horrible chance that when they were finished feeding on the locksmith, the two beasts would turn on one another the same way certain insects mate and then cannibalize each other.

The locksmith was all smiles when he greeted Mr. Botibol and his husband at the front door. He was a short man with a thinning hairline, carrying with him just enough extra weight to make him a sizeable enough morsel for Mr. Botibol and Bernard to share if it came down to it. Mr. Botibol, of course, secretly hoped he would never know whether or not there was enough of the poor man to share between the two of them.

"I hope you'll excuse the casualness," the locksmith said, gesturing to the red flannel pajamas he was wearing. "I got the call late and didn't want to keep you waiting."

"We're glad you rushed over," Mr. Botibol said. "Please. Right this way."

Normally, politeness would be at the forepart of Mr. Botibol's mind when receiving company, even a guest he was paying. But he could scarcely keep himself from thinking of the bunker in the cellar, the lock that wouldn't close, the ticking clock thumping inside his head. Even worse, it was nearing three-thirty in the afternoon and he knew full well that darkness was approaching and threatening to draw its curtain over them.

Without hesitation, Mr. Botibol guided the locksmith down to the cellar. As they walked, he felt himself growing queasy, as if he were willingly leading a man toward his untimely demise, as if he were a mere servant to his hunger. He couldn't help but wonder if the locksmith had a family. Indeed, there was every possibility he was a married man with children. After all, most of the residents in Henley's Edge were growing families. Mr. Botibol flinched slightly, imagining the poor man's wife now a widow and his children fatherless because of his nocturnal famishment.

He had only killed a man once before.

This was many years ago, when he was a young, inexperienced, feral creature and wasn't as proficient in the art of self-control as he was now. Long before he had met Bernard, he had made the acquaintance of another wretched soul—a young stockbroker from Tarrytown, New York—who was a sibling of a related sorrow, of a comparable affliction, a similar curse.

In their foolishness, they had rented a small cabin in the Vermont countryside and thought they might cure one another—as if somehow two wolves in the same room would become as pacified as stray kittens with a dish of mother's milk.

Obviously, that hadn't been the case.

Their disagreement hadn't lasted long—claws unfurled, jaws stretched, teeth gnashed. It hadn't been long before Mr. Botibol's lover was reduced to nothing more than a crumpled heap of wet fur, his entrails strewn across the living room carpet like party ribbons.

Naturally, Mr. Botibol worried what might happen if he was left unguarded with Bernard when the full moon appeared. But he had taken every preemptive measure to make certain that they were both contained during nighttime and that if one of their lights was snuffed out, the other would have to follow suit. Mr. Botibol knew full well that if the moment ever came when he and his husband couldn't be protected from one another and poor Bernard had perished because of his unappeasable hunger, he would shove the gun loaded with silver bullets into his mouth and gleefully pull the trigger. But, for now, like every other living creature—like every primitive and thoughtless creature to burrow through time and space—Mr. Botibol and his husband merely wanted to survive.

They came upon the bunker's entrance and the locksmith immediately set down his toolkit.

"You see, it's activated by the electric system," Mr. Botibol explained. "So, the door won't lock when the power's out."

"This was so urgent?" the locksmith asked. "Expecting a break-in tonight?"

Mr. Botibol shuddered slightly, as if his thoughtlessness had been caught. "It's for peace of mind. We—wouldn't want to be caught if something did happen. It's our first winter in the house, you know?"

"Guess you never can be too careful," the locksmith said, opening the door and carefully inspecting the frame.

Mr. Botibol's eyes flashed to his husband watching them from the top of the cellar steps, listening to their every word as if his livelihood depended on it. Mr. Botibol reasoned that it did.

"Can you fix this soon?" he asked the locksmith. "Before dark?"

"Eager, aren't we?" the locksmith teased, opening his tool kit and fishing inside for a screwdriver. "I'll have to replace the entire door's handle. But I should have everything I need in my car."

"Can you please hurry?" Bernard called from the top of the stairs.

The locksmith paused slightly, his eyes appraising Mr. Botibol and his husband. "Is—something going on here? Something I'm not being told?"

Mr. Botibol swallowed hard, the muscles in his throat flexing. "Nothing at all. We just – don't want to keep you. That's it."

The locksmith glared at Mr. Botibol, challenging him for a moment before finally releasing him from his gaze.

"I'll have to go out to my car quick," he explained, maneuvering out of Mr. Botibol's path and heading for the steps.

Mr. Botibol was already shadowing him, trailing his backside. The locksmith turned to him, visibly unamused.

"I work better without supervision," he said, imitating a polite and yet forceful tone he had probably captured from one of his superiors. "I assure you—the work will get done."

Mr. Botibol recoiled slightly, embarrassed. "Yes. Of course. Whatever you need."

As the locksmith passed him, Mr. Botibol's nostrils flared at his scent. He had starved himself for so long that he had forgotten what human meat tasted like. Stomach gurgling, he couldn't help but wonder if tonight would be the night he would finally remember.

Mr. Botibol and Bernard retired to the living room while the locksmith dashed to and from his vehicle outside. Normally, Mr. Botibol would be a nervous hen when thinking of all the snow and dirt his guest might be traipsing through the house. But spotlessness was the last thing on the poor man's mind right now.

He sat across from his husband, staring at him as if they were both prisoners about to be administered their final rights and led by armed officials to the electric chair. Perhaps that would serve them right. Perhaps that was what they deserved, after all. He and Bernard were a dying species—a rare kind of creature that the world would be far better off without.

Of course, he entertained the thought of taking the gun, loading two bullets in the chamber, and delivering a single shot to Bernard before ramming the barrel down his throat and thumbing the trigger. But there was hope, wasn't there? There was the faintest glimmer of hope that the locksmith would repair the door in time and that Mr. Botibol and his beloved would be safe from themselves for another night.

"What are we going to do?" Bernard asked him, his voice delicate and childlike as if lost.

For the first time, Mr. Botibol wasn't sure.

After all, what could be done? They were mere slaves to the locksmith's productivity. If only the poor man knew how dearly his safety depended on his efficiency. It would either save his life or end it.

Mr. Botibol climbed out of his chair and moved over toward the windows overlooking the driveway and the small cluster of nearby homes—neighbors they had come to know and care for in the short time they had lived there. He loathed to think of what they might be to him when all light was bled from the sky, when the moon hung there like a bowl of freshly picked cotton—they'd be nothing more than nourishment, they'd be the unsuspecting victims of his appetite. He winced when he thought of poking through his excrement the next day and finding specks of broken bones like bits of sea glass.

"It's getting darker," Mr. Botibol said, drawing the curtains as if hoping to momentarily stave off the darkness a little while longer.

"I'm going to hurt you," Bernard said, covering his mouth as his voice quivered. "I know it."

Mr. Botibol knew time was running out. It would be dark shortly and then he would be a mere puppet, a servant of the lowest order to the moon's every capricious whim.

Glancing at the cellar door for a sign of the locksmith, his eyes darted back to Bernard.

"I want you to go upstairs and barricade yourself in the guest bedroom," he told him.

"I don't trust myself," Bernard said. "I'll break the door apart."

"All of these things can be bought again. You're the thing that's most irreplaceable."

Bernard sank to his knees, pleading with his husband. "I'm not—I can't go without you."

"You know we can't be together at night if we're not protected," Mr. Botibol explained to him. "We'll hurt each other."

"I just—I want to be with you forever," Bernard said to him, kissing his hands. "I don't ever want to leave your side."

As Bernard buried his face in his husband's chest, Mr. Botibol glanced at the small handgun he kept on the coffee table. Perhaps there was a way for them to be together and to never be apart. After all, he conceded that there were no wolves in heaven. Their curses wouldn't follow them there. Even if they did, he had been told many years ago by his mother that everything in heaven is beautiful and nothing bad can ever happen there.

Just as he began to reach for the handgun, the locksmith appeared in the doorway with his toolkit.

"You're all set," he said, wiping strands of snot from beneath his nose. "The handle's fixed."

"Everything's working?" Mr. Botibol asked, glancing at his wristwatch as if in disbelief at the paunchy little man's timeliness. "You had no problems?"

"It was an easy fix," the locksmith shrugged, passing Mr. Botibol the yellow copy of a receipt. "You can call the office and pay over the phone."

"Yes, of course," Mr. Botibol said, glancing at the receipt and back to the locksmith as if he had been handed the precious egg of an extinct animal. "You have everything you need?"

"All set. I'll get out of your hair," the locksmith said, ambling toward the front door. "You two have a good evening. I hope your power comes back on soon."

Mr. Botibol held the door open for the man as he meandered out of the house and down the pathway toward his car blanketed with snow. "Thank you very much. Drive careful."

Without waiting to see if the locksmith made his way safely down the snow-covered pathway, Mr. Botibol slammed the door shut and sprinted toward the cellar door with Bernard fast at his heels. As was their custom, they filed into the small shelter and began undressing until they were completely naked. Then, when they had discarded their clothing in small piles on the floor, they began to handcuff themselves to reinforced steel shackles dangling on opposite ends of the chamber.

"Think we'll get some sleep tonight?" Bernard asked, jokingly as he fastened the cuff around his wrists and tossed the key on the nearby table.

Mr. Botibol's smile suddenly began to thaw the way snow melts in the afternoon sun. He regarded the weighted door of the bunker as it swung close and locked. Something in particular had changed – the door's handle.

It had been replaced with a lever made of solid silver.

Mr. Botibol gently approached the doorway, as if he were approaching a small, frightened animal caught in a steel trap. Against his better judgement, he leaned a finger against the handle and his skin began to sizzle like strips of bacon on a stovetop before a tiny flame exploded from the tip of his fingernail. He lurched back, screaming and blowing air against his finger seething red-hot.

Glancing at his husband, he possessed no ability to maintain a stiff upper lip, no capability to show him that everything would be okay.

Because it wouldn't.

They were trapped.

As soon as the weighted door had slammed shut, the bunker—the only place in the world where they felt safe from themselves and from one another—had become their tomb.

Perhaps once he might have loaded the gun and used it. But he had realized only too late that he had left it in the drawing room.

There was nothing that could be done now.

"How are we going to—?"

But Bernard didn't dare finish the sentence. Mr. Botibol's eyes begged him not to ask, the answer far too horrible to reveal.

Of course, they had some provisions—some food, a few gallons of water—stored in the chamber. But not enough for more than a few days. Even worse, the telephone line hadn't been arranged yet. After all, they had never anticipated needing to call for help when inside the room. Their most fervent desire was to keep everyone, everything out—to protect the world from the monsters that they were.

Mr. Botibol's eyes commanded his husband to remove the shackles from his wrists. His eyes told him that they wouldn't be needing them now. Bernard understood and obeyed without comment, his eyes never leaving him.

They circled one another for a moment like nocturnal creatures shamelessly introducing themselves with smell. Then, following the other's command, Mr. Botibol and his husband lowered themselves until they were lying on the floor and they swallowed one another in an everlasting embrace. This would be the end for them—the night when creatures of their kind were obliterated from the earth and sent sailing into the cosmos for an absolution they might never earn.

As they laid there and waited for the end to begin—for their claws to sprout, for their hunger to grow—Mr. Botibol listened closely the restful sounds of his husband's body. He listened to the gentle purr in the back of his husband's throat that slowly began to harden to a growl, the crinkling of skin as it loosened and new, thick bristles of hair budded in its place, the quiet tide of blood murmuring from the wellspring deep inside him and carrying them both on a gentle current toward a faraway land where monsters wander freely and where he and his beloved would never be apart.

For as long as I can remember, I've always been bewitched by the idea of some poor creature serving as a reluctant puppet of the full moon—a servant to nighttime, a poor, wretched soul marked by an ancient curse. At its foundation, this particular story serves as a character study about the lengths to which some people will go in order to protect and care for their loved ones. On a lighter note, some readers (especially Roald Dahl fans) might be interested to know I used the last name "Botibol" as a reference to one of my favorite Dahl stories of all time, "Dip in the Pool." Dahl's story has nothing to do with werewolves and the reference may seem somewhat random, but Dahl continues to be one of my favorite writers of short fiction of all time.

Eric LaRocca
Boston, MA
June 4, 2021

Eric LaRocca is the author of several works of dark fiction and poetry, including *Fanged Dandelion* (Demain Publishing), *Starving Ghosts in Every Thread* (independently published), and *Things Have Gotten Worse Since We Last Spoke* (Weirdpunk Books). He is represented by Ryan Lewis/Spin a Black Yarn for Film and Television.

THE WISHING WELL

DANIEL BARNETT

How it happened is I went down to the well while everyone was sleeping. I filled my pockets up with fresh quarters, shiny bright from the bank, so that I couldn't take a step without making a jingle. Ten dollars in quarters is heavy, and it's only right it should be for such a heavy price.

I won't tell you how I got in. You know that already. All I'll say is chain link has got nothing on the bolt cutters you can buy down at Henry's, and you give them back to him for me, will you? They're just as good as new, and it'd be a shame to see them go to waste. Don't you go questioning him either. He didn't know what I was using them for, and he wouldn't have sold them to me if he had. Henry's a fine man. He's never had a whiff of what's in the well, and he never will. To look down into it, to stare into its black, dripping throat and make a wish, you need a few rips in your soul. Mine's nothing but rags and tatters now, and that's okay. I had my reasons, and maybe they were even fair reasons. I'll leave that for you to decide after midnight comes and goes.

You're wondering about Niner, I guess, and don't you worry. He'll be right back to his happy self soon enough, if he isn't already. That's sarcasm, if your ears don't work. I know you all trained that dog to know not a lick of happiness in his poor, sad life, and if you're bad to him for what I did I hope you burn in hell. I mean that sincerely. It's not his fault he likes chicken. Chicken is chicken, and you couldn't resist it either if you were cooped up in that little pen all day and night, with no company except for what's lived in that well since long before any of us were here. You think *I'm* cruel, but I'll bet you've never even wondered if he can hear it, smell it, down there in the dark. Dogs, they pick up on more than we do, they feel what we can't, and no guard dog you've put in there has ever become an old guard dog. Sure, they all look old after a few months, when their hair has gone gray and their gums have gotten so soft their teeth are falling out, but that's not age, that's *rot.* Your dogs, they go in big and strong and mean, and they molder from the inside out. How many have there been in the last decade? A dozen? Two dozen? Three? How many of them have you needed a shovel to scoop up when it's all said and done? Don't answer. I don't want to know, but you think about what I said the next time you look in the pen and see that dog twitching in his sleep. You look at his paws and you ask yourself if he's dreaming of chasing something . . . or something chasing *him.*

Well, Niner has got some kind of bark, as you know—his bark being his job and all. I visited him every night for three weeks, each night throwing him a morsel and taking a step closer, letting him get used to my presence, my scent. I was very careful not to push him too fast—I know how quick you folks come running when he sounds the alarm. It got so he'd whine when he saw me, and I tell you, if I had a heart he'd have broken it. I'd never known misery and hope could exist together, in one sound, until I heard him whimper. Eventually he let me up to the fence, and I'd sit there with him, slipping him piece after piece through the chain link. He'd lick the meat right out of my hands, and then he'd lick my hands, too, and if there's one nice part to this story, my story, it's this part, me and him sitting together in the dark, learning that there's still such a thing as a friend in this world. On those nights, when I got home, I'd crawl into bed next to my wife and fall asleep to the chicken smell of Niner's spit on my fingers. Helena never woke up to me leaving or returning. She's a deep sleeper. Or was, anyway.

For our last supper together, I prepared a feast. A full chicken, roasted and sealed in a pot so that the juices still had sizzle to them when I sat down at the fence. I pried apart the limbs and stuck the pills into the big boneless chunks, hoping that Niner wouldn't notice the lumps, that he'd swallow them whole. The last thing I wanted was to leave him a bitter aftertaste to remember me by. In about fifteen minutes, he was good and corked. I made a doggy door for myself with the cutters, then I stuck the cutters in the chicken pot for safekeeping and crawled into the pen, where I pet Niner on the head for the first time, the last time. His tongue lolled out between his teeth. I picked it up and brushed the dirt off it the best I could and laid it back in his mouth so it wouldn't get dry. I don't know if it stayed put. I didn't look at old Niner again. I had business to tend to.

The well seemed to smile, something about the curve of its crumbling stone ring, the lip of its wooden cap. It sat under a softboiled moon, foxtails shushing against its side. The night was quiet. Nights always are, in the Corner. Days too. Houses without people in them are like scarecrows, especially after dark. They come alive in their stillness. You can't help but watch them, like at any time they might move. I stood in the pen with all those shuttered windows on me, like the eyes of an audience that's only pretending to be asleep. When I was a kid, I used to dream that I lived in the Corner, alone in an empty house. In the dream I would wake up and look out the window and see the well, out there in the clearing where only weeds grow. I'd stare and stare, and quarters would begin to slip from my fingers, striking the floorboards around my feet, filling the house with awful, clacking echoes. It was the most horrible dream there was, and so I understand why you don't tear down the houses, why you let them remain abandoned. They stay so that the folks living on the next block over don't have to look at that well when they get up in the morning and go to bed at night. People can live with just about anything, as long as it's one street away.

I started toward the well. My pockets felt very heavy all of a sudden. The sound of jingling quarters filled my head with devil's music. Every step I took dropped my interior temperature, until I was a little pocket of winter moving through warm summer shadow. I was close. Closer than I had ever been in my entire life. Some part of me revolted then, gave my mind a dizzy backward shove, and it took everything I had just to keep shuffling. As a kid, starting when I was three or four, my parents used to show me pictures of the well and scold me, *NO, BAD MICHAEL, NO.* Sometimes they pinched me, made me cry. Other times they screamed in my face, startled the tears out of me. By my seventh birthday, my mom and dad could walk me through the Corner and trust that I wouldn't take a single glance inside the fence, even with the snarling guard dog throwing itself at the chain link. I learned to associate pain and disappointment and fear with sight of the town well before I ever learned what lived inside the town well—not that any of us really know. When some kids in school wanted to sneak off to the Corner and throw rocks at it (five points for hitting the side, ten for hitting the cap), I couldn't. The thought made my body clam up, my skin prickle.

At last I was there. Its stone wall reached higher than my

waist, made me feel small in my adult body, a child again. I looked down at the cap, at the wedges of darkness between its warped slats. I reached for it, *NOBADMICHAELNO.* Touched it, *NONONO*. My face flinched involuntarily, expecting a blow. No blow came, only the wind, a dry rattle through the foxtails. Splintery hangnails dug at my fingers. I lifted. The cap rose on rusted, creaking hinges. The sound they made, it was like a hundred old doors opening all at once. I couldn't just hear it—I could feel it, like something was opening inside me. And maybe something was. Yes, maybe something was.

My boy.

My wife.

My *boy*.

I lowered the cap gently to the side, then I looked down into the well, down into the weeping dark of its throat. A warm draft touched my face. Trickling water teased my eyes with subtle movement. They say it can feel us up here. They say it knows our intentions. That Hilford fellow from the fifties, the out-of-towner who caught wind about our dirty little secret and decided he was going to fix it for us, fill in our troublesome hole, he never got past one scoop. He tipped his shovel over the edge, and as the soil went sprinkling down, he fell to his knees, coughing up the same soft grit. Almost died, he did, and same for the Doochack twins that thought they'd straighten matters with a steel lid and a padlock. Couldn't pry their jaws open with a crowbar, not until they uncapped the well and set its weathered old lid back in place. All this and more was skipping through my mind as I stood under that bloated white moon, my pockets full of change. I wondered if it knew the name on my lips, if it knew what was in my heart. And I wondered if knowing wasn't the same as owning, just with an extra letter.

I took out a quarter. I kissed it. A wish made without love

is not a wish, even when the wish is a bad one, and I loved her then, as I love her now, as I will love her always. My wife. My darling wife.

"*Helena*," I whispered.

The quarter slipped from my fingers, over the edge, and I counted the seconds of its fall. On five there came a splash, far, far down. I took out another. One is all that has ever been necessary in the stories, but one was not enough for me. For what I had come to do. I let go of the quarter, counted again, and again got to five. For a long while I went on that way, dropping quarters down the well, whispering her name. Helena, Helena, Helena. I began to weep. To sob. When my first pocket was empty, I started with the next. I felt like I was letting go of myself, my grief, my pain. At first I didn't notice when my counts became shorter, when five seconds became four seconds became three. Then my ears picked up on a change. Each splash sounded louder than the last. I looked down and saw the water, saw it rising blackly up the well's stone throat. It was shining. Where the moonlight touched its surface, quarters twinkled, silvery bright in the surrounding darkness. They jingled like they had jingled in my pockets, and their echoes bounced madly off the walls, rising, rising, and beneath them in the water, surging upward, was a face. *My* face, or a shimmery estimation of it, with coins where there should have been eyes and a mouth like the mouth of a well.

I dropped the quarter I was holding, the last one, then I turned and ran. My jeans snagged on the chain link as I crawled through the fence, and I gave myself a nasty cut tearing them free. I didn't stop to pick up my things. But I did look back, just once, just for a moment. A dribble of water spilled out over the well's curved lip and ran slowly down the stones into the dirt. I walked home on legs that didn't want to hold me.

It was almost midnight when I arrived—about the same time as it is now, as a matter of fact—and I hope that clock of yours isn't running behind or I might not have time to finish. I went to the bathroom. Enough blood had dripped from my ankle to soak my sock and saturate the inside of my shoe. The cut itself was about three inches long, north to south, and oozing like a stepped-on PB&J. It needed stitches. Too bad for it. I washed it off with a soapy dishrag and stuck on a few Band Aids. Then I sat on the toilet lid and shivered, listening to every creak and shift around me. I knew all the sounds the house made, but tonight each one seemed unfamiliar and full of meaning. There were floorboards in the kitchen that groaned even when no one was walking on them. There was the rain gutter that had come loose outside and conspired with the wind to tickle and scratch the walls. Windows clicked in their frames. The chimney told secrets under its breath. I listened, and I listened, and I shivered all the worse until the only warm part of me was the blood leaking out of my leg.

Finally, I got up. This is where my story gets hard to tell. It's not what I did. It's what I didn't do. All of you know about my boy and his blanket. What you don't know is I still have that blanket. I keep it tucked in the bottom drawer of his dresser, and sometimes when Helena is sleeping, which is about all she does, I take it out and smell it. Smell him. Then I hold it to my face so I can't breathe. A minute is as long as I can go before my body makes me pull it away. The body is cruel that way. It won't let you have want you want. On this night, though, I went into his bedroom and I stuffed the blanket into my mouth and pressed it up into my nose with my fingertips. It's a blue blanket, dark blue, like water. I imagined I was drowning. I imagined I was in the well, down where light cannot reach and love cannot live. When Helena would not feed Isaac, when I had to pump her milk and give him the bottle on my own, I told myself she was tired. When she stopped looking at him, when the sight of him would cause her to burst into tears, I said she was sad and that sadness was normal for a new mother, that there's a special kind of grief that comes after birth, when what's been a part of you for so long separates from you and becomes a real thing, a person. It's like mourning, I told her, and when I came home and couldn't find him until I heard him crying inside the cold oven, I took him out and ziptied the oven's door so it couldn't be opened again. The heat wasn't on, I said. She never would have, I said. And so it went, my love for her lying for her, telling me I could do it on my own, keep my family safe on my own. Until the crib and the blanket and the stiff lump beneath, and oh it looked like an accident, one of those things that just happens, but I knew.

I *knew*.

The blanket came unplugged from my nose, somehow, because next I remember I was lying on my side on the floor. The inside of my head felt like the inside of my mouth. My brain had been replaced with a bundle of dry cloth. I sat up groggily on one elbow, and that was when my eyes landed on the clock.

Midnight.

The front door whined open downstairs.

"*Heeellleeeenaaaa*," whispered a voice which I recognized all too well, for it was my voice, only wet. Dragging footsteps carried into the house, a sound like gulps and slurps. "*Heeeeeellllleeeennnnnnaaaa*," it called. Without thinking, I crossed the bedroom and stepped into the hall. It was coming up the stairs. Its shadow drooled up the wall ahead of it, rippling the way water ripples when a quarter strikes its surface. The thing in the well. The dark, beating heart of our little town. It was here.

"Michael?"

Helena spoke with dreamy softness. She stood in the doorway to our bedroom, her eyes open but not awake, and what had I done? Oh God, what had I *done*? I took her by her thin arms and led her back into the room, shut the door behind us, locked it. Out in the hall, feet slopped on the hardwood floor.

"*Heeeeellllllleeeeeeeennnnnaaaaaaa.*"

"My name," she said. "My name?"

"I'm sorry, I'm so sorry."

"Who's it?" She blinked as I walked her to bed. "Who's there?"

"It's no one, honey. It's no one." I pulled the covers up over her body, what little was left of it, and helped her head onto the pillow. "Go to sleep."

The doorknob clicked. She jolted upright.

"It's okay, it's all right, I'm sorry, it's all right." I wasn't making sense, but I couldn't stop. "Go to sleep, honey. It's okay, I'm sorry, you're okay, I'm so, so sorry."

Water dripped under the door, following the cracks in the floorboards and reaching toward the bed. I got up with a limp, numbly aware of the fact that I was dripping, too, leaving behind red spots wherever I went. The thing in the hall called her name again. Slobbered it. The door began to flex. Splinters popped. Cracks split the frame. I threw my shoulder against the wardrobe, once my mother's, now my wife's, now no one's. Its stubby peg legs screeched as I wedged it in front of the door.

"Go away!" I said. "Get out!"

But it wouldn't go away. I had made my wish, I had invited it in, and there was no sending it back. Perhaps that is why I summoned it in the first place. Because I knew that I would want to, that my love would never allow me to give her up on my own.

I went to her. I got up into bed where she was sitting, the

sheet balled in her hands. Her face was a confused smear. I kissed it, like I kissed the coin. I kissed her forehead. I kissed her cheek, her lips, her chin. I told her it was okay. I told her it was my fault. I told her I was sorry. Behind us, the wall between the hallway and bedroom was growing wet. Water seeped through the plaster, which began to fall away in soggy clumps. Through the holes slid long white fingers, skin as wrinkled and soft as raisins. I hugged her to me. Her body was still against mine. She asked me what was happening. I told her not to look. She asked me if Isaac was sleeping. I said, yes, yes, safe and sound, snug as a bug in a rug, and all the while grasping hands reached across the room toward us, attached to arms that stretched and sagged and quivered eagerly. Between the arms the wall began to bulge, to mold itself around a nose and eyes and gaping mouth. As its face pushed through the last wet membrane of plaster and was born into the bedroom, Helena looked at last. Recognition dawned in her eyes.

"You," she said.

"Yes," I answered. "Me."

I held on for as long as I could. She did not struggle as it pried her from me, as it wrenched her apart limb by limb and sucked each dripping piece down its throat. I wish she had struggled. I wish she had screamed. But she made no sound at all, as if she did not quite understand what was happening to her, or why, and that was somehow so much worse. It feasted on her, like Niner and I feasted on our chicken, and when it was finished it fixed its blind quarter eyes on me. Both were shiny bright, fresh from the bank. Both were spotted with blood. Then its arms retracted and its face, which was still my face, withdrew from the wall. I never glimpsed the rest of it, and for that one small mercy I am grateful. It left the house and went home to sleep—assuming it sleeps at all, down there in the dark—and I know it closed up shop behind it because coming over here this morning I strolled through the Corner and saw the well sitting in its little lot with its cap down like it had never been any other way.

That about covers things, and good timing, too, if that clock up there is right. You folks had better run along now unless you don't want to have a nice dream again for the rest of your life. And leave the door open behind you, so you don't have to buy another one tomorrow. Don't worry about me. I'm okay with it. See, the thing about coins is they have two sides. You can't have just heads or tails. They come together. Wishes are the same, at least when it comes to wishes in our well, and it's only fair. It's the price that keeps people away, more than the fear, and do you hear that? Listen. *Listen.* Can you hear the hinges creaking? Like a hundred old doors opening all at once, just like I told you, and I wonder . . .

Oh, I wonder . . .

Whose face is it wearing tonight?

The fun thing about "The Wishing Well" (at least, I think so) is that I don't remember much about its conception. Going in, I had the first line, some stuff about coins having two sides, and maybe a hint of the ending. Or maybe not. I really don't know, and I like that. It's nice when a story puts a leash on you and takes you for a walk in some new neighborhood and pats you on the head when you're done.

Daniel Barnett
Portland, OR
June 6, 2021

Daniel Barnett is a lover of stories—especially the scary ones. He has four published novels and is currently hard at work on the *Nightmareland Chronicles*, an ongoing serialized adventure horror epic following one man's journey to reach his daughter in a world claimed by eternal night.

CLOSING THE FIGURE EIGHT

BOB JOHNSTON

Saint Andrew's Day, 30 November 1990, with all the darkness, dampness, and weariness that is just a part of living in this cold wet part of the world. But we had found a way to throw the world out and beyond the single room and bathroom apartment. Here there was only us, this was the only world and it was warm, it was dry, and it was safe. For a first-ever stab at love for both of us, it was going to do very well indeed and with that long, dark, wonderful night came a commitment never to lose it. Saint Andrew was just going to have to share his day with us from now on.

"What are you thinking?" Anna's voice was quiet against the almost completely muted monochrome TV in the corner. I was thinking about spaceships, which was what unaccustomed periods of proper relaxation deserved. Spaceships or fantasy landscapes, but my mind was young and sharp so I adapted quickly.

"I was wondering how we keep this night with us forevermore. How do we find it in the future if things aren't working out for us?"

"Things will be good, Tommy. We'll get it right."

I smiled in the dark, thinking of all the people and generations I knew who must have had this same conversation at some time in their pasts. Lying in the dark, uncharacteristically happy in a society that valued only work, compliance, and money, they must have let their youth overwhelm their intelligence. Lying in the dark indeed, lying to themselves, lying to their futures. But faced with the blank, black wall that is the future perhaps, this type of lie is acceptable.

My mother, wrapped up in her romance novels and TV dramas and blithely unaware that we all knew about every one of her indiscreet trysts with everyone from salesmen to plumbers to the husbands of family friends. My father, more discreet but every bit as lost in the excitement of the chase and the capture. Siblings beginning to find their ways in this world of lies and casual, effortlessly forgotten betrayals.

Friends beginning their own tentative, first adult steps out onto the ice of infidelity. What truth any of us knew we knew from the movies, and it would be years before we discovered what unreliable teachers screenwriters are. And not even the vaguely understood consolations of religions abandoned by the generations who came before us, all eager for the next material improvement in their lifestyles. All carefully juggling what truth they could bear to throw away in return for a dishwasher or a wood-paneled wall.

Sorry, God, it was always going to be you first. You're just too damned judgmental about stolen kisses at wedding dances or nighttime visits when the husband is away for a few days. And Sunday morning is surely better spent redecorating the house in the latest gaudy, soon-to-be old fashioned abandonment of taste. My disagreement with God had nothing to do with the deplorable state of the world. It was entirely about how he let all these little lies and infidelities poison the waters of what should, by any reasonable reckoning, be a pretty good place to live and thrive.

"I read that with enough focus you can go back in time." Anna seemed determined to keep me from my spaceships tonight, but I didn't want the night to ever end.

"It would take one hell of a lot of concentration. How would you block out everything that's going on around you, the TV, the traffic, the neighbors?"

Anna rolled round and I kissed her forehead lightly.

"Well," she said, "you could switch off the TV. Other than that there isn't much going on anywhere close to the apartment."

I seem to recall having to make my naked way across the room to physically switch the TV off, but I may be misremembering. I'm sure there were remote controls way back then.

And there in the dark two souls, not yet calloused by the trivial daily thousand cuts that eventually crush your soul, made the jump back to our meeting some days earlier. On a bus, both vaguely remembering the other from school and a moment when things just click into place. Anna and I stood, phantoms, at the back of the bus and watched our days-old relationship begin again.

Finding our way back to the apartment turned out to be harder than leaving it, and we were drawn past many sights and situations on that return. Some were mundane but some were troubling. The best place to view any city is from the hills surrounding it. The darkness within parts of it are best avoided. But in time we found ourselves back in bed and it was morning and Saint Andrew could have his day back for another year.

Saint Andrew's Day, 30 November 1995, and uncommonly bright, mild, and sunny. Which was typically ironic because this was the day we had decided to throw in the towel after a year of setbacks and disappointments. I had managed to keep off the infidelity train while everyone else seemed determined to follow in their parents' footsteps as quickly as possible. Relationships that should have been straightforward and finding their slow ways forward and into the future were unravelling everywhere.

We both realized one night that the movies might be poor guides as to what constituted a good life but our parents and peers were a thousand times worse. Five years on and I felt lonelier than even those awful early years in high school.

We had gone back to the bus a few times, more often as things became worse between us, but the trips back showed more of the hard, unkind foundations of the city on our return trips. Of course we had become older, sadder, and a little harder and could see cruelty in things we would never have noticed before.

And so we pecked one another on the cheek and, under the harsh rays of wall-mounted sodium lights, Anna walked north toward the station and I walked west to the bus stop. It was night and the rain had begun, turning the city into its more typical early winter guise. An old man walked past and said, "It can't be that bad, son." A well-meant piece of cutting cruelty that I suspect is still lodged in my spirit, right next to the still not fully healed wound from Anna's last word: "Goodbye."

Time is a frighteningly flexible thing. Those rarest of things, days I want to last forever, charge past. Days filled with hate, fear, and the sour rage to destroy everything that has ever existed, well they just amble their merry way by, taking as long as they damned well please to end. But time does have one redeeming feature, and it is not that nonsense about it healing.

Nothing heals, ever. That scar tissue on your belly, your

chest, your arm. It looks so neat, so tidy against your proper skin color, but just you try going without food or vitamins for long enough and watch as those scars open up again. And those have the virtue of being physical scars which will kill you given enough time. Inside scars just suppurate forever when denied their sustenance, because most of the time we don't know what we need to keep our souls healthy until we are too old for it to matter anymore.

I could always go back if I could just find the concentration, but my life after Saint Andrew's Day 1995 was less a life than a walking exercise in worry and fear. Women came and went, all seeming to favor my outward appearance, the shell left behind, if you will. All fleeing from the dead darkness inside, the cold true me. None ever said goodbye again. They were just gone one day, days which were not worth remembering or recording.

Where, I often wondered, would I go back to if I could just find the peace and the concentration Anna and I had found in that small apartment so many years ago? So many years galloping past and yet filled with days that took forever to be done with me. How can the years pass faster than the days?

All through this I grow darker and the world drifts further from me even as I become more and more adept at playing a part in its trivial dramas. My father dead, my mother ill, family scattered to the four winds and never missed, friendships maintained and strengthened all against a growing sense of the utter pointlessness of every cue we follow on this horrible stage. I stand on my marks, I deliver my lines perfectly, and I *endure* because the word *live* long ago lost any real meaning.

But which Saint Andrew's Day to go back to? 1990 or 1995. The beginning or the end. Hello or goodbye?

Saint Andrew's Day, 30 November 2020, dull and overcast but mild. The rain used to mirror most of my moods but I find these days that a little cloud and a fresh breeze actually cheer me. The COVID-19 lockdown earlier in the year was hard as it forced me to stop blocking the past. Oddly, and despite all the pain of those months, I made the best of something awful. I stopped feeling old, which suggests to my contrary spirit that I must actually be old. But I can think again after so long and I am again contemplating the journey back, but to which date? To the room or the bus?

The symbol for infinity, the figure eight on its side, fills my thoughts these days. On the left 1990, loop down and up to the center, 1995, and then over the top to the right and today. It has to be today that I go back because I know there is no more future to the right. I have to close this figure eight and I have to do it now. Of course there will be a journey back, but I am pretty inured against the horrors of the city. A bleak resignation has replaced depression and I can now look without being hurt by it any more.

The room is quiet, the house a distance from the road and detached from its neighbors. There are certainly the distant sounds of sirens, helicopters, children playing, but all far away. This is the best opportunity in twenty-five years to make the jump back, but part of that deep concentration has to be the decision about where to go. I let my mind drift, give up control, and the answer arrives using Anna's voice.

Surely a trick of my mind, as it is the voice of a very young woman.

"You cannot close the infinity symbol without going through the center point. Close the circle instead."

What circle? But there is no further voice to help me out. Circle to where? Circle to when? Circle to. . . 1995. It is the only route possible. I realize even as I relax deeper into this journey that any attempt to take another route will throw me off the figure eight and I will be lost forever.

"Would that be such a bad thing?" I whisper to myself, but my own inner voice saves me from this thinking. Of course it would. Pain can be recovered from. The sort of lost I am facing here is lost never to be found or looked for. Simply gone.

Saint Andrew's Day, 30 November 1995, and I had forgotten the rain that followed the sunny day. I leaned against a closed shop door across the street from the building with the strangely mounted sodium lights. An hour earlier, Anna had walked away to the left and Tommy had crossed the street in front of me on his way to the bus stop. His face looked older than I remembered, and there was an anger I did fully remember because I was only now managing to throw it off my overburdened shoulders.

I wanted to follow him and talk to him but I also wanted to follow Anna and, for all I could travel through the years, the minutes would elude me here. Her train would come when it came as would Tommy's bus, and whichever of them I followed I would end up standing alone on a platform or a street.

I was twenty-five years away from home and it dawned on me that there was not a soul I could reach out to, not even myself or the woman whose love had proven impossible to forget or get over. Different world, different technologies, different ways, even the language would mark me as different. Was this the ultimate lost, lost in your own past?

"Tommy?"

I looked up from the pavement at the woman standing

close to the curb. It took a moment to adjust for the years but then I smiled. How else could the circle ever have been closed? I stood up.

"Anna."

"Closing the Figure Eight" draws on a variety of real events, all unrelated other than their effect on my emotional state through the years. It also uses Glasgow, Scotland as its background, a city of astonishing (and too often ignored) beauty; but a city that can be sombre and dark, particularly at the time of year described in the story. There was no break up under wall-mounted sodium lights, but those lights do exist. And my wife and I met by chance on a bus, after twenty-five years of just missing one another.

Bob Johnston
Glasgow, Scotland
June 5, 2021

Bob Johnston has been a fan of science fiction and horror since childhood. Starting with the *British Pan Books of Horror* series, he moved onto Michael Moorcock, Algis Budrys, Robert Silverberg, and a mass of American magazines that became available at the time. When he's not scribbling stories he reads history and theology and rides a big silver motorcycle. A quartet of his stories can be found on his website: bobjohnstonfiction.com.

HOLDING

SIMONE LE ROUX

I used to live in houses like a ghost. I would run my fingers along hallway walls, looking for messages in the braille of the beige paint. I'd stop and stare at photos of family members I ought to miss but didn't. I would sleep in a room that was for me but smelled of someone else, in a bed with its imprint of a body that wasn't mine. I didn't unpack boxes so much as I spread their contents on the shelves, seeing only the invisible paths they would follow right back to their cardboard homes.

Even after I outgrew my dependence on my parents' stochastic lifestyle, staying put didn't often cross my mind. I'd only learned how to live in temporary states, and I could only plan around the absolute certainty of impermanence. Besides, there were always better reasons to leave than there were to stay.

I didn't see this as a problem for a long time. I suppose that, for some people, it isn't a bad thing if their feet never touch the ground. For me, though, I eventually looked down and found myself a parched, pale human being, all tangled up and exhausted by the breeze that had swept me about for so long. My hands ached to hold on to something—somewhere—long enough that I could sprout roots and anchor myself.

I knew that people make fickle handholds and can't be relied on. So I ignored all advice to the contrary and bought a house.

After the sale, I stood in front of 37 Lemongrass Lane, marveling at how even the address sounded fantastical. It was a fairy-tale house at the end of the lane, straddling the border between sleepy town and gnarly forest. With its exposed beams and climbing ivy, it could have passed for the home of a green witch or the hideaway of a secret princess. It needed work, but I was head over heels in love with every broken inch.

I was determined to infuse the entire house with the stability and comfort I craved. I wanted to sink myself deep into those creaky floorboards, grow upward into the cracked mouldings, and fill the wild garden with perennial plants whose growth would mark the passing of years in one place.

After sorting my boxes into the correct rooms, I got Carlotta settled in the bedroom. She hopped around her cage, full of curiosity. I whistled her a tune and reached my fingers through the bars to stroke her downy chest. She was too agitated to enjoy it but obliged me with a little song of her own anyway.

"I'll let you explore once there aren't so many boxes for you to disappear in," I promised. After five years with me, she knew the routine. Always patient, ever-optimistic even in the dreariest of houses: she would finally have a bright, happy place to call home. My heart swelled at the thought.

I decided I would start settling myself in by painting the walls any and every colour that wasn't beige.

That's where the trouble began.

I would turn my back to the room for a second and find that an important tool had gone missing, even though I had just put it down. The paint was separated and wouldn't mix properly no matter how much I stirred it. The drop cloths drifted away of their own accord, no matter how much I weighed them down. I ended up with one stripped wall, two litres of spilled paint, and a ruined shirt.

The can-do attitude from that morning was depleted by the time I went to bed that night, replaced by the flighty nervousness that came too easily in moments of difficulty. It whispered to me about a new town with a boring apartment that I wouldn't have to paint.

I slept uneasily. I'd come to expect this on my first night in a new place, although this felt different. Carlotta, even with a blanket draped over her cage, was anxious too. She tweeted little querying melodies throughout the night, which wasn't like her at all. When she wasn't courting my attention, I started awake several times at what sounded like footsteps around my bed or something dragging across the floor downstairs. Exhausted and demotivated as I was, I convinced myself it was just the old house settling. If there was an intruder, they could take my things and I'd deal with it after some sleep.

What I found that morning was worse than a robbery. The boxes I had emptied the day before had been neatly packed up again and piled in the entrance hall, as though the careful thought and delighted organisation of yesterday had never happened.

I sat on my bottom step and cried. I couldn't understand what was happening or why, and I yearned to load the boxes back into my car and forget about this ill-fated experiment. It made me hate myself. Surely a normal person wouldn't have such an overwhelming urge to flee?

In the end, I called my mom.

"Anna! How's the move going?"

I took my time on the inhale before answering, scared my

voice would break as I talked. I didn't want her to worry. "It's hard!" I exclaimed, forcing a laugh to push through any tremors.

My mom joined in and the sound cheered me a little. "You've done this so many times before. I'd think you'd be a natural," she said.

"Well, I've never had to worry about paint and repairs and things. I always had a landlord to sort that out for me, and you and Dad before that."

"I guess that's true," she admitted. And then, more carefully, "Are you feeling okay, though?"

She always knew. The comfort of it made hot tears press at the backs of my eyes. I took another breath to collect myself before answering.

"Um, yeah. I'm okay. I just. . . "

"What, dear?"

"Have you ever felt like something just isn't meant to be?"

"What do you mean?"

"It feels like this house doesn't want me here. I know that sounds crazy."

My mom took a second to consider before answering. "Are you sure it's not just your itchy feet? You're taking a big step here—it's normal if you want to go back to what you know."

I paced around the empty living room, trying to ignore the dried paint stain on the floor. I looked out the window at the lush forest close by. The view had been one of the big selling points of the house. I'd loved the idea of watching the forest grow and change over the years from the comfort of my couch.

"I don't think that's it," I said. "I really want to make this work. It just feels like I'm fighting for it every step of the way. You should have seen me try to paint yesterday, Mom. Everything kept going wrong." I attempted to inject humour into my voice, but I must have missed the mark because my mom didn't laugh along.

"You know, when I was a girl and we moved house, we used to leave out little gifts," she mused.

"Gifts?"

My mom laughed. "It sounds silly, but my grandmother told me they were for the fairies. She said they get mad at disruption and cause all kinds of trouble. So we'd leave out cakes and saucers of cream so the fairies knew we were friends. I think it was her way of trying to make me feel comfortable in a new place."

I found myself smiling. "That's cute! How come you never did that with me?"

"Oh, I guess doing it just felt too permanent. You were already so upset about leaving your friends whenever we moved and I didn't want to add fairy friends on top of that."

My mom's tone was light, but I could hear the strain behind it. It can't have been easy for her to drag around a crying child and, later, a moody teenager, especially when she had her own friends to bid farewell.

"I turned out okay, Mom," I assured her and continued before I could ask myself whether that was true. "So, you think leaving out food is the answer."

"If you want an ant problem too."

My chuckle was genuine this time.

"But seriously, dear, take some time to get used to the house and let it get used to you. You're starting a long-term relationship—your first one ever besides Carlotta—so it's bound to be a bumpy road. If you need to bake some cakes to smooth things out, then do it. I won't tell."

I sighed. "Do fairies have any flavour preferences?"

"Not burnt is a start, knowing you."

"So funny!"

I ended the call a few minutes later, feeling better and

already explaining away the events of the last twenty-four hours. Maybe there *was* some deep part of me that was terrified of taking this step. Maybe it had caused me to sleepwalk and move the boxes around. It seemed I would just have to keep going until my brain got used to the idea of staying.

Less enthusiastic about painting than before, I decided to start unpacking the kitchen. It would be a good symbolic gesture if I cooked myself a meal this evening instead of relying on takeout.

It went well at first, and I thought that maybe I had jumped some psychological hurdle—until I heard the first plate crash.

I whipped around to stare at the shattered porcelain on the floor. I couldn't fathom how it had fallen from its secure spot on the shelf above, but I tried to take it in my stride. I went to fetch the broom, and that's when the sound of the second crash shattered its way through my grim positivity.

"Stop!" I yelled. I wasn't sure who I was addressing but, when I returned to the kitchen, all was still. I reached up and tried to wiggle the shelf that held the stack of plates. It held firm. I realised my heart was pounding and worried for the first time whether I really was losing it.

The rest of the day was more benign, but still unsettling. I would find books I'd set on the shelf scattered across the floor. While I unwrapped picture frames, I felt something brush across the back of my neck. After shrieking and letting the frame I held clatter to the floor, I realised it was a curtain I had hung earlier, floating back down to the ground behind me. It had touched my neck during its descent. On closer inspection, it looked like moths had eaten all along the top of the curtain, which I was surprised I hadn't noticed as I was hanging it.

I baked the damned cake. The feel of the curtain dragging down the back of my neck lingered on my skin and pulled my spine into a tense line that I would have done just about anything to relax. Baking had been an unpleasant process—I kept misplacing spoons and I burned my wrist taking the tray out of the oven – but I had six bran and lavender muffins on the table by bedtime. Feeling a little silly, I placed a saucer of cream next to them for good measure.

Despite my cynicism, I felt better. Something had been set to rest in my mind. Perhaps it had been following the old motions of baking, but something made the house feel lighter. This was the perfect moment to try out the bath.

The bathtub had also been a major selling point of the house: it was enormous, with claw and ball feet and brass taps. It looked like something a romantic heroine would use to daydream the afternoon away. I lit some candles and sank into the hot water with a moan. Perhaps today hadn't been as bad as I'd thought. After all, I had gotten quite a bit of unpacking done and, who knows, maybe I had just made some new friends.

With the warm water, flickering candlelight, and tranquillity of the evening, I sank into dreaming like a stone.

In the dream, I packed all my things into the car and left a lit match right in the middle of the house's fluffiest carpet before driving into the night. The house burned in my rear-view mirror and the smoky wind combed through my hair and brushed away the dried paint flecks on my cheek. I drove until the darkness swallowed me up, only to find myself right in front of the house again. It stood whole and unharmed.

That's when I realised that the smoke was coming from inside the car. A fire spread across the back seat. Carlotta screeched, wings beating out a chaotic rhythm on the rungs of her cage. I tried to open the car door but it wouldn't move, nor would the windows roll down. Smoke filled the car. I banged on the window, yelling for help, for the key, for air that didn't hurt to breathe. My skin blistered at the intense heat.

I awoke with a cry that amounted to little more than bubbles. I was under water that was hot, too hot, and I couldn't get my face above the surface of it. Something held my hair down, pinning my head to the bottom of the tub. I bucked and kicked, clawing at the sides of the tub to find purchase that wasn't there. The tap was running, fiery, onto the water above my belly. I screamed again, a futile gesture with no air to put behind it and no one around to hear. I was going to die alone in this bathtub, in this place that hated me, and I didn't know why.

All at once, whatever had held my hair released. When I at last got my hair above the water, Carlotta was screeching like a banshee in the next room, as though she had seen it all. Spluttering, I joined in with her cacophony.

My brain was numb with shock as I sat on the edge of my bed, wrapped in a bathrobe. My hair hung in strings around my wet face. The blisters on my stomach and thighs twinged. I knew I would go buy aloe in the morning, but I couldn't decide what to do at that moment.

I picked up the phone.

"Darling? It's late. Is everything okay?"

"Hey Mom. Yeah. Yeah, I'm okay. I just. . . " My voice wobbled. "It didn't work."

"What didn't work?"

"I know this sounds stupid but I—I put out some cakes like you said, but it didn't work. I still feel so unwelcome here. And so alone." My voice broke and I cried into the receiver, still the little girl crying to her mom because she felt lonely in a new place. Still the child waiting for the next place to be better. "Is it always going to be like this?" I asked between hitched breaths.

"Of course not, sweetheart." There was a long pause and, when my mom spoke again, her voice was low. "So they didn't accept the cakes?"

"I almost drowned in the bath just now," I sniffed. "And when I checked the kitchen, the cakes were just crumbled up and thrown everywhere. Cream all over the floor." I felt another sob coming on and swallowed it back.

"That's. . . not good."

"I know, I know. You're going to say I'm just resisting being here on some psychological level. I feel like I'm going crazy, Mom. Maybe I should just leave."

"Absolutely not."

I was surprised by the ice in her words.

"I'm going to say this once, Anna-Beth, and if you ask me about it again I'll deny it. There is a reason I don't like staying in one place for long. The folk in your house aren't the fairy-tale kind. They won't accept food and drink. They want sacrifice."

"Sacrifice?" I blinked at the fog the tears had created in my eyes and mind. I didn't understand any of what she meant, couldn't follow along fast enough. What did this have to do with cakes? With what was wrong with me?

"Blood. A life."

"Mom, I couldn't—"

"Then leave. But you need to decide soon or you're not safe. You won't ever be."

She hung up, leaving me to stare, open-mouthed, at the receiver.

My first thought was leaving this house and never looking back, money be damned. The moment I committed to the idea, though, I was heartbroken. I'd had so many plans and ideas. I'd framed pictures of all the people and places and things that I loved so I could hang them up and add to them every day. I'd wanted friends who would check in on me and invite me to dinner for no reason at all. I'd wanted to know my neighbours, attend their potlucks, watch their kids grow. I'd wanted to meet someone who would stay in this house with me and love me. I wanted to be part of a place, not just a guest.

"I'm so tired of being alone," I wept to the empty room, head in my hands. My shoulders shook with grief and dread for the future I would throw myself back into: a long road with nowhere waiting for me at the end of it.

Carlotta twittered at me in her reassuring song, the one she used every time she heard me cry. This sweet little bird, who wanted only to see the world and be with me, who had learned how to sing to me in my sadness, was my only friend.

I looked at her sky-blue chest, long tail feathers, and bright eyes through my tears. My hands shook.

My family had a mantra we used to throw around whenever we moved to a new place: the first six months are the worst. You just have to put your head down and get through them. I should have guessed that the same would apply at my new home: obstacles always arise and adjusting is difficult. Six months down the line, though, it's all become part of life.

Yes, having to consistently offer up gifts to the fairies infesting my house is hard, but no harder than saying goodbye to friends or packing belongings into cold boxes or walking into a new place that could never be my home. It just takes some getting used to.

I'm glad I stayed. The house is a joy to live in: I have all kinds of colours and pictures lining the walls. I filled each room with lush carpets, soft pillows, and silly accessories that never would have fit into my car. I bought a brand-new bed.

When I have visitors, which is often, we stay up late into the night, drunk on wine and laughter, breathing in the fresh scents of my garden. That's not to say I don't go out. In fact, my pot pie has become quite the commodity at community potlucks.

And the best part is that I always wake up to a spotless home. My shoes are polished, my clothes unwrinkled. I know that I was excited to live close to the forest and its wildlife, but I don't miss the birdsong in the mornings. I enjoy the silence.

Neighbourhood pets have started to go missing. Not just the wayward cats, but faithful dogs and housebound rabbits too. Everyone suspects a crime ring, so naturally I've joined the neighbourhood watch to do my part. I patrol the neighbourhood and help people install security systems. We haven't caught anyone yet, but we're doing our best. After all, it's only a matter of time until these monsters set their sights on children.

I wrote this story as I struggled to come to terms with settling down after I'd spent my childhood moving from place to place. I felt as though I had to sacrifice bits of myself that I liked, and I couldn't shake the distinct impression of being an odd changeling child wherever I went. It's an ongoing journey, but putting those thoughts to paper in Holding has made it easier to understand.

Simone le Roux
Cape Town, South Africa
June 7, 2021

Simone le Roux is a third-culture kid still figuring out the culture part. A lover of all things dark and creepy, but not the cold, she has settled in Cape Town where the temperature never dips lower than chilly but the rainfall is spectacular. An admirer of all mildly wasteful things, she has a neuroscience degree that she uses only to fact-check her own stories and an accent from a country she barely remembers. Her work has been published in *Dark Hearts*, a Ghost Orchid Press Anthology.

THE THREAD THAT DREAMS ARE MADE OF

HAILEY PIPER

Belinda didn't belong here, and even her clothes knew it, her crimson suit sleeve squeezing as if to stop her when she knocked on the office door. A black R glistened in the window. Once upon some dream of her life, she was a fixer, and fixers didn't hire each other for help. She shouldn't have come.

But the dream had gone nightmare, and fixers belonged to crews, and hers was gone. A dry voice beckoned her through the door.

She found him at his paper-piled desk, dressed in slacks and suspenders, a wooden pipe spitting smoke from the corner of his mouth. He was shorter than she'd heard, or maybe his back had gone stooped from long days bent over a spinning wheel. Her older sister once said he could spin hay into gold, but her middle sister said that was a fancy way of calling him a good liar. Belinda couldn't guess the truth. She only knew she needed help.

"Summer, autumn, winter, spring, whad'ya need from Rumpelstiltskin?" he asked. His eyes studied her suit. "Rainbow crew?"

"I'm here about the Royals Syndicate," Belinda said. "Business soured between them and the Dark Fairies when you still ran with their leader."

"Lady Em, then?" Rumpelstiltskin spun his chair to the window behind him. Outside, a busker blew depressed notes through a saxophone. "Walk me through it."

This story seemed old now, and unlucky. "Sixteen years back, the head of the Royals had a daughter, Princess, and invited the crews to her baptism. My sisters and I had just joined the Rainbows, and we were asked to bless the baby. Wished her beauty, health. I was the last, but—"

"Lady Em interrupted." Rumpelstiltskin chewed his pipe. "Party crasher."

"Her invitation was lost," Belinda said.

"Or never sent."

To purposely offend the Dark Fairies' matriarch seemed ludicrous, but Belinda couldn't know. "She showed up anyway and gave Princess the kiss of death, a curse to prick her finger on a spinning wheel at age sixteen."

"But you changed it," Rumpelstiltskin said.

"Fixed. But a death curse, that's a big thing to fix." Belinda bit her lip. Telling this part didn't seem right, but how was a fixer to fix a problem he didn't understand? "I spread it into one big sleep, one hundred years for the whole syndicate. The Royals tried burning the city's spinning wheels, but curses being set, Princess found the wheel, its needle."

Rumpelstiltskin fiddled with his pipe's chamber. "Fair's fair in mob curses."

"Nothing's fair." Belinda strode toward the desk. "Em couldn't plant the death curse again, but she found a loophole. Nothing stopping her from putting herself in the sleep to torment the syndicate. The Dark Fairies smuggled nightmares with her."

"But she can't kill them." Rumpelstiltskin turned from the window, pipe cooling. "They'll wake, eventually."

"After one hundred years of nightmares. What kind of mob boss will Princess become after a century of horrors?"

"Dreaming, waking, working, dozing." Rumpelstiltskin tapped his pipe over a wastebasket. "Tricky, tricky."

"My sisters thought we'd balance nightmares with dreams, led the Rainbows into the sleep." Belinda's face tightened. She wouldn't cry in front of a fellow fixer. "We weren't under a death-made-sleep curse. Killing us breaks no rules. When Em hunted us in dreams, my sisters—dying in the nightmare meant never waking."

"Big cost to salvage one family. Big gambler. A roulette wheel, that's your life." Rumpelstiltskin set his pipe down; tobacco stained his fingertips yellow. "How can I help, Ms. Fixer?"

"You used to run with the Dark Fairies."

"Used to. You know I'm not a fixer anymore, right?"

Belinda slapped her worn hands on his desk. "But you were the master spinner. The curse began with a spinning wheel. Isn't there something we can work from there?"

"Spinning hay into gold is one thing. Curses?" Rumpelstiltskin stroked his stubby chin.

"The Rainbows can't have died for nothing. I need to fix it." Memories draped Belinda's thoughts with too many funerals, each drawing fewer colorful suits around the lowered caskets. Mourning fixed nothing, grief even less. She would lower herself to make the sacrifice worth it. Grovel, if she had to.

"Know what's more powerful than curses?" Rumpelstiltskin asked, drawing Belinda up from memory. "A trade. Your nonsense etiquette, blessings between rival crews. A gang's politeness is like any fairy, bound to disappear in a puff of disbelief."

"If we make a trade, you'll help me?" Belinda asked.

"Growing, aging, death, birth. Loopholes are good; loops are better. You come full circle, make a wheel of it? The master spinner can help you then." Rumpelstiltskin dug through desk drawers, drew out a spool of red thread, and placed it in Belinda's hands. "And only then."

Belinda chose the cathedral of St. Giambattista as her brief resting place. The site of Princess's fateful baptism seemed fitting to reach the Royals' big sleep, and the Rainbows had used its pews to smuggle good dreams into the great nightmare.

Belinda had no good dreams left, no crew, only a spool of thread and a four-word prayer. "I can fix it," she said. A vial of bitter fluid emptied onto her tongue. No going back now; sleep would soon take her. She reclined across a wooden pew, stared at the ceiling, and waited for darkness.

And waited. The pew was hard and pressed her shoulders. Someone's high heels pounded over the stone floor, making sleep impossible.

Belinda sat up. "Would you quiet—"

The ceiling had turned wooden, its walls squeezed together, the floor busy with dresses, suits, and hats. No cathedral, but some shop's backroom. The smell of fabric dye laced the air.

Belinda had joined the dream. Her hand squeezed Rumpelstiltskin's red-threaded spool. It had joined, too, same as her clothes, at one with the great nightmare.

A crooked spinning wheel loomed at the room's center. Cracks ran through its every inch, and its needle aimed an ancient point. The filthy thing likely carried every disease imaginable. Small wonder it had been destined to kill a mob boss's daughter.

And there she stood behind the wheel in a flowing white dress—Princess, sixteen years old. Her face hung placid, eyes clouded. Mixed curses had overtaken her will and reshaped destiny.

Belinda crossed the room. Thread unspooled from her hand in a red line, but she couldn't worry about that now. Princess had yet to prick her finger here, and Belinda could stop the curse before it began. A preemptive fix.

"Princess, don't!" she snapped.

Princess's finger tapped the needle. A crack ran up her hand and spread through her body, every inch crinkling like a folded paper doll. Creases leaked from shoes to floor to walls, every piece of the dream crumpling into a paper ball, doomed for a steel wastebasket.

A familiar cackle seeped through the cracks. "You can't fix this, fixer," Lady Em said. "Otherwise, wouldn't you stop me?"

Screams rang beneath a wrinkled doorway, the sounds of crewmates and sisters dying in a neighboring nightmare. Belinda followed the sounds, but they faded the moment she stepped from the backroom. A pleasant, polished office greeted her. Thread ran behind her through the doorway, and she hoped the master spinner had meant it to unspool.

A turntable spun piano tunes from the corner of a smooth desk, where Lady Em reclined in a plush chair. Black hair puffed up her head in a stormy cloud. Her pinstriped suit was sleek and pressed.

"Sorry, sweetheart," she said, tongue playing with each word. "The whacking's done. Rainbows? Dead and mounted."

One hand swept behind her, where framed photographs cluttered the wall. Here, Lady Em tossed one of the Rainbow crew into the river, cement shoes hugging his feet. There,

Lady Em gunned down Belinda's eldest sister with a Chicago Typewriter, its muzzle flare caught like the sun in the dream camera's lens. Elsewhere, a garrote and a grin haunted Belinda's middle sister. Her neck never saw them coming.

"A tribute to your failures." Em pointed to the center. "Did you note Princess's snapshot?"

Belinda needed no photographs. The memories burned clear in her mind.

"Might need to make some room, yeah?" Em stood from the desk, eyes wild with glee, and strutted through another door set in the far wall. "You got plenty more failures coming my way, see? Could fill a cathedral with them."

Belinda charged after her. Fixing didn't always mean cobbling together a solution or undoing a mistake. Sometimes fixing meant revenge. She couldn't unmake the wall of photos, but she could stop Lady Em and pacify the great nightmare.

The door opened onto the street, where St. Giambattista's cathedral towered. Parishioners filled its mighty steps. Above them, a pinstriped suit slipped between cathedral doors.

Belinda crossed the street, cars honking around her. If the drivers knew who she was, would they be so impatient? Or, was she anyone anymore without the Rainbows? Sisters gone, crew gone—she couldn't let misery distract her. Up the cathedral steps and inside, she almost expected to find herself asleep across a pew, Lady Em looming with a switchblade pressed to a sleeping throat.

Instead, the cathedral was filled with dark suits and colorful dresses, various crews attending a fateful baptism. Someone had carried a small cradle to the front, as if Princess might be too dainty to be held. So innocent and small, she couldn't imagine the curses to come. She didn't deserve a hundred years of nightmares, and the city didn't deserve her reign of terror should Lady Em have her way.

Smart of the Dark Fairy matriarch to hide here among the throng of well-wishers. One pinstriped suit in the crowd resembled any other.

Colors caught Belinda's gaze. Three sisters stood to one side, their suits teal, violet, and crimson. Once upon a time, they were a family. They couldn't have imagined the curses to come any better than an infant.

Slamming doors sent Belinda glancing over her shoulder. Red thread crept under the cathedral doors, still unspooling down steps, street, maybe through Em's office to the backroom. It began with a spinning wheel; it would end with a spinner.

"Master spinner, help me," Belinda whispered.

Rumpelstiltskin didn't answer. He'd told her to come full circle, and the curse had started here. If Princess's baptism wasn't the place and time, then where and when?

A creaking voice called down the cathedral aisle. "Nobody can help you, sweetheart. And you'll help nobody."

Belinda pressed through the crowd. Their eyes gleamed now, not well-wishers but smuggled nightmares wearing guests' skins as suits and dresses. She reached the wooden cradle and leaned over.

An infant lay inside, but not Princess. The swaddling was pinstriped, the face twisted with dark clouds and wild eyes. "Know what it's like to be spurned?" Em asked. "You will. When Princess wakes up, oof, they'll wish my kiss of death had ended her, age sixteen. Nice job, fixer. A city's load of blame and hatred, coming your way."

Flames erupted through the cradle and shot to the roof. Belinda slipped back, startled, but St. Giambattista's walls had melted away. She stood on the street now, between cathedral steps and a roaring bonfire. Wooden spinning wheels fed the blaze, the spoils of a city-wide hunt by Royals Syndicate goons. Their needles gleamed with firelight.

Belinda stumbled backward over her unwinding spool. Its thread wove up and down the cathedral steps. Did that matter? The spool seemed a useless trinket. Rumpelstiltskin's spinning really had been a pretty euphemism for lies. He'd been a fixer for the Dark Fairies once, and his allegiance must've held. Belinda had been too desperate to notice. She ran a sleeve across her dampening face.

A small girl approached Belinda's left. She wore Princess's face, but the Royals wouldn't have dressed their special daughter in a pinstriped dress, its silver buttons carved into the faces of Belinda's sisters.

"Too late to save her," they said. "Too late to save us."

Belinda scuttled back. At this rate of retreating, she'd find herself where she started, the nightmare coiling around her. "I can—"

"Fix it?" Princess's face split into Lady Em's smirk. "You can't fix this. If we're being straight, you can't fix anything."

Belinda's heart sank. She should have ditched the city, found a new home, new work. Her sisters might have died in vain, but at least any nightmares would be her own.

"Despair, huh? Maybe you're no Rainbow—no, you're a Dark Fairy-to-be. That's how this ends, see?" Lady Em shed her Princess skin and loomed over Belinda, her cloud of dark hair filling the sky with storms. "When Princess wakes up from her nightmares in a mad fit, her reign will ravage the streets. Guess who fixes that problem? Guess who absorbs the ravaged gangs? We'll be one big crew, a city for Dark Fairies. Better you join late than never."

Smoke stung Belinda's eyes. "But the Rainbows—"

"Yesterday's news." Lady Em reached for Belinda's hand. "Here's your shot to be our new fixer, sweetheart. Take it."

Belinda flinched back. She would rather follow in Princess's doomed footsteps, take the kiss of death, prick her finger on the cursed spinning wheel needle than join with her sisters' murderer. Her feet scuffed asphalt as she crossed the street to Lady Em's office. Its wall of failures begged for Belinda's attention, but she turned for the backroom door.

Creases covered every surface. The paper doll Princess was gone, but the cracked spinning wheel stood hungering for another fingertip. Belinda could oblige.

Lady Em leaned into the doorway. "A death wish, then?"

Belinda said nothing. The spinning wheel grew across the room to meet her, and one finger straightened toward its filthy needle. Three inches, and its point would prick flesh.

"Same fate, either way," Lady Em said. Victory wasn't enough on its own; she had to gloat too. "No Rainbows, no Royals. That baptism will be the last time anyone forgets to invite Lady Em of the Dark Fairies to a party."

Belinda's fingertip hovered two inches from the needle point. She couldn't look, couldn't fix this. Her eyes fell on a red line across the floor. Its tail seemed unperturbed by the creased room. The same thread still unspooled in two lines to and from the door.

Loose ends, waiting to meet.

"I don't got all day," Lady Em said. "You've come this far, see? Finish it."

Belinda could oblige. An inch from the spinning wheel needle, she slipped her hand underneath, slung the spool of thread toward its tail, and tied both ends into a knot. A tremor worked up her nerves, a new crease in the great nightmare.

Her lips quivered. "Begins and ends may spin the same, for Rumpelstiltskin is his name."

The ceiling groaned, and a familiar voice rang through the wood. "Midnight, morning, noon, and dusk. Come full circle, have you?"

Belinda staggered back as the spinning wheel shattered. Wrinkles infected the room's every surface, the walls shriveled from their foundations, and the ceiling tore loose. The sky spun with clouds—no, the room was spinning, caught on a tremendous wheel. A new center to the nightmare, built of days and nights, births and deaths, the cycling rim colored red as knotted thread.

"What's this racket?" Lady Em broke from the doorway, her footsteps uncertain against the swiveling world, and grasped at Belinda. "What do you got up your sleeve?"

"I'm fixing it," Belinda said. "With help." It began with a spinning wheel.

It would end with a spinner. Enormous tobacco-stained fingers prodded the room's edges. "Loopholes are good," Rumpelstiltskin said. "But loops are better."

Lady Em aimed her angry face at the sky. "You can't take over! It's my curse! My revenge!"

"Sure, you've cursed their nights and days, round and round." Rumpelstiltskin's face filled the sky, far taller than Belinda remembered. "But before I was a Dark Fairy fixer, I was the master spinner, hay into gold, nightmares into dreams. And these cycles? They're all one big spinning wheel."

Yellow-tipped fingers gave the room another twirl. Lady Em staggered to where the wheel once stood in a whirl of dark hair and pinstripes. Wild eyes begged for mercy, and one desperate arm snapped from the storm, snatching for a helping hand.

Belinda didn't reach back. A wall of photographed deaths could explain why, but deeper than revenge, she was a fixer. Helping Lady Em wouldn't fix this. Only consequence would.

When the spinning slowed, no Dark Fairy matriarch stood at the room's center. A new spool wound in Belinda's hand, its thread pattern with pinstripes.

"I'll be taking that." Rumpelstiltskin's great dream-fingers reached down. A chimney-sized pipe smoked from the corner of his mouth. "Fair trade, yes?"

Belinda handed over the spool and watched him pocket it. "What will you spin her into?"

Rumpelstiltskin shrugged hilly shoulders. "Rare material, and powerful. I'll sleep on it, yes? Perhaps for a century." He tapped a knowing finger against the chamber of his pipe. "Take care, fixer. You've got your own nightmares to fix now."

He turned and thundered away, a dark silhouette on a dim sky. The great nightmare was coming unthreaded without its mistress, and Belinda sank through shadowy dreams of her own. Memories flickered, some pleasant, others not. She supposed that was normal. Princess and the rest of the Royals Syndicate would face the same, like any dreamer.

Belinda awoke lying on a pew. The stone ceiling of St. Giambattista's cathedral stared at her. No one else awoke nearby, the pews empty. Her part in the nightmare was over, but its toll remained. No Rainbows, no sisters. For all the safekeeping of the Royals Syndicate, Belinda was still alone.

She could only wait another ninety-nine years for Princess to awaken and see if she was worth the cost.

While recovering from a hospital stay and weird dreams brought on by painkillers last autumn, I dreamed of someone chasing me like Freddy Krueger, except not him, and not through Springwood houses or boiler rooms, but a fairytale castle. This idea got stuck in my head the next day and over the months, about Sleeping Beauty and ties to other stories, in this case A Nightmare on Elm Street, and later Rumpelstiltskin, and then Sleeping Beauty's baptism mixed with the infamous Godfather scene. All these threads knotted up inside me, and I had to write them out.

Hailey Piper
Maryland
June 5, 2021

Hailey Piper is the author of *Queen of Teeth, The Worm and His Kings, Unfortunate Elements of My Anatomy,* and *Benny Rose, the Cannibal King*. An active member of the Horror Writers Association, her short fiction appears in *Year's Best Hardcore Horror, Daily Science Fiction, Flash Fiction Online,* and elsewhere. She lives with her wife in Maryland, where they spend weekends raising the dead. Find her at www.haileypiper.com or on Twitter via @HaileyPiperSays.

MOS TEUTONICUS

BRYSON RICHARD

She was dead, finally.

There were seven of them, spread out in a crude circle. Their feet pointed toward the center. They'd been sitting together when the poison took effect, engaged in some ceremonial prayer; something communal with chanting and smoking. They writhed and squirmed in their final, agonizing moments, leaving crude scrawls on the ground like drawings etched in dirt by bored, grubby children.

Gregoire didn't care about the rest of them; only her. Only the Priestess.

He could not bear to put her in the earth, to cover her and leave her for the vermin. Nor could he stomach setting her pretty flesh aflame and her bones to soot, regardless of how eagerly she would have encouraged such things.

The others he would burn, but she. . . she deserved something special.

She deserved remembrance.

Preservation.

The trek home was long and arduous. Gregoire could not fathom packing up her corpse and tramping back to Europe over the many long months. It had taken him a year to reach the Holy Land from France, and though he was burdened then by travel among regiments of soldiers, mercenaries, and various self-professed righteous men, he was now alone and free to move on his own. This made travel faster, but not altogether safer. He could sneak, yes, he could move without being seen well enough, but to do so with a corpse in tow, and to do so over the course of eight or nine months, was impossible. She would not last the journey. He wished to avoid all confrontation on his way. Direct conflict rarely worked in his favor. It was a matter of strengths; his were not in his arms or breast or lungs, but in his mind, voice, and mannerisms. His strength was not physical confrontation, but mental manipulation.

He needed to hurry.

He cursed himself for not thinking it through in the first place. He'd acted impulsively by poisoning the sect's communal pipe. Now, he needed to discard of their bodies.

First, he rolled the Priestess's remains in a fine, ornate rug that lined a section of floor. He set her outside, then fetched a bow and quiver he'd discovered on the battlefield among the Muslim dead. He fired every arrow at the remaining corpses. Each impact made a solid, meaty *thwack* in their lifeless flesh.

Then he set the tent on fire.

Whoever found the inferno would doubtless find those inside. The arrows provided enough cover to deter any suspicion from coming his way.

He skulked into the night with the rolled-up rug slung over one shoulder.

Father of Flies the Priestess called her deity. The decaying one that feasts upon the dead. The *Father* that consumes the freshly slaughtered and the long rotted alike, the sick and murdered, the lost and lonely.

The sect danced through the lines of regimented men on the battlefield, ensuring them that, though their souls may be protected, their dead flesh belonged to the *Father*, and it would not go to waste.

Neither Muslim nor Christian wanted anything to do with the pontifying cult. Neither side knew where they'd come from, or where they'd go when the fighting was finally over. Perhaps wherever the next fight was. . .

The sect painted themselves in excrement, which drew flies and other insects. They did this intentionally, so their bodies were infested with crawling vermin and a symphony of insane buzzing announced their procession. They wore bones as jewelry, dirty feathers in their hair, but otherwise ran naked through the ranks. They babbled, chittered, blasphemed to all who had ears.

The Frenchman initially stalked them out of morbid curiosity, but then, trailing them to their tent and peering in undetected, he saw the Priestess cleanse herself of the excrement. Her beauty stood in stark contrast to the ghastly garb she wore in her ministries. Her hair was dark and her skin the shade of sand on a sun-soaked beach.

He watched her on the battlefield and intentionally positioned himself for an encounter. When she came upon him, addressing him in tongues, free and unhindered by her madness, he saw her eyes shone a strange indigo, a swirling, hypnotic shade that made him feel sick after peering into them for too long. It was like gazing down into the dark, shimmering abyss of a well.

She was, he saw, quite insane.

And it was that insanity that drew him to her. The undulations of her body stirred his lust, but it was her complete and utter madness that called to Gregoire. Her uninhibited actions, her mad prattles, it all contributed to a sense of ignorance that seemed much more akin to fearlessness to the Frenchman.

He certainly feared her, but was also infatuated with her, and the two conflicting emotions created an obsession within him, and he knew he must have her.

He never thought he would do it, but in the privacy of his own tent, Gregoire was overcome with passion for the Priestess. The poison had stopped her breath, stopped her life, but the rest of her remained unchanged, all except the twisted grimace left from her agonized death throes.

It was only after inserting himself that the shock of how stiff and cold her body had become made him fall back in disgust. But his passion ran hot, and he found his revulsion became tolerable after a while.

He had her in death and acted upon his impulses.

Afterward, he found that death was already spoiling her beauty. The corners of her lips were blackened. Most of her nose too. Large sections of her back and buttocks took on the semblance of a massive, purple bruise.

He rolled her back in the carpet out of shame, for himself as well as for her. He didn't like how her dark, empty eyes seemed to follow him around the tent either.

So quickly, he mused a short time later, so quickly is the flesh ruined. Wise it is to indulge it while it lasts. Yes, while it lasts.

In the early hours before dawn, Gregoire unrolled the carpet again.

This time he covered her face with an old, stained garment.

The Frenchman met the Teuton mercenary on the battlefield some time before he was even aware of the Priestess.

Gregoire had been swept up in the promise of glory and divine justice to be met out in the Holy Land. If the justice enacted included death and madness, then he'd seen plenty of both spread out to the deserving and undeserving alike. He knew not what would happen to him beyond the initial march to the desert, but it was there, among the bloodshed and brutality that he truly found himself.

He became adept at scavenging through the dead and dying, searching for wealth, weapons, and treasure, and was doing just that when he encountered the Teuton on the field. He mistook the mercenary for a corpse, initially, because he was reclined upon a pile of dead combatants. The Teuton was a giant, his arms long and gangly, his upper body stooped dumbly under the weight of his old, rusted, and dented armor. His face a mass of warts and scars. He stank worse than the dead who propped him up.

Gregoire nearly lost his head while rifling through the piled dead. The Frenchman begged for his life. It wasn't the first time he'd had to do it. The Teuton, maybe because he was tired from all the slaying, or maybe because he did not see the Frenchman as a threat, backed off from the cowering little man.

Later, Gregoire stalked the Teuton as he roamed upon the battlefield. It was while witnessing him barter the garments of a fallen enemy soldier in the market that the Frenchman realized he and the Teuton were in the same business. Only, the Teuton did not wait for the battle's aftermath as Gregoire did, when the roar of the victors had ebbed away and only the wailings and whimpers of the dying remained. No, the Teuton waded into each battle, armored, sword whistling through the hot air, and slew his prey so that he might pile their corpses and pilfer their remains. The Teuton only took from those whose lives he ended himself.

But then the Frenchman saw the Priestess, and her sect of insane doomsayers and all thoughts of the Teuton, of wealth, of gaining anything other than her, were lost.

The Teuton came to him as if he'd known all along that Gregoire had the Priestess in his tent. Later, when he was able to reflect on the situation, the Frenchman thought it likely that the Teuton was watching him, just as he had been watching the Teuton.

Inside the tent the carpet was unrolled. The Teuton looked upon the Priestess with seeming indifference. Finally, after a long moment of observation, he licked his scabby lips with a white, ragged tongue, a gesture Gregoire took as acknowledgement of her beauty.

He showed the Teuton her pendant, the sigil of a carrion bird, the only indication of her role as a Priestess in the sect. She had not been painted in filth when death took her. Without the excrement, it would have been nearly impossible to identify her. The pendant seemed to be recognition enough for the Teuton.

"What shall become of her?" the giant asked.

"I wish to take her back to France with me, if only I was able to maneuver her across such a distance. Perhaps only her head."

"Such a waste," the Teuton mused. "I can help you if you wish it. I know of customs that can separate the flesh from the bones. The bones will be much easier to transport than the whole woman."

"Only her bones?"

"The bones are the last thing to remain. Everything else rots and becomes putrid, dripping off the carcasses like dribbles of stew from a spoon. Flesh is of the water; supple, fluid, malleable. But the bones are of the earth, fashioned from the earth, and they endure."

Gregoire considered this, "What will happen to her flesh?"

He was hesitant to destroy her wholly, but then, what good was the flesh anyway? It would continue to swell, darken, and eventually burst. The flesh was limited.

"I want her flesh," the Teuton said.

Gregoire eyed him suspiciously. Even though he'd engaged in several taboo acts himself, his stomach cramped with disgust at what he imagined the mercenary would do with her flesh.

Yet, what choice did he have? If he wanted to keep her, some semblance of her, better her bones than nothing.

"Fine," the Frenchman agreed, "But give me one more day."

"Don't you mean one more night?" The Teuton gave him a knowing look, a grin that seemed to Gregoire to have too many teeth.

"I will need wine and salt," the Teuton said.

Gregoire gestured at a bottle he kept in his tent.

"More," the Teuton said. "Enough to fill a cauldron. I will return tomorrow evening and our work will begin."

The Teuton brought the cauldron, a large bronze thing that he carried on his back like a pack.

The camp was settling down for the night. There had not been any fighting for several days. All were resting and weary.

Gregoire showed him the bottles of wine and bag of salt he'd been able to procure. It cost him much, but she was worth it. Seventeen bottles would surely fill the Teuton's cauldron, he supposed.

The mercenary bid him build a fire outside the tent. Gregoire hesitated, wary of passersby who might witness their grisly task by firelight, but the Teuton waived these concerns away.

After Gregoire stoked the flames, the Teuton balanced his cauldron over it and began pouring the wine. It took all but two bottles to fill the vessel. One Gregoire kept for himself. The other he offered to the giant, who declined.

They retreated into the tent while the cauldron boiled. The Teuton unsheathed his notched sword and instructed the carpet be unrolled.

Gregoire lifted his bottle to his lips with shaking hands and watched as the Teuton worked. He flinched at each swing of the tarnished blade, grimaced as the Priestess's arms and legs were parted from her torso, then her innards removed and placed in a wrap with copious amounts of salt. The mercenary dug around under her rib cage until he brought forth her heart, which he gazed at hungrily before also dusting with salt and wrapping firmly.

Then the Teuton separated her head from her body.

Together, they carried the pieces of her to the bubbling cauldron and dumped them in.

"Why this woman?" the Teuton asked as they waited for the flesh to boil from the bones.

"She had no fear of death," Gregoire admitted. "And I've feared death since I first realized it would someday befall me. I admire her fearlessness and wish to have it for myself. To possess her for myself." He paused, then added "And she was quite mad. Her mind would never be knowable, never be repaired, but the rest of her, her body, well. . . " He didn't finish the sentence, didn't have to.

"Grant me this one favor," the Teuton requested.

"After all you've done for me? Certainly."

"Allow me to prophesy for you."

"You have such abilities?" Gregoire asked.

"I see you in a great hall surrounded by a host of royalty, gentry, nobility akin to a king's throne room," the Teuton began without pause. He bent down to Gregoire's height and set his wide, heavy-jawed, warty face in front of the Frenchman's own, studied him intently with glowering, dark eyes, murky, like black puddles on a moonless night. "You will be wealthy beyond reason," the Teuton continued. "And if I come to you then, in all of your splendor and success, seeking sanctuary, assure me now that I will be welcomed into such a place."

"Most welcome." Gregoire, smirking, agreed without hesitation.

"And if I do come, I would ask that you honor your word with a toast," the Teuton said.

"I toast you now." Gregoire lifted his near-empty bottle of wine to the Teuton, then threw his head back and glugged it down. "And I will certainly toast you then."

When at last it was time, the Teuton used a long, wide paddle to lift the pieces of flesh out of the liquid. They hung off the end like wet laundry on a stick. He made sure to collect it all before tossing handfuls of salt upon the remains. Then he bundled them up tightly.

Gregoire, eager to collect her bones, was dismayed when

the Teuton bade him wait while he drained the liquid in the cauldron into the empty wine bottles. It was a tedious task, and dawn was on the horizon once the Teuton had packed up his reward and the bottles of putrid wine. He then hefted his cauldron and dumped the still-steaming bones on the ground.

Gregoire fell to his knees in worship, and touched the boiled bones gingerly, running his fingertips across the smooth whiteness of her skull.

When he looked up again, he was alone in the tent.

He went looking for the Teuton.

He asked around the merchants but was only met with sincere silence. Finally, he found one he recognized as frequently visited by the Teuton. This merchant, consumed by leprosy, told him the Teuton was not to be trusted. He claimed it was the Teuton who had cursed him with the disease. He warned that such a man would rot anyone he encountered.

Gregoire presented the merchant with a bone.

"This is all that remains of Saint Genevieve, the patron saint of Paris. It is holy. It heals. It has kept me unharmed in this haggard land, in these violent times." The Frenchman let the merchant examine the bone, the bold, clean white of it, like a jewel, or a hunk of clean, pure ice in the otherwise brown and dusty desert. "Tell me, where is the mercenary? Tell me and it shall be yours," Gregoire tempted. It was all a lie. He did not live in Paris, and the bone belonged to the Priestess.

It took further peddling, but not much. The merchant was desperate, and the Frenchman succeeded in attaining the information he needed.

He went to where the merchant said the Teuton dwelled; a discarded and tattered tent near the mass graves where the insignificant dead were shoveled, unceremoniously, after each battle.

Venturing in, Gregoire was aghast to find the corpses of the mass grave had spilled into the Teuton's dwelling. The dead, Christian and Muslim alike, littered the tent, stacked, piled in mounds, the highest of which was like a throne. The stink surely made it inhospitable, Gregoire deemed, and the horrid buzzing, the same he associated with the Priestess and her cult—incessant, idiotic, maddening—filled his ears and his mind.

The Teuton, however, was not among the clutter of corpses and funerary artifacts.

Gregoire fled the tent, afraid that he would become lost among the piles of teetering cadavers and ceaseless buzzing.

In time, Gregoire amassed wealth and respect among his peers. His tales of chivalry and divine justice in the Holy Land were evidenced by the relics he brought back with him. It was shown to all that he was blessed with the sacred remains of saints, knights, martyrs, and holy men.

Of course, it was all pieces of the Priestess.

He kept her skull and the finger bones of one hand. He had a necklace fashioned from the finger bones, set with rubies and gold beads. Everything else was sold as a relic, a charm, a talisman of power. She was dispersed among witches, warlocks, alchemists, and monks. Her knuckles were sold to a seer, individual ribs and vertebra were passed out to lords and nobles as good luck charms. Her femurs were used in the construction of an ornate chair used by a bishop. One skeletal foot was kept whole and encased in glass, where it was presented as a relic to Spanish royalty.

He was granted a château in the French countryside and made it his own. He filled it with servants and invited peasants to work his fields.

The Frenchman kept her skull in his private chambers and spoke to it.

Oftentimes, he lovingly pecked the grin of exposed teeth with his own pursed lips.

When the first reports of the stranger came to him many years later, Gregoire convinced himself it was just some wandering vagabond.

The stranger was seen on the borders of his land initially, a giant sighted among the forest trees, then on the edge of fields and vineyards. When livestock disappeared, Gregoire changed his mind and suspected a simple bandit. Men were sent to confront the stranger but returned empty-handed.

Some livestock were eventually discovered mutilated and gnawed upon. He demanded a watch be implemented and recruited a band of the most hardy and superstitious of the peasantry.

The stranger was spotted skulking through the old tombs and burial mounds of the lords and cavaliers who originally inhabited the château in times past. Reports of the animalistic noises that came from the tombs chilled Gregoire's blood.

He commanded the peasants apprehend the stranger.

But they did not. They approached the stranger, and many were slain. Those who fled were unable to retrieve the bodies of the fallen.

Desperately trying to ignore his own certainty of who it

was, Gregoire finally took it upon himself to ride out to the tombs and drive off whatever *creature* had infested them.

In through damp rooms stuffed with the remains of nobility he shared not blood, life, or spirit with, the Frenchman stumbled into a nest. It was made of the bones of those that had lain in the rooms, and of the remains of his own peasantry and livestock.

The infernal buzzing of flies filled his ears.

It reminded him of the tent on the edge of the mass grave he'd wandered into all those years ago in search of the Teuton.

As if his thoughts were a mental summons, the Teuton presented himself to Gregoire from among the dead once again. The mercenary seemed much the same as he had in the Holy Land. Tall and yet gangly, like his arms and torso were too heavy for his frame. Same rusted and pocked armor. Toothy, his jaws hideously enlarged, constantly working, gnashing.

"Why do you come to my lands?" Gregoire commanded. Authority had been his for so long he no longer remembered how to be subservient to anyone.

"I come where I am welcome," the Teuton chittered.

"I have not welcomed you here."

"Oh, but you're mistaken," the Teuton assured him. "I told you a time would come when I would need refuge, and you eagerly agreed that I would be welcome."

Gregoire recalled the exchange but waived it away absently. "That was long ago. Things have changed. I recant my offer." He swatted around his head, trying to clear it of the maddening buzzing of the flies. They murmured around in clouds and crawled across the corpses and the Teuton and, much to his disgust, Gregoire himself.

"But you can't recant the taint that's blackened your heart," the Teuton said, showing all his teeth. "You can't recant the life that you ended in your selfish greed to possess it. The sin with which your fortune is founded." He splayed his dirty, scarred hands to indicate, apparently, the bowels of the old tombs. "I foresaw you surrounded by all this splendor; you recall."

The Frenchman balked. "You consider this ossuary a place of splendor?"

The Teuton licked his lips in answer, a gesture Gregoire remembered with a shudder.

"I've come," the mercenary continued, "just as I prophesied. And here you are, and now our deal can be fulfilled."

Suddenly a bottle was in the Teutons hand and Gregoire recognized it as one of the many he'd procured all those years ago, on the battlefields of the Holy Land, filled with the leftover wine-sludge from the cauldron.

"A toast is owed," the Teuton uttered.

A strange certainty came upon Gregoire then, a sense that no title, no amount of wealth, nor his reputation could assist him now. Escape was futile. The Teuton would certainly run him down like a predator does its prey. He was apprehended.

The Teuton lifted the bottle in the tomb. "*I toast to you now,* as you said all those years ago." Gregoire turned away from the man's ugly, wart-riddled face. The swish of the swill in the bottle told him that the Teuton drank greedily.

The bottle was thrust toward Gregoire. It reeked of vinegar and decay. He took it in his old, frail hands, shaking uncontrollably now. His other hand went to the necklace of white polished bone around his neck.

"Tell me," the Teuton asked, seeing the gesture, "does she free you from the fear of death, as you hoped?"

"I don't even remember what she looked like," the Frenchman croaked.

The Teuton leaned back, satisfied, with far too many teeth in his wide, wet grin.

"And what name should I toast?" Gregoire asked, already lifting the bottle toward the Teuton in salute. It shook violently. "Lucifer?"

The Teuton guffawed, a choking, barking sound that made the Frenchman jump.

"Not he, no." The Teuton seemed to consider something for a moment, then leaned toward Gregoire, his acrid breath consuming the Frenchman's head like a cloud. "Who did your Priestess serve?"

Gregoire blinked in thought. Then uttered the words, "Father of Flies."

"Drink," the Teuton boomed. A fly scurried across the surface of one jaundiced, bloodshot eye.

The Frenchman tilted the bottle to his lips and squeezed his eyes closed as the filthy liquid spilled down his gullet.

The Teuton took the finger bone necklace with him as a souvenir. "She was the most enthusiastic of them all," he mused thoughtfully. "And I assure you she would be delighted with the fate of her mortal remains."

The Teuton left him with the vague suggestion that he'd return, someday.

A change took hold of Gregoire, now left to his fate. A madness consumed him. His language reverted into savage grunts and guttural howls. He paraded across his lands as if possessed by the devil, smearing excrement and filth upon his person, consuming it and delighting in it. A bloodlust drove him to attack the peasantry and servants of his house. Those he failed to murder fled. Those he killed he feasted upon like they were savory morsels served to starving children.

His home and lands fell into utter disrepair.

He took to creeping out at night and scouring through the old cemetery, descending into the ancestral tombs to rifle through the scraps the Teuton left behind. He consumed the dried, mummified flesh of the dead, his jaws growing strong on the dusty, leathery remains. He gnawed upon bones with teeth that had become horrifically large. Not even the burial shrouds were spared his constant mastication.

After he'd pilfered all the dead from his lands he preyed on the occasional passersby or official sent to investigate the abandonment of his château. He wandered among the wilds where no living man had walked for generations, and no living man walked still, for he was no longer of the living, no longer of the spirit, or the mind. He was of the mastication, of the biting, and of the ceaseless need to gnaw and gnash and chew.

He could never bring himself to part with her skull. No matter how the need to chew crippled him, he would starve before consuming the last relic, though he did not think he would perish from such a misery any longer. He was beyond such mercies.

He no longer remembered the Priestess who'd exalted the dead and prostrated their rotting flesh. He saw the white perfection of her grin and remembered that it was put to him to chew, to bite, to rend. She was a symbol now, a talisman of his cursed existence.

It became known to avoid the ruins of the château. For nothing but encroaching wilderness and feral beasts roamed there.

Yet if one were to brave the decrepit darkness and decay of the château, creeping through unlit and dusty halls, up through creaking stairwells and into filthy chambers where the chittering of disturbed bats mingled overhead, and into a side room filled with moldering old books and scrolls written by secret hands, one might encounter a horrid, loathsome creature surrounded by a cloud of black, buzzing flies like a pile of carrion, the form of a man ruined, decayed, cursed into an inhuman travesty.

And in its slender, dirty hands, held like a child's precious to the exposed ribs of its chest, a skull, grinning in pristine whiteness.

Mos Teutonicus, Latin for the German custom, came about when I was doing research for a separate story and I stumbled upon the term. I knew immediately, upon learning the meaning, that it would make a great title. The story came effortlessly, almost writing itself.

Bryson Richard,
Black Swamp, OH
June 1, 2021

Bryson Richard is a writer from the Black Swamp area of Ohio. He's interested in books, monsters, ghosts, superheroes, folk tales, legends, mysteries, and all things weird, eerie, and fantastical. He and his wife and children live in an old house that they've filled with books and other physical media on those very same subjects. You can find him on Twitter @BrysRichard.

THEY DON'T EAT TEETH

JENA BROWN

It's a dry heat. That's what they say, as if it softens the blow. It's still miserable. Deadly. At least with humidity, you feel yourself being smothered. Not like the desert. By the time you realize you're in trouble, it's too late.

Ali rolls down the window, letting the hot air blow through the car. She breathes a sigh as the sweat on her neck cools and dries. It's a relief, but in the heat of the day, the wind is as dangerous as the heat. Dries your sweat, which forces the body to produce more. A vicious cycle.

Hydrate or die, that's something else they say. Nik, with all their slogans and catchphrases. They even stickered the phrase on the Hydro Flask Ali grabs, sucking in cool gulps of filtered water. She winces at her split lip, probing it with her tongue. Peers at her face in the moonlight. Her eye is swollen, and the entire right side will bruise.

It's not the first time she's been hit. Probably won't be the last. Working the streets is never safe, no matter how careful you are. Violence lurks behind closed doors. At least this time, she's the one in control. At least this time, she gave more than she got.

She shoves her arm out the window, letting her hand float in the blow-dryer breeze. The fight will cost her, no matter how satisfying it is to win. No one wants a beat-up escort. Not even the ones who do the beating. Which means no more hunting for now.

Ali sighs at the thought, pushing down her impatience. When they first started the hunt, Ali was impulsive. Angry. All she wanted was revenge, to make the man who nearly broke her pay. To make them all pay. But Nik helped. Showed her vengeance was an expensive meal and a fine wine. Better to be savored.

It's just past one in the morning and the heat continues to rise in oscillating waves off the endless concrete. The neon lights glow beyond the hills in her rearview mirror.

Ali pulls off the highway, a dirt road barely visible through the cacti and creosote. The tires crunch on the baked soil, rocks ticking up and down the undercarriage.

When Nik first brought her into this wild expanse, she was overwhelmed with the vast emptiness that surrounded them. The undulating expanse carved in violent swathes took her breath away. Still does when she lets it.

She's learned how to navigate this treacherous land. How to avoid the raging floods that come out of nowhere and the importance of watching for creatures the color of sand. It's the deadly side of nature that appeals to her. There's no bullshit here. Only life. Only death. And a blink between the two.

The car jolts and jumps along the uneven path, creating a thumping rhythm that roars in the quiet night. When she hits bigger ruts, dead weight bangs inside the trunk. She listens, wondering if he's awake. But there's nothing.

These roads crisscross the valley, the state, the entire Southwest. A secret language carved, dirt scars leading somewhere and nowhere, and god help those who don't know the difference. Ali navigates them expertly, having driven this path so many times she's lost count.

The farmhouse crawls from the shadows, a muted glow nestled against the hills. Joshua trees reach for the stars, their pom-pom ends throwing menacing shadows into the gloom.

A low squeal echoes as Ali stops the car. Her shoes crunch into the sand. She cracks her neck and elongates her spine, grabbing the duffel from the back.

The desert adjusts to her intrusion, coming alive with every footstep. Predators hunt and prey tries to hide, both following instincts centuries old. She does the same.

"How'd it go?" The squeak of the screen door punctuates their sentence.

Their face is hidden in shadows but light dances across their blond curls. They're slightly taller than Ali, with a similar frame. But where Ali is willowy and sensuous, Nik is nothing but wiry muscle.

Ali slips into their hug, inhaling the scent of dirt, sweat, and sun baked onto their skin. Nik frowns, pulling away to see her face, but Ali shakes her head and disappears inside.

In their bedroom she shimmies out of her cocktail dress and steps into a worn pair of coveralls. Nik watches from the doorway, studying the bruises rising to the surface.

"I'm fine," Ali says, meeting their eyes.

She knows it's hard for them. That it reminds them of when they found her. Battered. Dying. Hardly more than tenderized flesh covering broken bones.

"I know," they reply. And Ali knows they mean it. They have a way of never making her feel small.

Nik follows her to the car, snorting at the body shoved inside the trunk.

"Come on." Ali grabs the feet as Nik grabs the head. "One, two, three." They heave the body out and waddle to the barn.

They strip him naked before strapping him to a steel

gurney, securing his head and limbs. Ali slathers shaving cream all over his body.

"What. . . where am I?" he sputters, waking up.

He tries to move his head but can't, his entire body jerking at the realization. Or trying to, anyway.

"Hey!" he yells. "What the f—"

"Hi, Wayne," Ali cuts him off. "Remember me?" She points at her lip and then at her eye.

For a split second, his eyes flare uncertainly before arrogance comes rushing back.

"I'm going to ruin you," he snarls. "You have no idea."

Ali slaps the rest of the cream on his leg. "No, Wayne," she says, picking up a razor. "You have no idea."

He hurls obscenities, but without his fists, without his drugs, he's impotent. Ali ignores him, humming to herself as she works. A close shave is important, and she relishes how nervous he gets as she works up towards his more delicate bits.

"If you watch movies," she says, scraping the blade in tight, controlled swathes. "They always make it seem like burying a body in the desert is the best way to dispose of them."

She chuckles, remembering the dozens of invisible scars marking her previous failed burial attempts.

"It's not so easy," she continues. "They told me," she points the razor at Nik, "but I didn't listen."

Wayne cranes his neck, trying to see where she pointed. "Who else is here?" he demands.

But Nik stays quiet, remains out of his line of sight. They let the clang of buckets and tools build an orchestra of tension.

"Turns out, there's this thing called caliche," Ali says. She pauses her shave to mime pickaxing the ground. "It's a clay. Rock-hard and hurts like a bitch. Almost dislocated my shoulder." She widens her eyes and rolls her arm. "And it's everywhere. Good luck digging with a shovel."

Ali abandons his leg mid-thigh, almost laughing as he exhales a sigh of relief. Men. So simple. So fucking predictable.

"The other problem with burying a body," she says, glancing up at him. As if they're chatting, just two friends discussing the ins and outs of homicide. "Is the flash flooding."

The first time she experienced a desert storm was waking up to thunder clapping like percussion grenades. She'd never known that sound could be so violent, could rattle windows in their panes and shake the farmhouse on its foundation. Nik held her as rain drops the size of silver dollars pelted the roof, the ferocity shrinking her, bringing her back to other cruel storms. In the morning, the sky was blue, the desert dry. But evidence of violent waters couldn't be erased entirely. Ali understands that too.

"Easy to bury a body in those natural waterways," Ali muses. "But that water takes no prisoners. Which means bodies don't stay buried."

She takes the razor to his toes, needing to get every inch of skin nice and smooth. Reflex has him flinch, opening a thin line in his skin. He sucks in a breath as blood drips down his foot.

"Oops." Ali frowns. "It's important to hold still, Wayne. You should know better than that."

"You fucking bitch," he snarls. "I'm going to make you pay."

Ali pauses, her anger pulsing through her blood. Her bruises throbs as she relives his fists colliding with flesh. Wayne thought he drugged her, but her sleight of hand was better. His arrogance making him believe she was something he could break. Never imagining she could fight back. That she could break him.

She goes back to work.

"It's not that the water raises the corpse. No. The real kicker is that it can carry it hundreds of miles, ending in drainage ditches or the side of the highway. And that's never good for anyone." She pauses, bobs her head from side to side. "Well, maybe the dead guy."

Nik smiles as she talks, remembering her burials and how close they came to disaster. They had tried to explain, but Ali didn't always listen. Didn't want to rely on anyone but herself. Not after being so vulnerable for so long. But they were patient. And let her make mistakes. Always willing to help clean them up while never, ever saying they told her so.

They showed her how to trust. How to love. What true partnership looks like.

Ali cleans the blade, a smile unfurling as she catches Wayne's eye. She cups his balls in one hand, the blade hovering in her other.

"Now, Wayne," she croons. "I'd say things got a little out of control earlier, wouldn't you?"

Her tone is nonchalant, casual. But her eyes drip venom and for the first time, she sees fear flash across his face.

"What is it about hitting women that gets you off?" she asks. "I mean, really." Her eyes drift to what she's holding. "You do know that it's all in how you use it, right? I'm sure if you wanted to learn how to please a woman"—she purses her lips—"or a man for that matter—you could. It's not like it's that hard."

"You're all a bunch—"

"Don't be a bore," Ali says, letting the razor nick the wrinkled skin. "You're all a bunch of what? Hmmmm? Worthless whores? Sluts? Mouthy bitches?" She rolls her eyes. "God, you're all the same."

Nik appears above his head, a roll of duct tape in their hands. Before Wayne can sputter anything else, his mouth is covered.

Ali lets loose a deep sigh. "That's better."

Wayne trembles, rage and humiliation flooding his veins. She finishes his pelvis, works her way down both of his upper thighs.

"So the real question becomes: How do you get rid of a body in the desert? Or anywhere, really."

The uncertainty blossoms in his eyes, though the anger is still there burning her alive. If only she cared. Except that's not right. She cares. There's an order to how she unravels these men. A drama she's perfected with Nik over the years. A way to make them truly understand the pain and humiliation they've inflicted on others throughout their lives.

"The problem with men like you, Wayne, if I can offer a diagnosis. You're just an insecure man. Getting off on hurting others because someone hurt you. It's actually quite pathetic. They say people show their true colors when under duress. That who you are during difficult times is who you are all the time. What do you think?"

Wayne simmers, impotent from shackles and a gag.

"For example. Have you ever considered how you want to die?" She gives him an unimpressed once-over. "Probably not." The razor cleans his stomach, moving up toward his chest. "Like, I bet you've never thought about what it would feel like to be beaten to death. Or strangled."

The black void of panic tightens in her gut. Bile crawls up her throat, its sour taint filling her mouth. Even now, in the safety of the barn, the helplessness and pain surges.

Nik senses her distress, pressing their hand against the small of her back. Ali leans into them, taking strength from their strength.

Wayne watches, eyes squinting and calculating. Even

though he's sweating, his body is racked with chills. It's almost admirable, how he fights against his fear. Which is why she leans in, her hand resting on his forearm. Creating an intimate moment, just to shatter him whole.

"You ever worked on a farm, Wayne?" Ali twirls the razor around the barn. "I'm guessing not." She uses her closeness to shave under his arms. "Did you know that pigs will eat anything? Well, mostly. They don't eat everything. Hair, for one."

Her hand whips the excess cream and clumped hair into the small steel bucket at her side, a sickening splotch reverberating around the barn.

Wayne's eyes bulge as the blood drains from his face. She moves the razor to his head, taking off his silky, thick mane. It's pathetic that this, finally this, is what releases his fear, adrenaline a slight tang Ali can smell because she's so close.

Her smile bites. "Don't worry. I'm not as cruel as you, drugging women without their knowledge. Raping them. Beating them. As if they were things you owned instead of people." She leans in, whispers in his ear. "Because we're never people to you, are we?"

His body is taut, but still, his ego refuses to see himself as the victim. Refuses to believe there could ever be consequences from his actions. Refuses to break.

"Which is why I'm going to be honest with you. This next part is going to hurt."

She clicks a pair of pliers for dramatic effect, a gleeful smile erupting on her face. His eyes go frantic, pupils blown, and he tries to thrash through his restraints.

"Because they don't eat teeth either."

Wayne starts screaming, muffled through the tape but a meat mallet shatters his words along with his jaw. Ali rips the tape off, plucking teeth from softened bone.

Nik works in the background, preparing the feed. They'll

help prepare the body, but not now. Not yet. This is Ali's time.

"They do eat bone," Ali tells him, dropping the bloody pliers into the bucket. "But it's always better if you break the big ones up."

The mallet comes down on the tibia, crushes the humerus, pulverizes his femur. Gurgled screams taper off into a howling mewl. She runs her hands over his shaved head, almost looking sorry. Almost.

"The thing is, Wayne." Ali unbuckles the strap holding his skull down. "I've been hurt by men like you my whole life. Nik has, too, in different ways." The metal clangs against the steel as she releases his arms, his legs. "But what you fail to realize, is we're all the same in the end. We all live. We all die. And nothing makes you any better than anyone else."

Straps free, Ali steps back. Tears stream down Wayne's face but the fight is still there, still refusing to believe this is his reality. He lifts a shaking arm, crying as he fumbles to sit up, eyeing Ali warily before searching for Nik.

He finds the barn door, sensing freedom. This is the only chance he'll get, and though his predatory side knows this is a trap, he finally understands what it feels like to be prey. The desperate urge to flee.

One foot hits the concrete, eliciting a whimper. But the scream erupts when he tries to steady his weight. As he collapses on the ground, he rolls over and gives in. His sobs fill the silence.

Tears trickle down his face, mixing with the blood and saliva pooling on the concrete. He pleads with his eyes.

"I know," Ali coos, squatting down in front of him. Her head is cocked to the side, her eyes filled with ice. "You're sorry. You'll never do it again. You'll never say a word." Her voice is flat but Wayne grasps at pity, is desperate for hope.

He nods, barking a cry.

"Well, two of those things are true." She rises, using her legs to kick him onto his stomach and crack his spine, mashing each vertebra.

Nik rolls open the door, throwing feed into the troughs to wake the animals. The squeal of pigs wanting breakfast fills the barn.

Ali hacks his limbs at the joints, throwing them into the feed. They burn the hair, along with the clothes. Blood hosed down the drain. The teeth go into the pestle to grind into powder, then spread to add calcium to the soil.

Nik brews coffee as dawn breaks. Streaks of magenta and fiery orange light the sky, and the desert sighs to sleep while the farm wakes.

"If they ever trace these men here, who knows what evidence they'll find," Nik says.

Ali knows the terror of too many questions with no good answers. But they don't make mistakes, not like Ali once did. Nik made sure of that.

Ali shrugs. She's not worried. Never has been. "No one ever sees women like me. They see whores and sluts and women who deserve our lot in life."

They're quiet, frowning their disagreement as their eyes scan the budding day.

"I know." She squeezes their arm, leaning her body into their side. "You saw me, Nik. Now we see them. All of them. And we're going to keep making them pay."

It was Nik who bought the farm, raised the pigs. They said it would be better this way. And it is.

The desert stretches outside my office window. It's a harsh place, where the things you don't see are the deadliest. Rattlesnakes, scorpions, the heat. They strike fast, and you rarely see them coming. Las Vegas sits behind me, and is a different sort of deadly. Where money and power overshadow violence and control. I pictured an escort, someone unseen by society. A woman familiar with being used, abused, good only for fulfilling someone's twisted fantasy. Invisible. Deadly. It's a myth that it's easy to bury a body in the desert, but it can be a great place to raise pigs.

Jena Brown
Las Vegas, NV
June 6, 2021

Jena Brown grew up playing make-believe in the Nevada desert, where her love for skeletons and harsh landscapes solidified. A freelance writer, she currently contributes to *Kwik Learning, Truity, The Portalist, Insider,* and *The Nerd Daily*. In addition to writing, Jena blogs at www.jenabrownwrites.com and is active on bookstagram as @jenabrownwrites. When she isn't imagining deadly worlds, she and her husband are being bossed around the Las Vegas desert by their two chihuahuas.

THE OLD SWITCHEROO

CHRISTI NOGLE

Calvin and I have been happy here, all told. With both of us orphaned early on, we were lucky to find each other, lucky to get out of the city and find this valley. We were luckier still to find this house well stocked with board games and books, space to spread out, a good woodshop and pantry, a fine roof, and a well-stocked gun cabinet. We had the orchard out back and the tools to tend it, even some supplies of fertilizers and sprays. A late-model truck in the garage, insurance in case we needed to leave in a hurry sometime.

In twenty years, we've never needed the truck. I can't remember how many years ago it quit starting. That's all right.

Our happiness could have been more perfect in only one way: we could have finally gotten together. We could have made a family. It seemed like it was going there once or twice, so why didn't we follow through?

Calvin's walking around the deck one last time before bed, scanning the tree line beyond the fields, scanning the bare patches higher in the hills. We know the patterns of these hills like we know each other's faces. We've always spotted *them* before they could get to us, not that there are so many still walking now.

"There's a lost soul in the bear trap," Calvin says sadly when he comes in. He moves his chin in its direction. "I hate to leave it, but I'm going to wait until morning."

I've already seen it but don't say I have. Calvin likes to point out things to me.

"What are the chances?" I say, parting the curtain. We haven't seen one in months, and it walks straight into the trap. Does this mean more of them coming?

"It's fresh as hell," he says. Disgust and pity cross his face.

We could hazard a shot from up here, but the smarter thing is to put it out of its misery up close with the axe and retrieve the trap at the same time. For that we need plenty of daylight, and so we'll wait.

We'll sterilize the bear trap, get it back out there. I suspect we'd catch another of *them* easier than we could catch a bear, but there's still a chance a bear or something might stumble in, get infected—and wouldn't it be a shame to have to bury all that meat instead of eating it?

"The trees have gone celibate," Calvin says. Because so many people are gone—or "wiped off the planet," is actually how he puts it—the planet needs to cut down food production or else there's going to be a big mess of rotten fruit, and all the little animals and bugs who eat it will grow out of control.

"A lot more animals? I guess that seems like a good thing," I say.

"Does it seem like there are more animals? Traps fill faster than they used to?" he says.

No, there are way fewer animals. I don't know what Calvin's getting at. I say, "Anyway, the fruit isn't just to feed animals. The tree makes fruit to make seeds. The trees would want to make more trees even if there's nothing eating the fruit, wouldn't they?"

"The *earth* makes the trees produce seeds. It's not up to the trees. I bet they're as upset about it as we are."

The trees are upset? Calvin's been getting weird lately. He never would have thought this way back when we were kids.

I got mostly through eighth grade, Calvin sixth. Though I still remember some of my friends and teachers and the general feeling of going to school, I long ago forgot most of the actual content. Maybe I'd not learned those things deeply enough because I'd always thought I could look them up again, or maybe I just wasn't all that smart. That's possible.

Or maybe I was smart enough to begin with and then I got too traumatized, what with the whole world dying and all. I think it was that.

Calvin, though, tried to hang on to what he knew for a lot longer than I did. I remember him journaling about things he didn't want to forget. He remembered little facts about the seasons and weather, stuff about survival. He made sure we kept track of birthdays and holidays. He taught me how to shoot. That was probably the most important thing I learned in my life, what with all the headshots we had to take early on.

"Anyway, we're not 'wiped off the planet,'" I say some time after his whole tree-celibacy spiel. "You and I are still here. We're not smarter than *every*body else. There could still be lots of people in the cities."

"Do you want to go to that city again? Is that it?" he says. Defeat or contempt in his tone, can't be sure.

We don't call the city by its name. It's the only city that exists as far as we're concerned, certainly the only one we could ever hope to reach.

"I don't want to go anywhere," I say. I'd rather die

comfortably here, as I know Calvin would. I wish I knew it would still be comfortable, though. It's not going to be if we can't keep eating.

This *place* makes me comfortable. I know we'll never find its match. Everything scannable, all but the depths of the orchard. We've always feared them coming upon us in the orchard where they could get close before we saw them. When we harvest, when we prune, one of us stands guard. I hate to think that this fear has kept us from caring for trees as well or as often as we should.

Harvested, pruned, cared for, I should say. Past tense. The trees still live, but they've flowered less each spring for the past twenty. This spring, there are no blossoms. The trees must be turning off, just as Calvin says they are. I decide I'd rather believe that because then it isn't our fault.

Just before dusk, I stand outside with the binoculars, scanning at first but then lingering on the trapped corpse who's trying to crawl to us. So fresh, this one. He has long hair and a beard, but they look recently washed. The poor thing doesn't feel the trap cut across his midsection and even if he did, he would not have the intelligence to reach down to try to free himself, so he simply claws at dirt still muddy from last night's rain. I can't hear from here, but he's probably moaning, scaring off all the other animals, not that we've trapped an animal in the past few months. We haven't even seen an animal on the ground since the last snowmelt. Even if there's nothing he can frighten out there, he may pull free of the trap if enough time goes by, so we ought to get out there soon.

It's likely he smells me. I should get back inside.

He wants to eat me. Not my brain—that turned out to be

myth—but the rest of me. If he were to take me, he would eat my arms or legs or my guts first and stay there gnawing the bones clean, leaving just the top part of my head.

I've seen it more than a few times. It's not what I want for myself, though better that than to escape with a bite.

Just before dark, we do a last sweep of the tree line and make our way up to sleep in the attic. It's boarded shut, hot, and inconvenient, but it makes me feel so safe. It always has. We've slept here from the very first night, though usually not at the same time. Up until the past few years, there's been too much risk to leave no one standing watch. More and more now, we go up together, and we no longer expect that we'll open the door in the morning to a crush of zombies on the second floor. It's still possible; it's just no longer the focus of our worries.

I suppose we visualize starving to death now. That's what gets us in the gut now, not that it's urgent. There's a sack of dried apples and a tin of dried meat in the attic, odds and ends in the kitchen and basement too.

When we've gotten into our beds, Calvin turns to me and says, "The consciousness never leaves them, Abbie. They don't control the body anymore, but the brain keeps working just like yours or mine. They're horrified at what their bodies do. They're suffering."

"We don't have any way of knowing . . . but we never used to think that," I say. Calvin's been circling around this idea for a while now, but this is the first time he's spelled it out. It sounds crazy.

"That was before . . ." he says.

"Before what, Calvin? We don't know anything more than we ever did."

He says, "I just feel it. I felt it, looking at that man in the yard today."

I don't have anything to say to that, and after a while he yawns. I think about moving into his bed. I often think of this but can never make myself do it.

If Calvin and I ever would have gotten together, maybe—probably—we'd have had a baby. Maybe the baby and I both would have died in childbirth, who knows? Or maybe we'd have had a half dozen kids, some of them nearly grown by now. We'd have been happier, maybe, but now there'd be a whole herd of us facing starvation instead of just Calvin and me. Would they all be thinking strangely now, as Calvin is?

I'm all right with the choices we've made.

"We've had some good times," I say, but he's already drifted off. He doesn't answer.

Does he still remember the finding the horses and all those trips we made to the nearby farms on them, the times we stayed up all night making sure they were safe? Does he remember the fear that this place would be overrun when we returned? Does he remember that one, long heroic journey we made to the city? The fear of running out of ammo, the swarms of them even in the farthest suburbs. How we used to shower every time it rained? All the prairie dogs we trapped those first couple of years?

We were kids. We had to tell ourselves how to act.

I think we did well for ourselves.

When we've bothered to get us both to bed at the same time and all of the barriers are up, we sometimes will stay up there for a day or two. It's our vacation. We'll use a sealed pot. Seal or not, we'll be sitting up here in a bit of a farty smell, reading in candlelight, and when we tire of the reading, sleeping—not in shifts but both at once. It's the safest I ever feel. This time, though, it's just for one night.

We come out armed, check the second floor on our way down, check the windows. They're shuttered, and Calvin long ago put a bell system in so we should hear any breach, but we don't leave it to trust. All the smaller rooms are locked. The basement's locked. Once we've checked the windows and given a brief glance into the locked rooms, we know the house is clear. It's out to the porch to check the areas closest to us, then we use binoculars to check all the way to the tree line.

Anything could be in the orchard. That's always a risk.

This morning, the man has dug a wide trench around the trap. He hasn't torn himself in half. Calvin dons the welding mask and the raincoat. On the way out, he picks up the axe and a thin log.

"Be careful," I say.

He answers my command like always, "Yes, dear."

I follow at a distance, covering him. "What's the log for?" I call.

The man's digging grows more frenzied as Calvin approaches. I'm thinking, *Circle him. Good. Find out what his reach is.*

When Calvin has a clear angle, he's supposed to use the axe to split the skull and then lean back and do a few more cuts for good measure. That's not what he's doing, though.

"What are you doing?" I yell.

Calvin's dropped the log and is kicking it close to the zombie. Oh my god. I know what he's doing. It's not what we agreed.

He's lingering over his shot. He's chopping off the head. The man keeps mouthing the dirt, hands keep digging. Calvin's careful, rolling the head with his foot until it's face-down. He picks it up by the hair and with his other hand, pulls a white garbage bag from his pocket and shakes it open. He drops the head in there. The face still writhes.

I know what he's doing.

"You forgot the trap," I say as he passes me on our way back to the house.

"When do you think another animal's coming by here?" he says.

"What are you doing with the head?"

"You know what I'm doing."

I follow. In the workshop, he's getting a vise ready to hold the head.

"It's the old switcheroo. The mythology of it was all wrong. We are supposed to eat *their* brains," he says.

I'm not surprised by this, actually. His thinking has been going in this direction.

"That's not what 'the old switcheroo' even means," I say.

"It means what we say it means unless we can look it up. Can we? Do you think it's in the Scrabble dictionary?"

"All I know is this is how we get infected," I say.

"It's not, though. Not as long as I clean the brain. The brain's not infected. Even now, this poor guy is seeing us, hearing us. He's locked in there. It's the blood-brain barrier."

I have no idea if this is a thing, no way of finding out.

Calvin pulls the head out of the bag by its hair, raises it face-to-face with him. The zombie's lips stretch in a scream, but he can't make any noise without his lungs.

"I'm putting you out of your misery very soon now, sir. I'm so sorry this happened to you," Calvin says, all solemn and grave, and then he sets the head gently into the vise and begins to tighten. The head mouths a scream as before.

"This," Calvin says, tapping the head, "is the vaccine. If we eat *their* brains, we'll be immune."

Calvin has, hasn't he? Lost it. We'll be infected, or I will refuse, he will be infected . . . and I will strike into Calvin's dear head with an axe?

That's one thing that will not happen. I'm thinking through the various scenarios and decide the worst scenarios are those where he's wrong about this vaccine idea but right that we'll be locked in, spectating while something else propels our dead bodies. Both of us shuffling away from here, strangers. Or one of us eating the other and then shuffling back to the city.

"What reason do we have to think that the brain is the vaccine?" I say.

"I saw it. I saw it in a vision, all right?" he whines. He's finally had enough of worry and stress and doing things the best way every time. I don't blame him.

He's got the gloves on. The hand tools are all arrayed. This conversation is over, so now I must go and scan the hills.

"I stuck it in the pasta strainer in the creek," Calvin says. While the brain washes clean, we sit on the deck drinking cool peppermint tea. Everything is beautiful, the hills and the trees and the bit of the orchard all greener than they have ever been, all without a single flower. The man's body still digs at the dirt and will do so until his brain is sliced and seared.

Calvin says, "I wish I would have gotten more of them. Every bullet that's on the shelves of some store is a bullet that could have put one of those poor souls out of its misery. I wish I'd been brave enough to go out to the city and take down all the ones I could."

I say. "You were brave enough to stay here with me so we could have a life. That's enough."

Calvin leans forward in his chair, clears his throat. "Can I ask you something, Abbie?"

I nod. Of course. We've talked about everything else, our families and friends and homes, the journeys that brought us together, all the death. We've shared every little thought we've had during this time together. There's only one thing left.

"Why didn't we ever . . . you know?"

I laugh. "I can tell you, but it's kind of stupid."

"I'd like to know," he says.

"Were you old enough to like girls, before all of it happened? Did you have a crush?"

He considers and says, "Not really. I guess I was a little delayed."

"Well, I had a crush, or two actually. I'm sure I've told you about one of them, the one from the boy band? And then there was a boy who came late in my last year of school that looked like him—I mean a really uncanny resemblance—and I'm not saying we were boyfriend and girlfriend, but it was headed that way, right before everything."

"What happened to him?"

"What do you think?" But I never saw him, not between the time he was standing by my locker all sweet and beautiful and the time I learned he'd been taken down, and so he lived on for me.

Calvin nods, looks like he's holding back some remark.

I say, "It isn't that I was being faithful to him. That's not it. I guess I just had this really strong idea of my 'type,' and then you didn't fit because you looked different."

Calvin just looks at his hands.

"You're handsome, just in a different way," I say. "Anyway, I told you it was stupid."

"It actually makes me feel better," he says. "Sometimes I

wondered if it was because I was too much of a smartass, or too much of a nerd."

"You *are* a nerd, but I love that." I reach over and scratch his back. "I love your mind, Calvin."

"I guess it's as clean as it's getting," he says, rising.

I can't tell if this has helped Calvin at all, but I feel a little better. "It'll be good to put that poor guy out of his misery," I say.

Calvin's crouched out back by the fire pit turning the slices in the pan.

I'd half resolved to let him be, but I can't keep quiet now. "We have options. We could go into the city. Or if we're killing ourselves, aren't there easier ways?"

"This isn't going to kill us. There's no risk," he says.

Of course there is.

"I know you don't believe it, but I had a vision," he says.

A dream, he means.

I say, "I have dreams, too, Calvin, but they're not real. Don't you see that? There are a million things you dream, and when you don't have that much else to think about, you can fixate on things, but that doesn't make them real."

"It'll be good to have fresh meat for a change, anyway," he says. "I saved some to eat raw, just in case the cooking kills off some of what we're after, but this batch I want to be just right. Crispy edges and all."

It smells like food from a long time ago. It makes my own mouth water, for sure, but that's not a reason to risk us.

I say, "There are fewer of them every year. If this is the vaccine, Calvin—think about that—if this is the vaccine, what use is it even? They might be gone already. Almost gone."

"I think you ought to go scan the hills a while, Abbie," he says in a small, shaky voice. "Look way up high. There's a bunch more of them up there by now."

Goosebumps rise on my arms. I know he's right even as I rush in the back door, up the stairs, and out on the deck. Even before the binoculars.

The guy in the trap is still now, but the tree line ripples with dead. The bare patches aren't bare. I'm shaking, trying to still myself enough to look through the binoculars, and Calvin's calling from the backyard.

Come on back. Nothing we can do now. Dinner's almost ready.

I ate it, the cooked and the raw, all he gave me. We watched the hills while we ate. Now we sit cross-legged in our attic bedroom with all the barriers up and all the locks locked. We're here because I couldn't be anywhere else and because he owes me this much at least, after all the trust I've put in him. I could never stand terror for very long, always hid in this hidey hole, didn't I?

The fire's still going out back; we risked that. We've always been so careful with fires, but now I guess it doesn't matter.

We're holding hands, left in right and right in left, knees to knees. "I lied," I say. "It wasn't just about the boy."

"Shh. It's going to be all right," Calvin says.

"It was my mom too. She had a lot of trouble with my little brother. They were in the hospital a long time. They had to. . . and it wasn't you who was always too afraid to go back to the city. It was me. Every time I'd push to go, then when you'd start to agree, I'd back off. I've been a terrible. . . "

"Shh," Calvin says. "We've been happy. We're going to keep being happy."

What wouldn't we do to stay happy and safe, just a little while longer?

A bell begins to ring.

"They're in the house," I say. "Or could that be something else, wind on the windows? A bird?"

"They're in the house," Calvin says.

Something makes a dull crash far downstairs. More of the bells set to tinkling.

"They can't get up here. You promised."

"They can't. They'd have to do so many things you know they can't do. But I'm feeling it a little now, aren't you?"

I am. The whole attic is pink in the candlelight, warm and safe as always but different somehow. Calvin looks a little different, in a way I can't quite pin down.

Something crashes on the second floor, just below us.

"So when are you going to tell me about that vision?" I say.

"Are you sure you want to hear?"

I nod, and he scoots back to his bed, pulls me up against him. It isn't anything—we're like a brother and sister by now—but it still feels good to finally join him in bed. He whispers all of what he saw:

"We ate the brain. In the vision, it came to us on a silver platter. The hills shook with lost souls. You reached for the rifle, and I said, 'We'll free them, but we don't have to do it now. You don't need to be scared. They can't hurt us anymore.' I knew we didn't need to hide anymore, either, but still I brought you up here so you could feel safe. We lay here as long as we wanted, as long as it took to lose the last of the dread, and then we moved the furniture away from the hatch."

My body tenses at this. The bells ring, all of them now.

"We moved the furniture and let down the ladder. We watched them for a while until you felt safe again. They looked different. They looked like what they are, just poor, lost people."

"And they weren't coming after us, were they?" I say.

He says, all in wonder, "No, it was like they couldn't smell us anymore."

I say, "But they still smell us all over the house."

They're moving down there now. We keep hearing things crash.

He says, "They smell how we used to be. We aren't the same people because we don't have any fear anymore."

"I still do. Just a little bit," I say.

"Me too, just a little bit," Calvin says softly, "but it's almost gone. And when we've entirely lost it, we'll go down the ladder. We can walk right past them if we want, or we can put them out of their misery so easy then. Something, the meat thermometer I'm thinking, just punch it through the eye into the brain, and that's it. No drama. Just free them one by one."

"Or since we're immune now," I say, "we could even put our fingers—or some kind of a hook—into their eyes and pull out part of the brain." My mouth floods with water at that thought.

I'm not sure, though. *Will our hands still pick up tools? Will our hands know anything more than to dig and pull?*

But he says, "That was in the vision, too, something like that."

"Or, since we're immune, we could even go out to the bear trap and eat what's there—even that—and we wouldn't get sick?" I say.

He says, "That's what we did, actually. We sat down in the grass out there and cleaned up the trap."

"Was it good?" My mouth gushes again as I think back to

that time, years ago, when we had all that meat from the last of the horses.

"It was so good," Calvin says, hugging me tighter, "and we realized that we didn't need the trap anymore, or the orchard, or the guns, or anything but each other."

"What did we do then?"

"I don't know. It was the end of the vision."

"We walked all the way back to the city, don't you think?"

But did we walk together? Did we veer away as strangers?

He says, "I don't have any idea. Looking forward to finding out."

"Calvin?"

"Yes, dear?"

"I'm ready to go down now, I think."

When I wrote "The Old Switcheroo," I suppose I was feeling nostalgic about my grandparents' spacious house with its orchard, attic, and clear views of the hills. When the world seems threatening, the idea of a defensible and nurturing place has special appeal. I wished to go back to that place (to that time), but then of course I began thinking of what might go wrong there.

Christi Nogle
Boise, ID
June 7, 2021

Christi Nogle's debut novel, *Beulah,* is coming in early 2022 from Cemetery Gates Media. You can find more of her work in publications including *PseudoPod, Vastarien, Fusion Fragment, Boneyard Soup,* and *Dark Matter Magazine* and in anthologies such as C.M Muller's *Nightscript* and *Synth,* The

Dread Machine's *1986: Mixtape,* and Flame Tree Publications' *American Gothic* and *Chilling Crime.* Christi is an active member of the HWA, SFWA, Codex Writers' Group, and HOWLS. She teaches college composition and lives in Boise, Idaho with her partner, Jim, and their gorgeous dogs. Follow her at christinogle.com or on Twitter @christinogle.

NOTE FROM THE EDITOR

So many to thank, and only pages to do it.

Many thanks to Laurel Hightower for writing the introduction. You've been privy to this project since its inception, and I appreciate your words and encouragement along the way.

Many thanks to the contributors for giving me a part of yourselves for this project. Each piece seeped deep into my bones and wouldn't let go. They're still there, with me now.

Many thanks to all who submitted. After all was said and done, there were 423 submissions, which is mind-boggling to a first-timer like me. I was just a guy with an idea, and to see that sort of response was humbling. Know that there was enough material I adored for an anthology twice this length, and though the spirit was willing, the wallet was weak.

Many thanks to Gabino Iglesias, Max Booth III of Perpetual Motion Machine Publishing, Brhel and Sullivan of Cemetery Gates Media, Sam Richards of Weirdpunk Books, Samantha

Kolesnik of Off Limits Press, and Doug Murano of Bad Hand Books, for their willingness to answer my questions and keep me sane through all this.

Many thanks to Ellen Datlow, to whom I've rarely spoken but whose willingness to share her wisdom and tricks of the trade on Twitter, various podcasts, and interviews helped immensely in the curation of this anthology. If you see this, thank you. You are legend.

Many thanks to George Cotronis, for the phenomenal cover art.

Many thanks to Rachel Oestreich of *The Wallflower Editing* for your keen eyes. Thanks for catching all I've missed over the years. To many more books together.

And many thanks to you, the one reading these words now. Thank you—yes, you.

I'd always wanted to wear an editor's hat, and now that I have, I'll be damned if I don't have a taste for it. Now, I'm a writer first and foremost, but I *may* already have an idea for another anthology, and. . . well, I heard somewhere it's best to leave on a cliffhanger. So—

Scott J. Moses
Baltimore, MD
July 7, 2021

Printed in Great Britain
by Amazon